"Intrusion alert," the Zor hologram that was the SDF-1's new interface said with unusual intensity.

"Don't these hackers ever sleep?" Lazlo Zand asked.

"Intrusion. Code Alpha: highest priority. The source is scrambled and heavily encrypted."

Zand lifted an eyebrow. "Getting clever, are they? Take your best guess at the source."

Mirroring the apprehension rampant in its quantum circuitry, the holo was clenching its hands and pacing about. "The ship should be reconfigured. The main gun should be armed."

Zand's brow furrowed. Sometimes the thing didn't even realize that it had been removed from the ship. "What good are guns if we haven't located the source?" he asked, playing along for a while.

"The source has been fixed." Numbers scrolled inside the holo field and across several display screens.

Zand was baffled. "State the source."

"Approximately five hundred million miles from the present position of Neptune," answered the holo.

"The SDF-3?" Zand asked in sudden misgiving.

The holo shook its head. "The Masters."

Published by Ballantine Books:

THE ROBOTECH™ SERIES:
GENESIS #1
BATTLE CRY #2
HOMECOMING #3
BATTLEHYMN #4
FORCE OF ARMS #5
DOOMSDAY #6
SOUTHERN CROSS #7
METAL FIRE #8
THE FINAL NIGHTMARE #9
INVID INVASION #10
METAMORPHOSIS #11
SYMPHONY OF LIGHT #12

THE SENTINELS™ SERIES:
THE DEVIL'S HAND #1
DARK POWERS #2
DEATH DANCE #3
WORLD KILLERS #4
RUBICON #5

ROBOTECH: THE END OF THE CIRCLE #18
ROBOTECH: THE ZENTRAEDI REBELLION #19
ROBOTECH: THE MASTERS' GAMBIT #20

Also by Jack McKinney:

KADUNA MEMORIES

THE BLACK HOLE TRAVEL AGENCY:
  Book One: *Event Horizon*
  Book Two: *Artifact of the System*
  Book Three: *Free Radicals*
  Book Four: *Hostile Takeover*

THE MASTERS' GAMBIT

Jack McKinney

A Del Rey® Book
BALLANTINE BOOKS • NEW YORK

A Del Rey® Book
Published by Ballantine Books

Copyright © 1995 by Harmony Gold U.S.A., Inc.

Library of Congress Catalog Card Number: 94-69916

ISBN 0-345-38775-9

Manufactured in the United States of America

First Edition: April 1995

10 9 8 7 6 5 4 3 2 1

For Bill Spangler, whose comic book
series, *CyberPirates*, figures on the action

AUTHOR'S NOTE

This book is a reworking of the plot Carl Macek devised for the animated film *ROBOTECH: THE MOVIE*, blended with some of my own ideas and those put forth by Bill Spangler in his *CyberPirates* series for Eternity Comics. The addition of this book to the ROBOTECH/SENTINELS epic alters the order in which the novels are meant to be read. For what it's worth, here's how it should go: Robotech 1–6, Robotech 19 *(The Zentraedi Rebellion)*, Sentinels 1–5, Robotech 20 *(The Masters' Gambit)*, Robotech 7–12, and finally, *The End of the Circle*. A future book will probably be tucked between Robotech 9 and 10.

CHAPTER
ONE

With the Zentraedi menace ended—and that race's few survivors self-exiled on the factory satellite—humanity was free once more to wage war on itself. The so-named United Earth Government essentially served the needs of the Northlands and the sundry city- and nation-states that comprised the Western European Sector. Most non-allied regions had become self-sufficient and were loath to involve themselves in any global bureaucracy. Separatism prevailed. The thinking went that, should [the Masters or the Invid] arrive, the territory that played host to their planetfall would have the privilege or task of dealing with them. And so low-intensity conflicts flourished, particularly in the Southlands. Much as the Robotech Expeditionary Force had abandoned Earth, Anatole Leonard had abandoned the Southlands after parceling it up among his former lieutenants and cronies. By 2029, petty disputes between rival armies and polities had escalated to fullblown warfare.

Dominique Duprey,
Prelude to the Second Robotech War

I T WAS GOOD WEATHER FOR A BATTLE: A CLEAR SKY, tolerable heat, and an invigorating wind out of the northwest. Sated on weeks of rain, the lush forest south of Cavern City was vibrant, unblemished by mud or dust, charitable with outpourings of oxygen and floral scents. The lost-world tablelands to the north seemed near enough to touch. For a change, crafted warriors could perform without fear of suffocating in the cramped cockpits of their mecha, and foot soldiers armed with rifles and grenades had the planet's plush mantle to cushion their falls.

It was good weather to live or die.

Until noon, when the battle had taken a turn, most of the dying had been done by the severely outnumbered forces of Krista Delgado. But now it was Rawlins's crusaders who were crashing and burning and staining the savannah with spilled blood.

"You think I don't know we're killing children?" Delgado was telling her field officers in an underground command bunker not far from the ruins of the Southern Grand Cannon. "You think I've forgotten that there are ten-year-olds out there? But remember this: those *kids* would think nothing of massacring everyone in Cavern City." She paused to make brief eye contact with each of her lieutenants. "See that your teams are reminded of what Rawlins's People's Army did in Porto Velho, Leticia, and Manaus. Then order them to press the counterattack—even if that means employing Mongoose missiles against Wolverine rifles. This isn't an honorable fight, ladies and gentlemen. We're going for the win, whichever way we have to."

Delgado had to force the words from her mouth. A handsome, small-boned woman closing on sixty years, she had raised seven children, four of them members of the same orphaned generation Aaron Rawlins had conscripted into his People's Army and loosed on the strife-torn city-states of the Southlands. She could issue orders until she was blue in the face, but who could she point to as the source of her orders? Who was she answering to but her own conscience?

She dismissed her officers and turned her attention to an array of monitors, on which half-a-dozen battle views were running in living color. The expert-system computer tasked with coordinating the aerial counter-offensive put the morning's casualties at 4500; 3000 more were projected to die by nightfall. Remote cameras panned the bodies of the dead and dying, spread-eagle in the tall grass, entangled in precarious heaps, arranged like the numerals of a clock around the rims of blast craters. The battlefield was littered with the holed torsos and armored limbs of mecha as well: Gladiators, Excalibers, early-generation Veritechs, Hovertanks, and even a couple of Alpha Fighters—courtesy of the Earth Defense Force, which had dispatched a brigade to intervene in the fighting and had wound up taking part in it.

Colonel Tannen, one of perhaps fifty EDF soldiers who had allied themselves with Delgado's Cavern City militia, was in the command bunker just now. "You're doing the right thing, Krista," he announced. "Rawlins has to be stopped. It might as well be here."

Delgado swung away from the monitors with arms folded across her narrow chest. In place of a uniform, she wore a blouse and skirt, covered by a dun-colored battle apron. Black boots met the hem of the skirt, and her long gray hair was captured in a chignon. "And better still if the one hundred EDF siding with Rawlins die with him." Her pale blue eyes flashed. "I'm aware of your motives, Evan, so don't try to con me."

The colonel quirked a wry smile and bowed his head. He was younger than her by five years, but age spots and the dark pouches under his eyes made him appear ten years older. "Kris, you always could see through me."

"Then, now, and tomorrow," she told him.

Tannen's tight-fitting black pants and leather torso harness were standard EDF issue, but underneath it all, he was Robotech Defense Force through and through. Seven years earlier, the RDF had been incorporated into the EDF, but it lived on in the hearts and minds of those who had served. Delgado, too, had been an RDF officer during the war against the Zentraedi, though she hadn't actually gone to guns with the aliens until the final battle, in which the surface of the planet had been ravaged by plasma and directed light. Then, following the Rain of Death—and for reasons never fully explained to Tannen—she had thrown in with Anatole Leonard and risen to full-bird in Leonard's Army of the Southern Cross. Even so, Delgado had been openly critical of Leonard's actions in Cavern City in 2018, and might have resigned if he hadn't ultimately bequeathed her the city. The former Southern Cross now comprised the majority of the EDF. Only days earlier, when infighting had factioned the peacekeeping force sent to Cavern City, two out of three soldiers and mecha had gone over to Rawlins's side.

Rawlins had been one of Leonard's trusted lieutenants during the Reconstruction and the Malcontent Uprisings, spearheading numerous attacks on alien bases in the Zentraedi Control Zone. When Leonard relocated permanently to Monument City in 2022 and the Southlands was "compartmentalized," Rawlins received the southwest and Delgado the northeast, including most of what had been the Venezuela Sector. The two had fought on opposing sides in the Global Civil War and had rarely seen eye-to-eye under Leonard. But their mutual distaste hadn't flowered into enmity until Rawlins fell under the sway of HEARTH—the Heal Earth Hajj.

Founded by disabused members of the Church of Recurrent Tragedies, HEARTH had seized the orphaned generation of the Southlands, those born between the

years 2008 and 2020, some of whom had survived the
Rain of Death, and all of whom had been raised to expect a second invasion from the stars—from either the
Robotech Masters or the Invid swarm. HEARTH, however, was a reaction to the pervasive paranoia of the
times. Its founders posited that the United Earth Government had conspired to foster the fear of extraterres-
trial invasion as a means of maintaining power and
shaping a contentious future. HEARTH rejected all no-
tions of imminent warfare and most aspects of high
technology; to its tens of thousands of followers, the
launch of the SDF-3 to Tirol had been little more than
an elaborate and criminally costly ruse. HEARTH advo-
cated the overthrow of the UEG and the myriad bu-
reaucracies it had spawned, and worldwide commitment
to the healing of the planet.

Aaron Rawlins had been responsible for affixing
"Hajj" to the acronym and militarizing the movement.
Birthed in the provincial territories of western Argentina and southern Amazonas, the People's Army had begun a slow northward march through the Southlands,
gaining converts en route—overrunning townships and
isolated city-states, burning churches and temples, closing schools, butchering politicians, lawyers, doctors,
and any who refused to subscribe to the new order,
sowing vast killing fields wherever they ventured.

Krista Delgado hadn't felt threatened by the Hajj until it was clear that Rawlins had his sights set on Venezuela. She had never taken lightly to people who
thwarted her own designs. Ask any Zentraedi. On inher-
iting Venezuela's dubious throne, Delgado's first order
of business—following a precedent set by Leonard in
the early days of Brasília—had been to rid Cavern City
of the aliens who had clustered there. More dispirited

than they'd been on losing the war, the displaced Zentraedi had attempted to emigrate to the Northlands, only to find things so uncomfortable there that most had ultimately quit Earth for the factory satellite. Hundreds had starved themselves to death in protest; others succumbed to mysterious illnesses, or lost themselves in the still-radioactive wastes their own annihilation bolts had created.

Having rid her domain of one scourge, Delgado wasn't about to open Venezuela's borders to the likes of Aaron Rawlins and his army of mindwarped—some said narcotized—children. So, as a dare to Rawlins, she had massed her troops south of Cavern, near the site of the dismantled Grand Cannon.

The situation had been closely monitored by the United Earth Government, which was headquartered in the Northlands, in Monument City. The UEG had taken a stab at negotiating a truce between the two former allies, but no accommodation had been reached. Finally, when warfare seemed inevitable, a peacekeeping force had been ordered south, jointly commanded by Colonel Tannen and Colonel Laubin—another ex–Southern Crosser. The Earth Defense Force brigade hadn't been on the scene twenty-four hours before everyone began to choose sides.

Forty years earlier, when both had served aboard the supercarrier *Kenosha*, Tannen and Delgado had been lovers. But passion from the old days didn't count for much in the postmodern world.

"Don't think for a minute I'm dumb to why you were so quick to break ranks with the EDF, Evan," Delgado was hectoring him now. "You don't give a shit about Cavern City or the People's Army. It's Laubin's contingent you're after. The chance to kill a couple of dozen Southern Crossers."

Tannen shrugged it off. "Like Laubin isn't doing the same thing, Kris. I know for a fact he hates Rawlins. But he'd back Satan if it meant a shot at eliminating a handful of Robotechs from the EDF." He regarded Delgado mournfully. "It comes down to this, wherever we're sent. None of us have any commitment to the EDF. It was counterfeit from the get-go, something the UEG hatched to keep the RDF and the Southern Cross from trading fire before the Tirol mission launched. Hell, if the Masters or the Invid showed up next week, we wouldn't have a prayer. We're too busy fighting each other to take on a mutual threat."

Delgado's look had softened somewhat. "Chairman Moran should have sense enough to disband the EDF and start from scratch."

Tannen grunted noncommittally. "Maybe it'll come to that. But until it does, friendly fire is going to remain an EDF soldier's worst enemy."

Delgado held his gaze for a moment, then eyed the monitor screens. "I sympathize, Evan. But in the meantime, there's killing to be done." She thought once more about Aaron Rawlins's crusaders. "Even if we are making mincemeat of our own future."

"What happens in the Southlands is of no consequence to Monument City and its allies," Barth Constanza told the members of the Senate from his seat in the vaulted hall that was their workplace. The hall occupied center place in the classically adorned building that housed the United Earth Government; within were marble columns, adamantine floors, and fine furnishings, all under the protection of squads of towering military police armor.

Senator Constanza went on, "We didn't create the mess down there, and we're under no obligation to solve it. Those territories chose to secede from the UEG, and most elected to pursue a separatist course even after Wyatt Moran was elected chairman. If they're determined to wage war on one another, there's nothing we can do to prevent them, short of giving our blessing to a full-scale invasion and subsequent occupation by the Defense Force."

The remark met with vociferous opposition, and Constanza had to raise his voice to be heard over the tumult. "What we cannot permit, however—what we *must* not permit—is factionalism and the perpetuation of internecine fighting among the EDF!"

There was little point in continuing until the room quieted; when it did, Senator Grass, esteemed member of the old boy network of the Southern Cross, was on his feet. "Does the senator from Portland propose that we simply ignore would-be conquerors like Aaron Rawlins? That we allow ourselves to sink further into the medieval morass our previous inactions have fostered?"

"Rawlins isn't the issue," Constanza returned from the other side of the hall. "The People's Army would have been crushed months ago if it had been in our interests to do so. The point is that the EDF is using these so-called peacekeeping exercises as an excuse to settle old scores between the RDF and the Southern Cross. And such an army can hardly be trusted with defending the Earth from invasion."

Owen Harding, from Detroit, took the floor. "Skirmishes are inevitable at this point—whether between

Delgado and Rawlins or rival factions within the Defense Force. These conflicts are a by-product of tensions produced by years of waiting for an enemy that has yet to show itself."

"Tensions we inflamed by faking communiqués from the SDF-3," Constanza pointed out.

Grass took issue with him. "And if we'd admitted the truth—that the SDF-3 hasn't been heard from? That *wouldn't* have proved inflammatory? The people had to be given hope, something to hold on to!"

"*We* are the people," Harding shouted. "Or at least we're supposed to be. And our lies have kept the entire world on a war footing for almost a decade now. The truth wouldn't have been any more devastating. What's more, people have already begun to see through our fabrications. Take this HEARTH, for example. They doubt that the SDF-3 ever launched. To them, it's still sealed inside the factory satellite. We know it launched, but no one can say whether or not it ever reached Tirol. And where, I ask you, are the Robotech Masters? Where is this ultratech army we've been made to fear?"

A substantial portion of the Senate applauded. Constanza waited, then rose to his feet. "Some of you seem to have forgotten what Hunter and Lang said before the launch: silence should not necessarily be construed as a sign of success *or* failure, but rather as a signal to heighten our readiness. And this is why the EDF must be brought under control. It should come as no surprise to anyone in this hall that Monument will be the focus of any attack. Rawlins or others like him won't be factors in a global invasion; Earth will live or die by what happens right here."

"Commander Leonard has been saying that for years, Senator," Grass said. "If Alfred Nader, from Roca Negra, hadn't requested intervention, Leonard would never have ordered a peacekeeping force into Venezuela."

Constanza ridiculed the idea. "Leonard knew full well those troops would break rank and throw their support to Rawlins or Delgado. He'd like nothing more than to eliminate the RDF from the army he forged and brought here from the Southlands. The RDF has been a thorn in his side since the SDF-3 launched."

The hall was deathly still. No one rose to challenge Constanza or to pat him on the back. The senators lowered their eyes and studied their hands.

Constanza understood. "This is a secure room, people. We're supposed to be free to speak our minds here." Nothing. Not a voice, not so much as a cough answered him. He snorted in derision. "It's not enough we've had to watch the skies for fifteen years? Now we have to watch what we think and say, for fear of retaliation from one of our own kind?"

"Should I see to it that Constanza learns some manners?" Joseph Petrie asked. A small man with a squarish head and close-cropped hair, he had been Leonard's adjutant during the old days in Brasília and was now a kind of behind-the-throne presence in Leonard's cadre of EDF officers.

Leonard himself was sitting across the room, blunt fingers steepled, the hairless brow of his bullet-shaped head furrowed. A protracted exhale ended his long moment of silence. "Constanza's harmless. He's only saying what a lot of them are thinking. In any case, I respect a man who endorses the unpopular opinion, even when he knows that he's bound to lose. The rest of them are spineless."

"So I should let him be?"

"For the time being."

The two men were in what Petrie liked to call the "listening post" of Leonard's office in EDF headquarters, elsewhere in Monument City. The Senate meeting was coming to them real-time via A/V bugs planted throughout the allegedly secure hall.

Headquarters was a soaring megacomplex of high-tech needles, punctuated with crenels and merlons like some medieval battlement. The central tower cluster had been built to suggest the white gonfalons, or ensigns, of a holy crusade hanging from high cross-pieces. Leonard's chambers were luxurious, but he often longed for Brasília, for his palace by the lake, with its small rose-windowed chapel in which he had offered morning and evening prayers.

And just as often he thought of Seloy Deparra, the Zentraedi who had become his lover for a short time, a partner in the games of debasement and atonement he had devised—the female who had borne him a son, whom she had named Hirano. But Deparra and the boy were dead, dead ten years now, though Leonard shuddered nightly at the memory of their corpses, picked over by carrion birds in the jungle camp that had been home to the all-female Malcontent group known as the Scavengers.

He had discovered them on the day the Zentraedi rebellion had been crushed, during the battle in which he had sustained the wound that had robbed him of the full use of his left leg. Left leg and much more: his manhood. Despite doctors' claims to the contrary—that his impotence was psychosomatic.

Seloy, and perhaps Hirano as well, had been killed by Miriya Parino Sterling, seemingly lost in space with her husband and the rest of the SDF-3 crew these past nine years, whose daughter remained on Earth. One of a handful of aliens who remained onworld, and the only one of mixed Zentraedi and Human blood. But Leonard didn't feel vengeful toward Dana Sterling. There was no profit in it—not with the Robotech Masters long overdue. They were why he had come north, abandoning Brasília and the Southlands for Monument City. Few understood that he had undertaken the move for the sake of all Humankind; that the move was a holy undertaking.

Senator Constanza was correct in surmising that Monument City would be the focal point of an encounter with the Masters. Most of the UEG accepted this, but there was no consensus regarding Earth's response. Leonard knew through prayer and intercession that the sole viable response was war. And yet few were willing to stand by him. Even Patty Moran was weakening, often bowing to UEG demands. The chairman had become little more than a silver-haired figurehead, not at all what T. R. Edwards and Leonard had hoped for—too concerned with his own power base to allow his Minister of War much leeway when it came to dealing with petty dictators like China's Ling Chow, or with marauding hordes like the People's Army. Here Leonard had been successful in herding almost all the Zentraedi into the factory satellite, and instead of exterminating them, Moran was willing to let bygones be bygones.

Part of the problem was that there were too many players on the field: not only Moran and the UEG Senate with its numerous subcommittees and special interest groups, but people like Rolf Emerson, Moran's Minister of Terrestrial Defense, and Lazlo Zand, director of the former Robotech Research Center in Tokyo, Earth's preeminent city.

But Leonard saw the RDF as the principal problem—what remained of it, at any rate. Reinhardt, Hunter, and the rest had shown their true colors during the Malcontent Uprisings, when they had pursued a course of accommodation with the rebels, and Leonard feared that devout RDFers might take the same tack with the Robotech Masters, inviting them to share the Earth, for God's sake. If it hadn't been for the actions of the Southern Cross, half the world's population would be dead from the virus the Malcontents had attempted to spread in the final days of their rebellion. That alone was reason enough for winnowing the RDF from the EDF.

So, of course, Leonard encouraged his former confederates to engage the RDF at every opportunity.

He would have liked nothing more than to come out from behind the subtlety and order his troops to storm the RDF's private headquarters in Monument and on Fokker Aerospace Base—areas awarded to the RDF by the Accords of 2019 and 2022, in which the EDF had been created. But two things stood in his way: certain promises both he and Moran had made to T. R. Edwards, who had grown very powerful in the two years preceding the launch of the Tirol mission; and the unsettling possibility that the SDF-3 might return when least expected, equipped with even greater firepower than it had left with.

His caution on the second point always struck him as the sort of deal agnostics were wont to make with the universe: they accepted the idea of God not so much as fact but as a hedge against God's actual existence.

But Leonard was no agnostic. He doubted neither God's existence nor that he and God were frequently in direct communication. Indeed, on God's command he would dismiss his concerns about the SDF-3's return, along with his promises to Edwards, and rid himself of the RDF once and for all.

CHAPTER
TWO

Lang had already waged a two-year battle [with the UEG] over funding when the Hades Mission finally launched in 2017. For a time he was convinced that the [mother computer's missing components could be retrieved from Plutospace and returned to Earth] well in advance of the projected launch date for the SDF-3 [2020]. When, however, the Hades' robots still hadn't completed their objective in late 2019, Lang urged the UEG to fund a rescue operation, only to see his pleas fall on deaf ears. The mission was all but forgotten in December of 2028, when the ship at last touched down at the Tanegashima aerospace facility in Japan. So much so that only one newscaster commented on the story, dismissing its importance with the line: "Too little, too late; even ten years ago, scarcely worth the wait."

footnote in Zeitgeist, *Insights:
Alien Psychology and the Second Robotech War*

THE HARBINGERS OF EARTH'S FATE LURKED AT THE edge of the Solar system, twenty million miles beyond aphelion Pluto. There in that dark, frigid birthplace of comets floated six stupendous warships, five miles end to end through their long axes, bristling with weapons and sensors, the likes of which had never appeared in Sol's parcel of space-time.

The flotilla had originally numbered eight, but two ships had been cannibalized during the translight journey from Tirol—a journey that should have been near instantaneous but had instead required almost twenty

14

Earth years. Insufficient supplies of Protoculture had precluded the use of the ships' space-fold generators; in fact, it was the absence of Protoculture that had prompted the journey itself. For the only source of the transformative fuel that derived from the Invid Flower of Life now resided on Earth.

The source was the Protoculture matrix, a unique device created by the Tiresian scientist, Zor, who—as an act of rebellion against the empire that had spawned him—had removed the matrix from Tirol, concealed it aboard his dimensional fortress, and dispatched the fortress to Earth. One war had already been fought over the matrix, devastating to Earth as well as to Tirol, which had seen the defeat of its army of giant warrior clones, the Zentraedi. Some of the clones had since defected to Earth's side and were presumably prepared to defend the matrix with their lives.

Sixteen years earlier a combined force of Earthers and Zentraedi had attacked the Zentraedi outpost of the late Commander Reno and made off with a factory satellite, folding the moonlet-sized maintenance and repair facility to Earthspace. Though it was more accurate to say that Commander Breetai's mixed contingent had been *allowed* to fold the factory to Earth, in so doing revealing the space-time location of the world Zor had chosen to receive his fortress. The sacrifice of Reno's forces—the last of the loyal Zentraedi as far as Tirol's Masters knew—had seemed a small price to pay to learn the whereabouts of the planet that had eluded them for generations.

The flotilla's reemergence in the dimension of light had strategic import: normally dauntless, the Robotech Masters were reluctant to engage the race that had defeated the Zentraedi without first observing the world they inhabited—a blue-white, water-laden gem, rife with life, in spite of the destruction visited upon it by the five million crafts of the Grand Fleet. As well, the Masters needed to reestablish contact with distant Tirol and the masters they themselves served: Tirol's triad of Elders, last heard from some ten Earth years earlier.

The Masters' ships were elongated lozenges, the dorsal surfaces of which were stippled with structures resembling segmented insect legs, two-tined forks, stairways, bridges, onion domes, ziggurats, and massive louvered panels. The bulk of their interiors were given over to living space for the clone population the Masters had brought with them, the cream of Tirol's vat-grown crop: contemplative, artistic, and submissive. There were also vast holds crowded with battle mecha, and barracks for the soldier-clones that piloted them.

The command center of the flotilla flagship was a cathedral of arching structures suggestive of neural tissue—axons and dendrites—or a kind of information-highway maze, which pulsed and flowed with the pure radiance of Protoculture. And all of it was quite literally at the nailless fingertips of the Masters, who controlled and accessed the flow via a hovering mushroomlike device five feet across, around which they stood, each upon a small platform.

Dressed in monkish gray robes whose colored cowls were modeled on the tripartite petals of the Flower of Life, the three Masters were of a type: fey and gaunt, with slender limbs, hawkish profiles, and flaring eyebrows. Though their gleaming pates were bald, they had fine blue hair that fell to their shoulders. Scarlike chevrons of skin under sharp cheekbones emphasized the severity of their laser-eyed faces. The mottled control device they seldom abandoned—the Protoculture Cap—

enabled them to communicate with one another telepathically. When they conversed audibly, their voices
resounded with vibrato, the result of decades of contact
with Protoculture.

In the same way the Masters served the Elders, there
were those who attended the Masters: triumvirates of
effete, scarlet-haired, blue-lipped clones, who advised
them on matters of war, politics, science, and other
mundane affairs.

One of those clones, Dovak, leader of a triumvirate
of scientists, was addressing the Masters now from the
floor of the command center, fifteen feet above which
the Masters and their Cap floated.

"All intelligence from the surveillance vessel has
been received and stored for future reference," the clone
reported.

Having materialized from translight nearly an Earth
year earlier than the six spade-shaped battle fortresses,
the flotilla's forward ship had spent that time analyzing
Earth's ceaseless outpourings of electronic signals.
Protoculture-enhanced communications arrays capable
of folding space-time permitted the signals to be read at
their source, thus allowing for real-time monitoring of
the planet.

"Several of the Humans' principal language groups
have been deciphered," Dovak continued, "and a chro-
nology of events has been assembled covering the past
twenty-nine Earth years, commencing with the arrival
of Zor's fortress. In addition, the surveillance vessel observed the final stages of what seemed to be a salvage
operation that took place in the vicinity of the small ice-
world known as Pluto. Recovery work was performed
by classes of nonsentient machines. The machines'

ship—also robot-controlled—returned to Earth seven months ago."

The Master called Shaizan, who frequently spoke for the triad, conferred for a moment with his confederates. "What were the machines salvaging?" he asked.

"Debris, my lord. Perhaps from the explosion of a spacecraft of some sort. Surveillance personnel report seeing what looked to be household belongings, electronic devices, and a myriad of vehicles, including several boats."

"Boats?" the Master Dag said, who was the more lantern-jawed of the three.

"Flotation vessels for use on water. Apparently there were many of these."

"Is there a shortage of boats on Earth?" Shaizan asked.

"Observations would indicate otherwise, m'lords."

"Then why? Speculate."

"The Humans were searching for one or several irreplaceable objects. Possibly objects destroyed during the Zentraedi Rain of Death—their phrase for the Grand Fleet's bombardment of the planet under the auspices of Zentraedi Commander-in-Chief Dolza."

Shaizan sent to Dag and Bowkaz: *A retrieval operation would suggest that these objects, whatever they are, are as important to the Humans as the matrix is to us.*

Agreed, the two Masters returned in mindspeak.

"Has there been any communication between the surveillance ship and the Elders?" Shaizan directed to Myzex, leader of a triumvirate of politicians and policy makers.

"None, Masters," the clone said, kowtowing. "All transsignal communiqués aimed at Tirol have gone unanswered."

Bowkaz, the strategist, barked, "Assessment!"

"Tirol has been abandoned."

"Explicate," the Masters ordered in unison.

"Surrendered."

"Elaborate."

"An Invid attack on the Near-Group worlds."

"Karbarra, Praxis, Spheris, Garuda—all defeated?" Bowkaz asked. "Ludicrous."

Myzex kowtowed once more. "Only a probability, my lords."

The Masters took a moment to deliberate in silence. *The Elders would never have allowed themselves to be captured,* Shaizan sent. *They would have departed Tirol on first detection of the Invid.*

If so, they will contact us, Dag assured him.

The Masters fixed their collective glower on Myzex. "Report on Earth's defenses."

"Forward observation bases on the planet's large moon and in stationary orbit; several orbital weapons platforms; a flotilla of deepspace frigates and cruisers; abundant surface missile silos, though nothing on the order of Dolza's description of the Grand Cannon. The factory satellite is anchored midway between Earth and its moon, but appears to be inoperative."

"And Zor's fortress?" Shaizan asked.

"Nowhere in evidence."

"Could it be concealed somewhere on the surface—submerged in Earth's waters, perhaps?"

Myzex inclined his head. "The suggestion offers some promise. Reports from Exedore Formo at the start of the Zentraedi campaign against Earth indicated that the fortress was apparently incapable of executing a space-fold. And it was surely further incapacitated during the Rain of Death. Or why else would the Humans have had to employ Breetai's ship in their attack on Commander Reno's outpost?"

"The Elders will apprise us," Dag said.

Bowkaz nodded. "Until then, we must assume that the matrix is safe within Zor's fortress and that the fortress is somewhere on the surface." He looked at Dovak. "Would we prevail in a direct engagement with Earth?"

"Only if it was brief and surgical," the military adviser stated flatly. "A protracted, all-inclusive war on the planet would deplete the fleet of Protoculture in a matter of months. Moreover, the Humans have had ample time to prepare for our arrival. If the matrix has been discovered, they will have ample supplies of Protoculture to fuel their battle mecha."

The Masters pressed their bony fingertips to the surface of the Cap and retreated into the sanctity of their communal thoughts. *We must wait for the Elders to advise us,* they sent in unanimity.

"Without specimens of the Flower of Life or a functioning matrix, we haven't a prayer of producing Protoculture," Emil Lang had told Lazlo Zand more than ten years earlier. "Our one hope lies in being able to synthesize it. I'm certain that the key to that process is to be found somewhere in EVE's databanks, but they're impermeable without the components the SDF-1 was forced to leave behind in Plutospace. If only we hadn't been so panicked by our miscalculated fold. Then, of course, there were the lives of Macross's fifty-six thousand to think of . . ."

EVE was Lang's name for the mother computer that had overseen the SDF-1 and had been removed from the fortress years before the ship's destruction at the hands of the Zentraedi warlord, Khyron. An acronym for Enhanced Video Emulation, the computer had provided sky effects—clouds, rainbows, and sunsets—for the citizens of the island city that had been inadvertently folded into deepspace and subsequently rebuilt inside the fortress. From 2012 to 2020, when the SDF-3 launched, EVE—a stand-alone system, isolated from the world's plethora of interactive computer networks—had merely taken up space in Lang's Robotech Research Center in Tokyo. Then, in 2023, Lazlo Zand, responding to requests from the city's Ministry of Human Services, had discovered a way to make the machine earn its keep. "EVE" was turned into a motherly, Big Sister telepresence that spoke to the needs of the orphaned generation, appearing on her own telecomp channel and on billboard-size screens throughout the burgeoning cities of the Pacific Rim. It was a source of mindless propaganda, much like the heartening Zand-authored messages allegedly received from the missing SDF-3.

But EVE had become little more than the public face of the mother computer since the scarcely noted return of the truant components from Plutospace some six months earlier. Lang's dream of accessing the system had been realized, only it was Lazlo Zand—tall, willowy, rumpled, and every bit as alien-eyed as Lang—who was reaping the rewards.

Lang's chief disciple during Reconstruction, Zand had inherited the UEG-funded research facility. In 2025, at the height of the anti-Robotech movement, it had been renamed the Special Protoculture Observations and Operations Kommandatura, or SPOOK, after the department Zand had administered under Lang. The new designation, however, was also indicative of deeper changes. By 2027, Zand had rid SPOOK of all Lang-loyal personnel. Gone were the research and development teams, the support staff, the cybertechnicians who had created the android JANUS M; in their place were scientists handpicked by Zand and *his* chief disciples, Joseph Petrie and Henry Giles.

But Zand had worked solo on reacquainting the components with their mother machine, and in the process had gone Lang one better. It had long been Lang's assumption that Zor had not only designed the ship but had programmed the computer as well. Why, then, not let the computer reveal itself as Zor? Zand had asked himself, envisioning a virtual telepresence—or better still, a hologram—that could be constructed by sampling the A/V warning message Zor had recorded for the finders of his fortress.

Lang himself had viewed the message during the initial recon of the crashed ship, shortly before receiving the mindboost that had catapulted him overnight to the apex of the pre-War scientific community.

Zand's mindboost had come nineteen years later, though not at the controls of a piece of unfathomable Robotechnology. His had come from a transfusion of ur-Protoculture drained from an Invid battlecraft found aboard the remains of Khyron's ship, mixed with a liter of blood liberated from Dana Parino Sterling, Earth's only Human-Zentraedi hybrid. And depending on where in the galaxy the SDF-3 had ended up, Zand had access to something else Lang didn't: Flowers of Life, recently discovered growing in the shadow of a rusting Zentraedi battlewagon in a remote area of the Southlands. Not in abundance—far too few to supply a Protoculture matrix, even if one could be built—but enough to numb Zand's palate and intoxicate his mind. Since ingesting his first Flower petal, he had almost passed beyond the need for sleep or sustenance, and his understanding of the Shapings had increased tenfold.

Locked inside his cluttered subbasement office, Zand had one of the petals in his mouth just now. And pacing a stretch of soiled carpet in front of the office's smart-wall was the Zor hologram the Protoculturist had conjured from the mother computer: a dreamy-eyed youth of average height, with handsome features and wavy locks of shoulder-length brown-blond hair. The faintly blue-green holo appeared courtesy of a projector imbedded in the floor. Data could be projected in 3-D or displayed on a large flatscreen centered in the smart-wall.

In the two months the computer had been permeable, Zand and the Zor holo had engaged in several introductory discussions, many of them pleasant, all of them enlightening. The machine knew English, but most of the conversations had been conducted in Zentraedi, which Zand spoke fluently. So as not to confuse it, Zand had allowed the machine only limited access to the world outside SPOOK, though it had learned quite a bit on its own through the celebrity telepresence, EVE.

The focus of that night's discussion—Zand was at his best after midnight—was Zor's secret rebellion against the Robotech Masters and his attempts at seeding worlds with the Flower of Life.

"Were those missions undertaken to ensure a ready supply of Flowers?" Zand asked.

In keeping with its emotive programming, the holo glanced at him with arrogant disapproval. "The seeding was done for the sake of the Invid."

"But if the Invid were Tirol's enemies—"

"The Masters made them what they were by harvesting Optera's Flowers, then defoliating the planet.

The seeding missions were an attempt to redress that wrong, and to provide them with a world that might nourish them."

"Obviously they rejected the offer."

"The Flower of Life owes much to the soil that supports it. Each planet that accepted it—Karbarra, Garuda, Spheris, and the rest—produced strains that diverged from those fostered by Optera. The Invid were unable to derive what they needed from the varieties I sowed. The Masters put a stop to the attempts, in any case."

Zand, seated at his desk, stroked his chin in thought. The computer didn't seem to realize that its creator had died on one of those worlds—murdered by warriors of the race he had been so desperate to rescue. "Dispatching your fortress was a way of retaliating for the action of the Masters?"

"Partly."

"But why to Earth? Why here, of all worlds? Not simply because of its distance from Tirol, I take it."

The Zor holo took a moment to respond. "There are matters I am insufficiently programmed to address, though I am aware of being referred to data concerning Haydon."

"What is Haydon?"

"A historical personage of great power. The seeding attempts were strongly influenced by my investigations into his life."

"Do you contain those data?"

"Those data are not found."

Zand sucked at his teeth. "Even so, you obviously *knew* what you were doing in sending your fortress far from the Masters' reach. You thought enough to include a message of warning about the Invid."

"Yes, I knew what I was doing."

"Then you deliberately targeted Earth. The fortress's controlled crash on Macross Island wasn't an accident."

"Earth figures strongly in the coming events."

"What events?"

"I can only address potential developments. What's more, the ship isn't important; its contents are what matter."

"The Protoculture matrix," Zand said knowingly and somewhat despondently. "Where was—*is* it concealed?" The computer was still unaware of the ship's destruction and burial.

The Zor holo started to reply, but stopped itself. It remained silent for a moment, then said, "Intrusion alert."

Zand straightened in his swivel chair.

"An attempt is under way to infiltrate my databanks."

"Locate the source of the intrusion," Zand commanded.

"The infiltration is being routed through a host of fiber-optic relay stations, but I have the source address."

"Here in Tokyo?"

"Yes."

"Hackers," Zand said with patent disgust. "Trying to ride in on a call to EVE, are they?"

"Through EVE, yes."

Zand nodded. "Then transmit the usual free sample. But be sure to append a reprimand. Nothing life-threatening. Just enough to give them pause before they try this again."

CHAPTER
THREE

*Spurred by Anatole Leonard, by then [2025] a permanent resident
of Monument City, public sentiment toward the REF and those
Zentraedi still living on the surface underwent a decided shift.
Leonard was able to use the SDF-3's encouraging though completely bogus transmissions—written at Chairman Moran's behest
by Lazlo Zand—to suggest that the members of the Expeditionary
Mission had had no real intention of reaching an accord with the
Masters and had made a new home for themselves in space.
Wherever it appeared, the once-esteemed fighting-kite symbol of
the RDF was slashed with a red diagonal; the term Robotech was
used disparagingly when used at all; and Lang's Research Center
was renamed SPOOK. Then, of course, there were the Klan attempts to drive the Zentraedi offworld, and the acts of cyber-
sabotage committed against the RDF Cobra Squadron's Alpha
VTs, which have come to be called the Giles Crimes.*

Zachary Fox, Jr., Men, Women, Mecha:
The Changed Landscape of the Second Robotech War

IF THERE WAS ONE THING THAT HADN'T BEEN AFFECTED
by the Rain of Death, the fiery ruin of Macross City,
and the apparent disappearance of the Expeditionary
mission, it was the belief that weekends were still for
putting aside the sometimes nasty business of the world
and focusing on the things that mattered: family and
friends, sport and avocation, the timeless traditions and
pastimes that kept the world turning through the harshest of reversals. Even dedicated public servants like

Rolf Emerson—recently elevated to the burdensome-sounding position of Minister of Terrestrial Defense—looked forward to weekends. Especially during August, when the Northwest's skies were clear, the air was warm and redolent with pine, and mid-October's chill winds seemed a long way off. And especially that particular August of 2029, with only a month to go before Bowie Grant and Dana Sterling, Emerson's teenage charges, were required to relocate to the dormitory of the Earth Defense Force Academy in the heart of Monument City.

For Dana, only daughter of the Robotech War's most able pilots, Max Sterling and Miriya Parino, the EDF Academy was the natural choice. But for Bowie, a talented musician of fragile health, enrollment struck Emerson as more punishment than privilege. Nevertheless, Emerson had promised Bowie's career-officer parents, Jean and Vince—unheard from these past nine years—that Bowie would receive a modicum of military training. Not that the boy had much choice, given the climate of preparedness that had dominated the '20s.

Emerson had conceived of a weekend of hiking and fishing for the three of them, with at least one overnight camp in the high mountains north of Monument. It was just the three of them since Ilan Tinari had elected to join her fellow Zentraedi in voluntary banishment aboard the factory satellite. Ilan had reentered Emerson's life a month after he and Laura Shaze had called it quits, but had only remained for a year. In light of the miserable conditions aliens had been forced into by Earth's xenophobic lawmakers, he didn't blame her for abandoning him a second time.

Emerson had just endured a week of meetings with the Senate Appropriations Committee, hammering out a budget for improvements to Fokker Aerospace, and had decided that a dose of wilderness would return him to sanity. But his plans had been thrown a curve by a phone call he had received at home on Friday afternoon. Major General Nigel Aldershot wondered if Emerson wouldn't meet with him in Monument City on Saturday morning to discuss a matter of great importance. No, not at the general's office, or at Emerson's either, but in town. If Emerson would check his e-mail, he would find the address of the place.

It had all sounded needlessly mysterious, but Emerson couldn't very well refuse the request. Aldershot was an old friend, in addition to being one of the living legends who had flown against the Zentraedi from the launch bays of SDF-1. Emerson suspected that the meeting had something to do with the Senate's recent passage of a bill that created a Special Oversight Committee on Military Deployment. The politically appointed members of the committee would be responsible for assessing proposed intervention by the EDF in territorial disputes among non-allied nations. The bill was in direct response to May's confrontation in Venezuela, in which factions within the Defense Force had fought one another. But while the bill granted the committee authority to override Commander Leonard's deployment decisions, few thought it likely that the veto would ever be exercised.

So Emerson was headed into Monument City. Aldershot had made a point of stressing the "informality" of the gathering, which Emerson had understood to mean no uniforms, no chauffeured cars, no entourage. So he was piloting the family solar, heavily dented along the left side from an encounter Dana had had with a moose, of all things. Their log-and-stone home—once the property of General Gunther Reinhardt—was nestled in a wooded valley about fifteen miles east of the city. Elsewhere, trees were something of a rarity. The northwest had enjoyed a short fling with fertility early in the decade, but a blight had since denuded the immediate environs of Monument, and the disease had been followed by a drought that had yet to end. It had gotten so bad that water was being flown, trucked, and piped in from the north of Canada.

There had been changes to the city as well. The Zentraedi battlewagon that had once risen spikelike from Monument's artificial lake had been cut apart and removed, putting a symbolic finish to "foreign" influence in a city that had been founded by Zentraedi. And of course there were the new and somewhat medieval-looking headquarters of the UEG and the Earth Defense Force, along with sundry substructures given over to the Tactical Armored Corps and Civil Defense. Even Fokker Aerospace had seen changes since the formation of the Cosmic Units, whose bases included the lunar bright-side facility at Aluce, the orbital platforms, and Space Station Liberty, in stationary orbit on the far side of the moon.

At nearby Macross, radiation readings had finally subsided to acceptable levels, and Monumenters frequently traveled to the overlook to gaze at the three Humanmade buttes that marked the resting places of the SDFs 1 and 2 and the cruiser Khyron the Backstabber had wielded. Emerson had made the pilgrimage with Dana and Bowie, whose Aunt Claudia had died aboard the SDF-1. The view had put Emerson in mind of a site in central Mexico where a city had been buried by the lava flow from a volcano that had literally grown out of a cornfield. There, amid a landscape of porous black boulders, only the steeple of a church had been visible.

Central Monument had begun as a copse of alloy-and-permaplex milk-carton highrises, and had gradually blossomed into a full-fledged metropolis, with building clusters rising on both the east and west banks of the river. Of all the Northlands' new crop of urban sprawls, it most resembled Macross in the days before its demise. From a distance, the city looked healthy and prosperous. What wasn't immediately apparent, however, was the murky darkness of its narrow streets, the shabby construction of the Quickform buildings, and the palpable sense of apprehension and uncertainty.

Driven out by vicious bigotry, the last of the Zentraedi had left the previous year, only to be replaced by thousands of indigent homesteaders who had been eking out an existence on the Plains. Assailed by droughts, floods, the eruption of two volcanos in Mexico, an earthquake in the West, and hurricanes in the south, the homesteaders suddenly had nowhere to turn to but Monument, Denver, and Portland. For a time, it was easy to believe that Earth was out to extinguish all life—or at least to make itself unfit for habitation by Humans, Zentraedi, Robotech Masters, Invid, or any other allegedly intelligent species with designs on the place. Some saw the storms and upheavals as the planet's delayed shock reaction to the ravaging it had suffered from Dolza and the Grand Fleet.

The place Aldershot had selected for the meet was in Monument's Gauntlet district, an inner-city pink zone where criminality was condoned and illicit goods were readily available: prostitutes, outlawed technology, designer drugs, violent contest. The Gauntlet served as a kind of proving ground for experimental pleasures, weapons, and cyberware escaped from research labs as near as those in Denver's "Protoculture Valley" or as distant as SPOOK.

Monument's police force didn't bother trying to control the flow of goods or the rivalries of the gangs, many of which had drifted north from Freetown, in Mexico, after the eruptions. The city's privileged denizens viewed the Gauntlet as a necessity of sorts—escape for the lumpen populace from the brutal realities of the everyday life. And perhaps that explained why the orphaned generation was so taken with the place. It appealed to the more nihilistic-leaning of Dana and Bowie's peers, with their taste for Zentraedi-inspired, body-hugging clothing and discordant music, their easy acceptance of violence, and their rabid fascination with EVE, who wasn't even a flesh-and-blood celebrity but a telepresence—a ghostly, digitally created Holy Mother–cum–Big Sister. The Gauntlet, and like enclaves of sanctioned self-destruction in Tokyo, Portland, and Paris, seemed to be the flip side of the Southland's Earth-First People's Army.

When, as per Aldershot's instructions, Emerson had searched his e-mail for the rendezvous site, he had found a listing of weekend events. But on closer inspection he had spotted, under brunch options, an ad for a restaurant called CUTE MEAT.

The eatery was located in a Gauntlet alley, tucked between a piercing parlor and a virtual-travel agency. Emerson eased in through beaded curtains and was halfway to the sushi bar when he was intercepted by a burly man he recognized as one of Aldershot's staff officers, the civvies notwithstanding. The officer touched his hand to his forehead in subtle salute and directed

Emerson to a blood-red doorway in the rear wall of the room.

Crowded around a circular table in a poorly lighted private dining area sat Aldershot and several other officers, all of them former members of the RDF. At the table's eight o'clock position was Evan Tannen, whose ex-RDF forces had taken on Laubin's Southern Cross contingent in what was supposed to have been a peacekeeping operation in Cavern City. Tannen and Laubin had gone to guns, but, in the end, the People's Army had pulled back to regroup, then struck off in the direction of the unfortified city of Roca Negra.

Emerson shook hands all around while the burly officer brought a chair for him.

"Nothing said here leaves this room," Aldershot announced straightaway. "It's been swept three times and sanitized top to bottom."

"Why the precautions, Nigel?"

"We'd rather the Oversight Committee on Deployment didn't get wind."

"I figured," Emerson told him. "But, for what it's worth, I support the aims of the committee. We can't have the EDF involved in every low-intensity situation that arises. And we certainly can't afford to have the Defense Force shooting itself in the foot every time it's assigned a mission." Emerson glanced at Tannen. "Not if we want to present a unified front to the Masters."

"If and when they show up," Tannen grumbled.

Aldershot was fingering his waxed mustache. "We agree with you about the committee, Rolf. In theory, it seems a reasonable idea to grant veto power to someone other than Chairman Moran. Our problem with it is that the majority of candidates suggested for committee membership have strong ties to the Southern Cross apparat."

"There hasn't been a Southern Cross apparat for nine years."

Aldershot lifted a bushy eyebrow. "I don't think you believe that for a minute. The Southern Cross might not exist as a titled entity, but everyone here knows it exists. Moran, Leonard, Zand ... each one of them is carefully positioned to influence the UEG, the EDF, and the Protoculture-research community. All thanks to T. R. Edwards. Admiral Hunter and the rest were too busy with the SDF-3 to realize what Edwards was setting in motion. Now, with control of the Oversight Committee, Leonard will be able to choose who goes where, and with what mecha. And before we know it, the 'disbanded' Southern Cross will be too powerful to counter."

"Against what, exactly?" Emerson asked.

"Ridding the Defense Force of all Robotech Defenders."

Rolf shook his head. "I haven't seen evidence of a calculated effort to wipe out the RDF. Besides, it's plain that Leonard doesn't need to engineer anything—not when the EDF is so adept at engineering its own catastrophes."

Aldershot was silent for a few seconds. "I was hoping you would drop your guard and speak to us as a confederate and not as a politician." He paused again. "Do you want to talk about the Giles Academy, Rolf?"

Emerson didn't. But he couldn't help thinking about it.

For a brief period in 2025, the Giles Academy had existed as an exclusive training facility for would-be Veritech pilots. But in fact the academy had been a front for a clandestine operation to sabotage flights of experimental RDF mecha, via remote control, by a select group of Giles-trained cyberpirates. Emerson had detected the hand of Anatole Leonard in the conspiracy and had sent Dana Sterling, then thirteen years old, to investigate the goings-on. Afterward, he had tasked an RDF lieutenant named Terry Weston with exposing the operation. Weston had succeeded, but Giles had either committed suicide or been murdered, and Leonard had escaped implication.

Dana and the ruggedly handsome—and much older—Weston had kept in touch after the penetration, and Emerson had always suspected that they had become lovers. Dana wouldn't say. But there had been no more talking to imaginary friends after Weston had entered her life. As for Weston, the last Emerson heard he was living in Tokyo.

"We just want to know where you stand, Rolf," Aldershot said, sparing Emerson the need to rehash the details of the covert operation he had mounted against Giles. "Everyone at this table is well aware of your past—in Sydney during the Reconstruction and in the Argentine during the Uprisings. But, frankly, your years of service as liaison between the RDF and the Southern Cross have left some of us a bit confused as to your present loyalties."

Emerson bridled. "My loyalties are to the Ministry of Terrestrial Defense and the EDF, and I refuse to contribute to increased factionalism. You people know damn well what Reinhardt and Hunter expect of us. Defending the Earth has to come before defending any parochial interests of the RDF."

"I don't think Reinhardt and Hunter gave a thought to what might occur in the absence of the SDF-3,"

Aldershot argued. "They assumed they'd be back within a year or two, and that they could straighten out any problems that had cropped up between the Southern Cross and the RDF. They didn't want to deal with the rivalry issue then, out of fear that a confrontation would delay the launch of the Expeditionary mission."

"And who knows what's become of that ship," Colonel Tannen interjected. "We may never hear from it again. Or from the Robotech Masters."

Aldershot studied Emerson. "It's time to begin thinking about the future, Rolf, and to concentrate on who the real enemy is."

Emerson held Aldershot's gaze. "Meaning what?"

"As things stand, units of the RDF are still well placed. We're strong in Monument and on Fokker Base, and we're at parity with Southern Cross contingents on Aluce and the weapons platforms. And, really, we're only talking about three principal targets: the Senate Hall, Leonard's wing at EDF headquarters, and the Chairman's Palace. It's just a matter of coordinating the timing."

Emerson considered Aldershot's words, then sat back from the table, stunned. "You got me here to talk about staging a goddamned *coup*."

In the Kabukicho apartment she shared with Census, Discount, and Gibley, whom they called Hongo, Misa Yoshida paced nervously while Hongo did what he could to ease Census's distress.

"Is he going to be all right?" Misa stopped to ask, nibbling at a fingernail.

Hongo glanced at her, sighing dramatically. "Standard Zand attack. Blinds you for a while and leaves you with one hell of a headache. But nothing untreatable."

With herbs, he meant, most of them mildly euphoric. Thriving right there under grow lights in a corner of the six-mat room.

Census, making moaning sounds, was lying on his back on the tatami, one arm thrown over his eyes, his long black hair configured in a ridiculous pompadour. His interactive goggles—a brand-new pair of All-Seeing Eyes—were beside him, inert by the milky look of the elongated lenses. The control deck itself, which Misa thought she had heard sizzle when the pirated data was coming through, was still on the table, but the apartment smelled of fried microcircuits or something.

Where Census had been pale a few moments earlier, he was flushed now, his round face looking like he'd suffered an allergic reaction to shellfish or bee stings. Hongo was fanning him with a coffee-stained faux-paper manual that had come with the pricy, ubertech control deck. Kneeling, Discount was proffering a container of citrus juice he'd run in from one of the lobby vending machines. Unlike some, the ones in their building didn't deliver.

When Census raised himself on his elbows and blinked, Hongo cut his spectacled blue eyes to Misa. "You heard me warn him this could happen."

Misa frowned at him. Hongo would know; he had once been employed by the facility Census had just tried to invade. But that had been years ago, before the name had been changed from the Robotech Research Center to the Special Protoculture Observations and Operations Kommandatura. "You warned him, Hongo, but I didn't see you try to stop him."

"Did we get anything?" Census managed to ask between groans.

Discount handed him the juice drink and hurried over to the printer.

"Doubt it's anything we can sell," Hongo commented.

As if sticking out its tongue at them, the printer had extruded a single sheet of hardcopy. Discount eased the sheet free of the machine's gentle grasp and perused it.

Squinting, Census stared in the direction of the printer. "Well?"

"A listing of EVE's guests for the coming week," Discount told him. He cursed, balled up the sheet, and threw it toward the sliding screen, which Census had tagged with the names of his favorite *manga* heroes.

Census exhaled loudly, but Hongo merely chuckled to himself. Misa wanted to smash both their faces.

EVE herself, audio muted, was running on their pathetic excuse for a telecomp, where, before Census had been knocked to the floor, she had been indulging in the usual cheerful futurecasting. How everything was going to be rosy when the SDF-3 returned, but until then Earth had to be ready to defend itself against attacks by the Masters—those evil Zentraedi-makers. And how the subsurface shelters in Tokyo weren't such awful places once you got used to them, and how people should always respect and comply with the drills and the commands of the *omawari*—the police—who had the people's safety in mind. Most of all, how Tokyo was a lot better off than most other cities, because if an attack did come, it would be Tokyo's fortunate citizens who would emerge unscathed from the shelters and underground malls to rebuild the world—like the people of SDF-1 Macross had done after the Rain of Death. In fact, Tokyo should be thought of as the new Macross,

EVE often said, and Earth as Tokyo's dimensional fortress—Tokyo's *Yamato*.

EVE was a ravishingly beautiful e-specter of mixed ethnicity. Her dark eyes were ever so slightly epicanthic; her nose was ever so slightly wide; her lips were ever so slightly full; her complexion was a shade past olive. Her height and proportions tended to vary, depending on whether she was alone or hosting guests—live or comp-generated. Of course, her creators could have written her any way they wanted. But—according to Gibley, at least—research into the psychodynamics of the orphaned generation had ordained what EVE should look like. Not too sexy, not too talented, not too intelligent, either. No *ii-dol talento*, for sure. More like the caring mother lost to a generation.

The world had come a long way since Lynn-Minmei and Janice Em.

EVE took questions from callers and dished out advice, gossip, and propaganda. She was accessed on the Lorelei Network, whose satellites had been used to monitor the movements of Zentraedi Malcontents during the Uprisings twelve years earlier.

Only young kids didn't clutch that EVE was a telepresence; for them she was a combo Santa Claus, Superhero, Tooth Fairy, Easter Bunny, and psychic adviser. But by the time you were eight years old, you clutched she was nothing but digitized data and pixels, birthed by a computer taken from the SDF-1.

Census was coming around now, sitting up and sipping juice. His real name was Shi Ling, and he was Chinese—from Beijing—but his family had been living in Tokyo when the Rain happened. He was good-looking and cut, but, at five eight, kind of short. Even so, he had an inch on Discount, whose real name was anybody's guess, but who was definitely from the Northlands, and who claimed to have seen the SDF-1 in 2011, when he was three and the ship had returned to Earth after spending two years in space. Discount was blond, blue-eyed, and cute when his face wasn't breaking out. Raised in the same communal home, he and Census shared the same last name.

Terms like *gaijin* and *chosen-jin* didn't apply much anymore; Japan was pretty much as multiethnic as anyplace else in the world now. The Rain of Death had seen to that.

Misa was the only *Nihon-jin* among them. Their nickname for her—Miko—meant vestal virgin, but she wasn't religious, and she sure wasn't a virgin. She was tall and shapely and maybe a bit heftier than most of her female peers, but no guy had ever complained about her size. She sometimes thought she could remember her parents, but she wasn't sure.

The three of them had gotten to know each other through the placement agency that assisted in moving teens from the communal homes into real homes, but, more often, shared apartments.

Hongo—Gibley—had come along later. He was eleven years older than Discount, who was thought to be twenty, which made Hongo more a doomsdayer than a member of the orphaned. But age didn't matter all that much for guys with a common interest in high-tech piracy.

"It was dim trying to tap SPOOK through EVE," Discount was saying, a little late, as always. "Calls to EVE are monitored by watchdog programs. You try to pull a fade from the line and the dogs are on your tail that quick. Hacker's hell, Census. Everyone I know who's tried has ended up dazzled by download jolts. Real dim."

"I warned him not to stray," Hongo repeated. "But I guess everybody needs to experience defeat firsthand."

Census was massaging his eyes with the heels of both hands. "I was only looking around in there. How'd I know security was watching me?"

Hongo shook his head in amused disbelief. "Security is what they *do* there, pirate. You think you're dealing with a telephone company or something?"

"We shouldn't even be doing this," Misa said when she'd heard enough.

The three regarded her like she was some XT specimen.

"I mean, we shouldn't be stealing and selling information. You guys have strong enough *mecha* to get jobs as software writers, and instead you're risking your . . . your *minds*, for secrets you half the time can't even sell."

"Oh, 'zat right?" Census said, thinking he was looking right at her when he wasn't. "Notice you didn't refuse the skirt I paid for outta the deal we made with that yak."

Yak was short for *yakuza*, which had once referred to *Nihon-jin* gangsters but now meant just about anybody wedded to a criminal tribe and hot to profit. "I never asked for that skirt," she said defensively.

"*Chu-gen*, Miko," he said with a mocking smile. "Christmas in July."

She stiffened but said nothing. She and Census were supposed to be love interests, but they had frequent gorounds, especially about buying things. She would accuse him of being *nowie*—hungry for hip—and he'd reply that if she was so correct and Earth First, why didn't she just run off to the Southlands and enlist in the People's Army? The arguments reflected the difference in the philosophies of the communal homes they'd been raised in. But the real problem was that she was push-pull about having and not having. Plus, Census was something of a *freeter*, which translated as "womanizer" the way Misa used it.

She could get with the idea that the boys liked their toys, but each acquisition, each possession, only had them working harder to score. As things stood, Misa, Census, and Discount each received an orphan allowance from the Ministry of Human Services in exchange for working in the shelters, the homes, the hospitals, or just about anywhere else they were needed. The three allowances combined were enough to cover food and the rent on the apartment and the tiny telecomp, but never much more than that. Most of the furniture in the place—from futons to the bathtub—had come from midnight raids on the geo-grid's rubbish heaps.

That was why the guys had turned their dubious *ki/bushido* talents with control decks and network-interactive goggles to rifling computer databanks for salable information. SPOOK, home of the SDF-1 computer, was of course the mother of databanks; not only did EVE originate there, but so did most of the vision papers that eventually found their way to the Chairman's Palace or to EDF headquarters in Monument City.

Not everyone knew that the SDF-1 computer was actually right there in Tokyo; most novice data pirates thought the system was in Monument or even inboard the factory satellite. The satellite was the abode of giants, kids were told; they could be seen at night, gazing up at the thing as if it were the castle Jack had climbed to by beanstalk. But then, not every data pirate had a roommate like Gibley. He'd even met Dr. Emil Lang once. But after Zand had assumed control of SPOOK, the whole cyber department had been fired, and Gibley had been sore about it ever since. Legend had it that he'd fallen in with some acid-head posse after the layoff and had eaten nothing but psychedelic mushrooms for two years. Which was how he had come by the nickname Hongo.

He was grinning at Misa just now. He was so tall, gangly, and gawky that fellow bathers in the *ofuro* would often stare at him as openly as they did any tattooed Modern Youth or horribly scarred or limbless survivor of the Rain. "Misa, think what it would mean for all of us if we *could* penetrate SPOOK."

"Yeah—more headaches," she told him, slipping into her clogs and storming from the room.

CHAPTER FOUR

*It is astonishing that Zand was able to learn as much as he did
[about Zor] in the short time that the SDF-1's mother computer
was operational—from January through October, 2029. What dis-
tinguishes Zand's contribution is the fact that his meticulous recordings of his sessions with the computer offer glimpses of the
Tiresian as he was in the year before his death, when even Cabell,
our primary historical source, was estranged from him. Had I not
been fortunate enough to be one of the first to enter Zand's compound near Monument City in the concluding moments of the Second Robotech War, these incredible documents would have been
lost to the explosion that obliterated his laboratory.*

Louis Nichols, from the introduction to his
BeeZee: The Galaxy Before Zor

IN THE COMMAND CENTER OF THE ALIEN FLEET'S FLAG-
ship, the Master Dag sent to Myzex, "Would we prevail
in a direct engagement?"

"Only if it was brief and surgical," the military adviser stated flatly. "A protracted, all-inclusive war on
the planet would deplete the fleet of Protoculture in a
matter of months. Moreover, the Earthers have had ample time to prepare for our arrival, and ample supplies
of Protoculture to fuel their battle mecha."

Exchanges of late between the Masters and the leaders of the sundry triumvirates had taken on the repeti-
tive nature of a litany. But Bowkaz suddenly broke with

convention by addressing the Clonemaster leader, Jeddar. "Suppose we brought our Triumviroid weapons to bear on Earth."

Jeddar considered the question. The most powerful in the Masters' arsenal, the clone-piloted Triumviroid fighting machine system had been developed rather recently—by their stagnated standards—and incorporated certain characteristics of the savage Invid. Costly to produce and engineered of mismatched horn, chitin, and sinew, the Triumviroids were high-energy spined spheres that looked as much biological as Robotechnological.

"Well?" Bowkaz asked after only a moment had elapsed.

The Clonemaster kowtowed. "M'lords, the Triumviroids were created primarily for intra-atmospheric contest. Thus, we would be required to insert our ships into orbit, or, better still, to make planetfall, which presupposes the launch of a comprehensive invasion. I submit that the Invid Fighters should be reserved to supply tactical support."

The Masters conversed in mindspeak; then Shaizan spoke aloud. "Perhaps we can make use of the Zor clone to fix the location of the fortress and the matrix."

Myzex responded. "That, too, presupposes a fullscale invasion of Earth. Unless you have sufficient confidence in the clone's loyalty to permit him to be surreptitiously inserted on the surface by a single, small ship."

The Masters kept their thoughts to themselves.

Of the twenty clones sprung from tissue samples taken from Zor's body upon its return to Tirol, only one had made the trip to the Solar system. The rest had either succumbed to experiments in accelerated development performed on Tirol or been left to expire in the stasis chamber that was their communal environment. All twenty had been grown in biovats, and all were possessed of their donor's elfin handsomeness. Only one, however, had been given the chance to grow naturally into a facsimile of the original Zor; but even that clone had yet to reveal evidence that the brilliance of the donor had been passed undiluted to its offspring. This was despite an upbringing that mirrored Zor's own to the greatest extent possible: the emotional deprivation, the surfeit of material luxuries, the seclusion from his peers, the forced feeding of scientific knowledge.

Zor Prime, as the Masters referred to him, had somehow matured into a more physically oriented being than his father/sibling, evincing an interest in the design of combat mecha and the contemptible companionship of the soldier-clones that operated them. Chagrined by the course the clone had taken, the Masters conceded that they had erred in underestimating the influence that Zor's mentor, Cabell, had had on his student. The wizardlike Cabell had been left behind in Tiresia to ease the Elders' burden of having to govern Tirol's non-clone population.

We must wait for the Elders to advise us, Shaizan sent at last.

Normally, the sending would have ended the session, but just then a radiance blossomed in the command center, close to where the Masters hovered at their Protoculture Cap. The radiance unfolded like the time-lapse roiling of a storm cloud until it was fifteen feet in diameter and had taken on the sapphire tint typical of a transsignal sphere. The sphere threw forth a brilliance that splashed off the keen, hawked-nosed faces of the Masters; inside it, enthroned in a circle around an identical Cap, sat the three Elders, Nimuul, Fallagar, and Hepsis.

Like their far younger counterparts, they were dressed in regal robes, though they looked less like monks than executioners. All had shaven pates, wide sideburns, and straight, fine hair. Under their sharp cheekbones were scarlike creases of skin, suggestive of tribal markings.

The Masters and the leaders of the triumvirates kowtowed. "We have long awaited audience, Elders," Shaizan said aloud. "That you now grace us with an appearance restores our faith in the expedition and in the future."

The words sounded sincere, but Shaizan's thoughts were troubled; mind-linked to him, Dag and Bowkaz understood why. The Elders weren't communicating from Tirol or from the surface of any world, known or unknown. The commo sphere showed just enough of the Elders' immediate surroundings to reveal that they were aboard a starship—and scarcely a ship, at that. Shaizan recognized it as the prototype a Scientist triumvirate had been working on when word of the Zentraedi defeat had first reached Tirol. The vessel was scarcely larger than the assault ships that carried the Masters' bioroids into combat.

In a disembodied voice as thick as syrup Nimuul said, "Your respect is well received, Shaizan, for we have events to relate that may cast a pall on the confidence our appearance has unjustly inspired."

And with that he began to recount what had happened on Tirol four Earth years earlier: an Invid swarm led by the Regent had conquered the planet.

Prior to the actual invasion, the Elders and an entourage of subalterns had indeed taken flight aboard the prototype ship, leaving Tirol's aboriginal population, backed by a battalion of bioroids, to fend for itself. The scientist Cabell and his young assistant Rem had been left behind. However, just when death at the hands of the Flower-hungry Invid seemed inevitable, Cabell and Rem had been rescued by a detachment of humanoid fighters, who had arrived in the Valivarre system aboard a purposely modified Zentraedi ship. It was Breetai's flagship, in fact, remodeled to resemble Zor's fortress, and commanded by none other than an alliance of Zentraedi and members of the army that had vanquished the Grand Fleet.

Earthers, in other words. In league with Breetai, Exedore, and some hundred other giants.

On receiving this news, the Masters' consternation was absolute. Had they journeyed for eighteen years only to learn that the object of their quest had been returned to Tirol?

No, the Elders assured them. The Earthers did not have the Protoculture matrix. The Elders were certain of this because the ship, while Protoculture-driven, had been crippled by Invid plasma fire and was unable to execute a fold. But the humans had had firepower enough to rout the Invid and liberate Tirol.

Then an even more curious event had occurred: the Earthers had joined forces with a ragtag group of former prisoners of the Invid, who called themselves the Sentinels. The band was comprised of Karbarrans, Praxians, Garudans, even a few Perytonians. And together the two forces had carried the fight to a host of Near Group worlds, liberating Karbarra and Garuda and ending the curse that had plagued Peryton since the time of Haydon. As a result of the Invid Queen's meddlings in self-generated evolution, Praxis had been destroyed. And something or someone had stirred the Awareness on Haydon IV. But, more importantly, the Sentinels had begun to move on Optera itself. A schism seemed to have taken place among the Earth forces, but it was clear that both sides were anxious to eradicate the Invid.

It was doubtful that Earth's population was aware of the Masters' journey. But cognizant of the fact that the flotilla of space fortresses was closing on their homeworld, the Earthers on Tirol had dispatched two battleships, though they wouldn't manifest in the Sol system for another three Earth years.

The Elders had learned all this by watching from various places of concealment, much as the Masters had been doing for the past few months. Just now—relatively speaking—the Elders' ship was concealed behind a moon of the T'zuptum system's fourth planet.

"Elders," Bowkaz said, "we must act quickly if we are to retake the matrix. If the matrix has been damaged and the contained Flowers have gone to seed, their presence will be detected by an Invid Sensor Nebula and the swarm will descend on Earth."

"Quickly but not rashly," Nimuul told him. Centuries of direct exposure to Protoculture had given his voice an eerie quavering. "First, we must await the cleansing of the Near Group worlds. Then, when the matrix is repossessed, we can return to Tirol without having to fear attacks from the Invid. Replenished and rearmed, we will rid the Valivarre system of Earthers and Zentraedi and turn to the task of reunifying our empire."

"We understand, Elders," Shaizan said, answering for the trio.

Hepsis nodded. "Now, tell us what you have observed thus far."

Dag spoke of the progress they had made in deciphering Earth's myriad of languages and of monitoring its steady stream of electronically generated noise.

"Transsignal all the data you have collected," Hepsis ordered.

"It shall be yours," the Masters responded in unison.

Dag also spoke of Earth's orbital defenses, the presence of the captured Robotech factory satellite, and the salvage operation that had been observed.

"All well and good," Hepsis said, "but have you learned the location of Zor's fortress?"

Shaizan confessed that they hadn't. "The fortress could be lying in wait on the planet, or it might have been disabled and abandoned."

"And the matrix?" Fallagar asked.

"With the ship, we presume."

The Elders deliberated for a moment. When Fallagar spoke again, his tone was blunt. "Have you given thought to attempting to establish contact with the ship?"

Shaizan glanced at his comrades. "How, Elders?"

"Through the computer Zor designed to function as his second self. No doubt you possess the necessary decryption codes." Fallagar seemed to lean forward from the commo sphere. "Surely you've succeeded in prying that much information from the clone's cellular memory."

"No doubt," Shaizan said quietly.

"Then reposition the fleet closer to the planet," Nimuul instructed. "Determine a way to reach out to Zor's machine without betraying yourselves or otherwise engaging the enemy."

Leonard handed Emerson a snifter of brandy, then settled back into the overstuffed couch with a glass of spring water in hand. "To creative solutions," the commander said, raising the glass.

The two men were in Leonard's riverside home a few miles south of downtown Monument. It was a rambling, turn-of-the-century estate, filled with massive pieces of wooden furniture and twentieth-century bric-a-brac. Dogs patrolled the manicured grounds; EDF sentries were posted at the gate.

Figuring he was going to need it, Emerson took a good-sized gulp of the brandy, peering at the bearish Leonard over the rim of the snifter.

Leonard set his drink down on a glass-topped table. "Rolf, I know we've had our differences over the years, but that's never stopped us from being open and honest with one another. Can we be open and honest now?"

"About what, Commander?"

"About the feuds that are plaguing our military. Chairman Moran is too busy kissing babies and attending state functions to grasp the seriousness of the situation. So I thought you and I better put our heads together and arrive at some strategy to nip this thing in the bud."

"It's already beyond the bud stage," Emerson said.

"All the more reason for us to hammer out a plan."

Emerson swirled the brandy and took another gulp, holding it in his mouth for a moment before swallowing it. "You should really be talking to Major General Aldershot, not me."

Leonard's ham-sized hands motioned dismissively. "I've never seen eye to eye with Aldershot. I've never trusted his judgment. Because he served on the SDF-1, we're all supposed to think he has an inner line on the enemy, when in fact he doesn't know any more about the Masters than the rest of us. And as for terrestrial combat experience, not even an SDFer can hold a candle to we Southlanders."

Emerson responded with a halfhearted nod. Of the two of them, only Leonard was the true Southlander, having been born in Argentina. Emerson had come to the Argentine from Sydney, Australia, and had served as an officer with the RDF South before being promoted to commander of the Argentine base. After the base had been closed and the Argentine ceded to the Southlands, he had acted as liaison between the RDF and Leonard's burgeoning Army of the Southern Cross, which was then restricted to Brazil's southeastern territories. Leonard, appointed governor of Brasília, the territorial capital, had lived like a king in a lakeside palace that had its own chapel.

"Commander, I'm a politician now," Emerson felt required to point out. "I don't see how—"

Leonard interrupted him. "What would you say to our having Zand author another communication from the SDF-3? As a means of reunifying the EDF, of course—and affording some hope to everyone else. We could write the message together, Rolf."

Emerson looked at the floor, asking himself what Leonard was up to. "I'd like nothing better than to give everyone hope. But I'm not in favor of giving them false hope." He lifted his eyes. "I voted against falsifying the earlier communiqués, and I'd do the same now. Disinformation is the ploy politicians have been using since the Global Civil War. For Alphonse Russo, the SDF-1 was simply a means to an end—an object he could get everyone to perceive as a threat—"

"And he was correct," Leonard said forcefully. "The aliens who sent that ship *did* arrive to claim it. And we could be correct in making use of the SDF-3, Rolf. For all anyone knows, the Tirol mission succeeded in establishing terms for an accord with the Masters, and has simply been delayed in returning to Earth. That's all we'd need to say in our message."

Emerson was shaking his head, masking his suspicion. "If they were successful, they would have already returned. What problems could have arisen that the Masters couldn't have helped them overcome? Exedore assured us that the Masters had a fleet of fold-capable ships."

Leonard narrowed his eyes, then softened his expression. "Look, Rolf, neither of us is a scientist. Maybe the problem didn't occur until after the SDF-3 folded from Tirol. The ship could be stranded between dimensions or in some star system billions of light-years from Earth."

Emerson said nothing. Worldwide, people had been debating just that point for nine years.

Leonard went on. "By the same token, if the mission was unsuccessful and the Expeditionary Force was defeated, where is that fleet of fold-capable ships Exedore kept warning us about? Why haven't the Masters arrived to reclaim the SDF-1 or exact revenge on the planetary race that humbled their clone army?"

Emerson's lips made a thin line. "I don't know the answer to that. Maybe the Masters have been monitoring us, and are planning to strike when we appear weakest."

Leonard spread his arms wide in a gesture of endorsement. "Perhaps our message should say just that: the Masters are on their way. If that doesn't unite everyone . . ."

"And what if the SDF-3 returns the week after we've issued that message? There's no way we could keep what we did secret. Think about how our tactics are going to be viewed. No one will see these messages as our attempt to foster harmony in the EDF. We'll stand accused of having manipulated world opinion to serve our own ends. Are you seriously willing to take that risk?"

Leonard was quiet for a long moment. "You're very smart, Rolf." He stared at Emerson. "I'm genuinely moved by your sudden concern for my military career and my place in history. But I can't help but wonder about it. I mean, I know that we've never agreed on policy regarding the Zentraedi. You blame me for chasing them offworld, don't you?"

Emerson thought about Ilan Tinari. And about Rico, Konda, Bron, and the dozens of other aliens who had become his friends while they had lived downside. And he thought about Leonard the xenophobe, who had ordered the massacre of a thousand Zentraedi in Brasília, who had destroyed Cairo and battled the Malcontents throughout the Southlands, who himself had gone to guns with the RDF in Cavern City during Jonathan Wolff's stint as commander, setting the stage for ten years of bitter infighting among the EDF.

The same Leonard who, while governor of Brasília, was rumored to have taken a Zentraedi female as a lover. Emerson had once tried to pry the truth from Leonard's adjutant, Joseph Petrie, but to no avail. Petrie had resigned his commission in the Southern Cross to become a partner in the Giles Academy—under Leonard's orders to do so, no doubt, though Emerson had never been able to prove it. The academy's cyberexperiments in remote control had resulted in a fatality: a young VT pilot named Amy Pollard, who had been Terry Weston's fiancée at the time. As for Joseph Petrie, he had become as elusive a figure as Lazlo Zand.

But Emerson had no desire to rehash everything now.

"The Zentraedi would have relocated aboard the factory satellite anyway," he mumbled at last.

"Yes, yes, perhaps you're right." Leonard regarded him broodingly from the huge couch. "I just want to make sure there's no bad blood between us."

"There's no bad blood."

"Then you'd tell me if you were aware of any rumblings of discontent?"

Emerson managed to field the question without betraying himself. "From what quarter, Commander?"

"Aldershot's. The RDF club."

"That's not a fair question," Emerson said angrily.

Leonard made a placating gesture. "Let me explain myself. The creation of this Oversight Committee on Deployment is a good thing for everyone involved, and I'd hate to see it jeopardized by the actions of a few disgruntled officers. I know it's been suggested that the appointees are all beholden to me in one fashion or another, but I want to assure you, Rolf, that I won't abuse my seeming advantage. Besides, it's clear that the Masters will center on Monument, if and when they arrive, so why should we be sending the EDF out to settle territorial disputes in Asia and the Southlands? Let them deal with their own turmoil. If it's city-states and polities they want, so be it."

Emerson shook his head in disagreement. "We'll only be drawn into it eventually. Local disputes will escalate, and what happens in one place will affect the whole. We won't be able to marshal a unified defense against the Masters if we're preoccupied being peacekeepers on our own planet." He glanced at Leonard. "Maybe that's what the Masters are waiting for."

"Then how do you propose we take care of the world

without creating an environment for incidents like the one in Venezuela?"

"I don't know that there is a solution. Southern Crossers outnumber Robotechs three, sometimes four to one. I don't see any way of being equitable without ending up showing favoritism to the minority."

Leonard was smiling. "That's what I've always respected about you—your candor and your integrity."

"Commander, we both want what's best for the EDF."

Leonard wagged his head in triumph. "That being the case, Rolf, *can* I count on you to report any rumors of insurrection?"

Emerson forced a weary exhale. He sometimes wished that he had enlisted in the REF and launched for Tirol with Hunter, Hayes, and Reinhardt. Ironically, the Sterlings had eliminated that option when they'd asked him to be Dana's guardian. Then Bowie's parents had asked the same of him. Dana and Bowie were the ones he wanted to be with just now. He wanted to be home. Away from Anatole Leonard.

"Give me some time to think about it," he said at last.

Leonard folded his arms across his massive chest. "Take as long as you need."

Tugging at his stubbled chin, Lazlo Zand eyed the Zor holo in vexed contemplation. The topic of the evening's session—a gentle interrogation, Zand called it—was the Protoculture matrix Zor had filched from the Masters and hidden aboard his dimensional fortress. But the machine was being evasive, and Zand was determined to know the reason.

In a notebook Zand kept in a voice-locked drawer in his office desk were stored the six hundred e-pages of his "Notes Toward a History of Tirol as Revealed in the

Biography of Zor." The notes reflected the hours of gentle interrogation the SDF-1's computer had undergone in the months since it had been made whole again by the addition of its long-absent components. Many of the files contained unedited recordings, in Zentraedi, of the Zor holo's monologues; other sections incorporated summaries of Lang's research notes on Protoculture and Zand's own research into the Shapings. Zor's personal history had not been delivered in chronological sequence, but in random bits. Zand, however, had tasked the computer with assembling the entries into chapters of a sort, covering everything from the minutiae of Zor's everyday life to the Grand Transition in Tiresian Society.

And quite a life it had been.

To have heard Exedore or Breetai recount it, Zor was superhuman—not merely the discoverer of Protoculture and the founder of Robotechnology, but in some sense the father of the Zentraedi themselves. But the computer, alternating between self-effacement and megalomania, had a different tale to tell: that of an obviously brilliant though flesh-and-blood man born into a civilization of already advanced rank, and well on the path to even greater glories. Zor was not so much the architect of Tirol's lofty pretensions as an agent of unforeseen and radical change. It was Protoculture that was largely responsible for Tirol's turn toward evil.

There was a lesson in this for Zand, though he would choose to disregard it.

Tirol's challenge in the era of Zor's birth and young adulthood—Aeon Lanak—was to discover some means of peacefully imposing its egalitarian dream on its brethren worlds in the local star systems. Consumed with implementing the dream on its own turf, Tirol's leadership had allowed the planet to grow dangerously dependent on those same worlds for energy and goods of all variety. Unless it could expand its reach and influence, Tirol ran the risk of finding itself absorbed into an empire forged by Karbarra, Haydon IV, or some other local world.

Tiresia's Grand Chair, comprising a triad of benevolent despots known as the Elders—could they have felt other than *fated* to profit from the tripartite Flower of Life?—had authorized a search for a new form of usable energy, one that would free Tirol from the economic tyranny of the Near Group worlds. However, the Elders' plan met with opposition from those who felt that Tirol's remaining funds should be invested in currying favor with certain worlds, thereby setting up rivalries that would gradually weaken the power of all and allow Tirol time to emerge from its financial trough. On the scientific side was Zol, who may or may not have been Zor's father—the computer was vague on this point, often implying that Zor was a ward of the state. Nimuul, the most vocal member of the opposition, would eventually ascend to the Grand Chair as one of the Robotech Elders.

In the end, both sides had their way. Even before the deepspace explorer *Aztraph* was launched, plans for the destabilization of the Near Group coalition had already been put into effect. Among the *Aztraph*'s crew, however, was the young genius himself—Zor. And, after years of disappointments, the ship would chance upon a world in the T'zuptum system, from whose gentle interplay of atmospheric gases and fertile surface had emerged the docile, sluglike Invid and the sustaining plant they knew as the Flower of Life.

Events of seemingly operatic proportion had occurred on Optera between Zor and the Invid—events the computer was either reluctant or unable to address. When questioned, the Zor holo had become confused, saddened, and angered, and would reveal only that Zor—convinced that he had at last found a new energy source—had ultimately returned to Tirol with specimens of the Flower.

In Zor's long absence, Tirol had already begun to deteriorate, a victim of its own machinations. By the time the *Aztraph* made planetfall, the world seemed to have been turned upside down: those who had been in positions of authority were now prisoners; those who had been loyal were now seen as traitors; those who had been peaceful were now the fomenters of revolution. Birth itself had given way to engineered creation. And at the helm of a crumbling society sat Nimuul, Hepsis, and Fallagar, the new Elders.

Zor was not oblivious to the reversals, yet he chose to ignore them so as not to jeopardize his research. Or perhaps he thought that the new energy he was about to unleash on Tirol—indeed, on the whole of the Fourth Quadrant—would eradicate all Tirol's social and political ills.

Prior to the *Aztraph*'s launch, another scientist, a Tiresian named Cabell, had been investigating the harnessing of bio-energy, so the Elders were not much impressed when Zor presented his findings to the Grand Chair. But their cursory dismissal only incited him all the more. And within a year of his returning to Tirol, he had succeeded in conjuring Protoculture, that animating enigma soon to guarantee the conquest of worlds and the rise of a near-immortal elite.

So began Aeon Robotech, whose hallmarks were the creation of a millions-strong army of morphable warrior clones, war on a scale never before imagined, the deflowering of Optera, and the eventual transformation of the Invid into a vengeful swarm. Through it all, Zor pretended to be under the influence of a Compulsion, though he was in fact engineering a subtle rebellion against the Elders and their hierarchy of Masters and clone triumvirates. He persuaded the Grand Chair to allow him to construct a dimensional fortress that could be used to locate even greater wonders than the Flower of Life—and into which Zor would secretly transfer the only existing Protoculture matrix.

The Elders weren't aware of what he had carried out until much too late. Zor had been clever to leave them well supplied with Protoculture. And while they luxuriated in their newfound sovereignty, he was out seeding worlds with the Flower—to afford the displaced Invid a fecund garden, it appeared, though Zand suspected a second, less evident purpose as well. Something that had to do with a mysterious being known as Haydon, and an even grander plan in which Tirol, Optera, and Earth were only subordinate players.

"I want to return to our earlier discussion about the matrix," Zand put to the computer now. "You explained how you arranged to have the matrix lofted to your fortress, which was parked above Tirol. But I'm wondering how you managed to conceal its presence from the ship's Zentraedi crew."

The holo, "clothed" in a tight-fitting jumpsuit, smiled in self-amusement. "Neither Dolza nor Breetai knew that the matrix was aboard. But there were several Zentraedi that did know. Much earlier, through the application of music, I had succeeded in corrupting the Imperative that ruled them. They became my confidential agents, assisting not only in the installation of the matrix but in piloting the ship to its secret destination."

Zand steeled himself. "Where onboard did you install the matrix?"

"Among the furnaces that drove the fortress."

Zand tugged at his lower lip. This was in keeping with the accepted wisdom. In fact, Zand could still recall a day fourteen years earlier when he had accompanied Lang on a final tour of the ruined SDF-1—one of the few times Zand had been aboard. Lang had shown him around the vast compartment that housed the Reflex furnaces and Protoculture drives. Lang had theorized that the matrix had gone missing with the fold generators that vanished during the SDF-1's first Human-piloted jump, the one that had sent it to Pluto.

"Was it part of your plan that the fold system would disappear if and when the ship executed a jump?"

"Yes," Zor answered. "The fortress has to remain on Earth."

"Why is that?"

"As the matrix deteriorates, the Protoculture will go to seed and the Flowers will take root. The Invid Sensor Nebulae will detect them and the swarm will come."

"Is Earth to become their world?"

"Only temporarily. Then they will depart."

Zand scratched his head. "But how is this to occur in the absence of the matrix?"

"The matrix didn't go anywhere."

Zand considered it. The computer was probably replying in the abstract. Without the essential element of time, hyperspace couldn't be thought of as having fixed locations—anywheres. Assuming the matrix was in hyperspace.

He suddenly recalled Lang's making a big issue of wanting to know if Zand *felt* anything from the drive compartment—the lingering presence of some then-unseen objects, presumably the fold generators and matrix. Unless . . . unless the device hadn't been concealed in the fold system but *among the Reflex drives themselves*. He was about to put the question to the computer when the holo interrupted him.

"Intrusion alert," Zor said with unusual intensity.

"Don't these hackers ever sleep?" Zand asked, more to himself than to Zor.

"Intrusion. Code Alpha: highest priority."

"Coming right at us, then. All right, let's do it by the numbers: locate the source."

"The source is scrambled and heavily encrypted."

Zand lifted an eyebrow. "Getting clever, are they? Take your best guess."

Mirroring the apprehension rampant in its quantum circuitry, the holo was in agitated motion, clenching its hands and pacing about. "The ship should be reconfigured. The main gun should be armed."

Zand's brow furrowed. Sometimes the damn thing didn't even realize that it had been removed from the ship. But overreaction was something novel. "What good are guns if we haven't located the source?" he said, figuring to play along for a while.

"The source has been fixed."

Numbers scrolled inside the holo field and across several display screens. Zand was baffled. "State the source."

"Approximately five hundred million miles from the present position of Neptune."

"The SDF-3?" Zand asked in sudden misgiving.

The holo shook its head. "The Masters."

CHAPTER
FIVE

My dear colleague, I am growing increasingly concerned about the mores of our young people—this group the media has seen fit to label the orphaned generation. They seem entirely too willing to embrace—or more often shrug off—whatever happens to the world. All this fascination with sex, mind-altering technology, piercing and tattooing . . . They don't demonstrate what I consider to be an appropriate fear for the future. To remedy this, I suggest that we attempt to codify their behavior by fashioning a hero or heroine capable of simultaneously addressing their wants and needs while indoctrinating them in a way that addresses our wants and needs. Give it some thought and get back to me. I am certain that Edwards would approve of the tactic.

Chairman Wyatt Moran in a communiqué to Lazlo Zand,
as quoted in Hopi Bushcraft's *The Two Faces of EVE*

MISA SAUNTERED THROUGH THE KABUKICHO, eyes on the sidewalk, hands stuffed into the pockets of her baggy trousers, with no particular place to go. The weather was typical for early September, hot and sticky, and she was dressed too warmly for it. She had left most of her clean, lightweight stuff back in the apartment when she'd walked out on her cyber-deluded roommates.

Again.

To live aboveground in Tokyo was to be considered one of the expendable. *Okage* was the word for you—

burned rice at the bottom of the cooker—a term that had once applied to women who hung with gay men. Now it referred to society's sacrificial discards. Power, wealth, and permanence resided underground in the geo-grid, which had been the centerpiece of Tokyo's post-Rain reconstruction. Plans for pyramid- and volcano-shaped cities, ultra-highrises, and multifunction polities had been dismissed as the demented fantasies of a bygone age.

Cluttered during the pre-Rain era with structures to house its twenty millions and plagued by traffic snarls that could last for days, Tokyo's surface had been turned over to the needs of industry, and to a Byzantine system of superhighways, along which moved the merchandise that fed the voracious appetite of the underground. Social scientists thought of modern Tokyo as an inverted Disney World, where the maintenance corridors were out in the open and the rides and illusions were hidden from sight. Down below, the world was newly made and pristine; goods and service personnel descended hourly by elevator, to reappear miraculously in shops, hotels, and restaurants. Waste and outmoded items were removed by stealthy squads of sanitation workers and returned to the surface, where they could be trucked to the Dream Archipelago landfill dumps that rose from the bay. Gargantuan factories that had arisen out of the debris of skyscrapers and luxury highrises were free to spew as they would, into skies scoured clean by the annihilation bolts of the Rain. Pollution was no longer a cause for concern. The Earth of 2029 was a world with fewer cars and fewer cows and fewer rice fields to poison the air; a world of fewer people to log trees, plunder the oceans, or demand greater and greater supplies of petroleum derivatives to fuel their machines or fill their lives with plastics. Neither were animal rights a concern; with so many species exterminated by the Rain, it hardly mattered if a few more died off in the process of retooling Human civilization.

You had to be either an avid EVE listener or a member of the People's Army to care about such things. The bulk of Misa's generation had never known a whole Earth, so how could they be expected to feel any real attachment to the notion of Earth First? Orphaned, they'd had no parents or grandparents to tell them otherwise, and they had no one to prove themselves to now. They were entirely free to foul up on their own . . .

At the start of the Global War, the Kabukicho district, west of the Imperial Palace, had been devoted to entertainment of the sexy sort, to the floating life: brothels, peep joints, strip clubs, soaplands, massage parlors, love hotels with rooms no bigger than kingsize coffins. It had been a typical urban haven for perverts, pink traders, gangsters, and artists. Once the City Hall complex had gone up, however, the place had been gentrified, the eroticism tamed—a response, in part, to Japanese families finally learning how to leisure. Goodbye to all-male, all-night drinking sessions, slurred *karaoke*, textbook cases of salaryman *karoshi*—sudden death from overwork. Families were suddenly doing things together, backpacking in Nikko or Chichibu, traveling to foreign lands, frolicking in amusement parks like Tokyo Disney and Seagaia. *"Hi-ho! Hi-ho! Shinpai nai utai tsuzukeyo!"*

Then came the Rain. And now that City Hall, that faux-Edo trio of two-toned granite and glass, was a memory, the Kabukicho had gone back to being what it was good at: a sleazy playground for the disenfranchised.

The reason Misa had been avoiding the apartment for the past few days was because of another blowup with Census and company about their peeking and poking into SPOOK. Fried the first go-round, the interface deck had been crisped as a result of their most recent attempt at riding into Lazlo Zandland on an EVE phone call. Only it was Discount who'd had the goggles on this time, and who was now wearing bandages over both eyes while hooked up to some kind of brain-wave monitor at the free clinic on Yasukuni-Dori.

Misa held Gibley responsible. The onetime-legit cybernaut claimed he'd had a guaranteed way into the heart of the SDF-1 computer, which someone—some former tech also cut from the facility when Zand took over—told him had been restored to mint condition, thanks to the retrieval of a bunch of peripherals that had come down the well to Tanegashima. Misa remembered hearing something about the overdue return of a mission launched back in the teens, but she hadn't tied the news reports to the SDF-1 computer or to SPOOK. She'd figured it was just another shuttle arriving from the factory satellite, or maybe from Space Station Liberty, which was in orbit out past the moon where it couldn't be seen from Earth.

So she and Census had gotten into it again, the issue this time being expenses that were a lot more than their combined allowances could cover—not to pay for Discount's health care, because Human Services provided for that, but to replace the interface deck, natch, and to score more of the black-market programs that afforded the guys access to other think-tank machines. And where was all that NuYen going to come from? Why, from criminal runs into corporate databanks. Which, if everybody wasn't careful, could end up with Tokyo's finest knocking on the screen someday.

It was a dizzy loop, not to mention dangerous, and Misa wanted out. Besides, all the money she'd been secretly pocketing from her allowance to buy some stupid bracelet was going to end up being used to bribe the landlord not to report the pirate run to the fiber-optics commission. Zand's counterattack had not only done Discount, but scrambled the building's FO hookup.

About the bracelet: it was just a strap of black leather, real, and studded with seven silver bears. Okay, you weren't supposed to want stuff like that, or anything more than what President Misui, out of the goodness of his heart, provided for you. You were supposed to eschew envy, trust ability, revere the future; maintain *wa*—harmony—by knowing your life-role and adhering to your place, all the while demonstrating integrity, honesty, goodwill, confidence, and selflessness in every gesture. But a new privileged class had begun to emerge the past five years, and sometimes it was hard to reconcile what you were taught to believe in the collective homes with what you confronted in reality, especially in the underground.

Meandering through the Kab thinking about it, Misa all at once had a destination. Even if she couldn't spree, she could at least go looking.

There was an elevator entrance to the Taisei-Shimizu geo-grid near Shinjuku Station, and she hastened toward it, indifferent to the heat and humidity for the few minutes' walk. Inside the rambling station, she made for one of the glass booths, jumped the detector, and rode thirty stories down into the cool comfort of the underground.

The geo-grid was actually a group of interconnected,

subsurface domes that stretched all the way from the grounds of the Imperial Palace to Big Bird, as Haneda Airport was known—Narita hadn't weathered the Rain. It was something like 4000 square miles of shops, offices, residences, sports complexes, cabarets, wedding chapels, and casinos—*sic bo* and *pai gow*, that year's favorite games. Giant atriums, like the one crowning Shinjuku, provided natural light for video gardens filled with palm trees, and shrines where you could get Shinto priests to execute punch-deck rituals or bestow blessings on just-purchased software or *paso-kon*—personal comps. Elsewhere, fiber optics brought in sunlight through small openings in the grid's ceiling; and throughout, the artificial light was adjusted in color and intensity to reflect different hours of the day. EVE was omnipresent, running on huge screens and checkout-aisle telecomps, as were robots of infinite variety. It was underground that the *robotto okoku*—the robot kingdom—had come true.

Misa had never made a purchase in the grid; invariably she came to gawk. The leather bracelet she'd had her eye on wasn't in a store down here, but in one on a shopping street up in Ueno, wedged between a noodle shop and a tofu place. She gawked at the robots and the kinetic sculptures and fish-stocked ponds, at the sand and stone gardens, at the displays in the Wako and Takashimaya department stores, with their brand-name items by Matsushita and Sony—the Mikimoto pearls, the Comme des Garcons men's suits, the past-century period videos running on the huge, high-def wall-screens.

And mostly she came to enjoy the people show. As she did now, Misa often found herself a bench near the waterfall in her favorite park to watch the career women nibbling at expensive lunches to the strains of chamber music. She saw the retired husbands trailing their wives through exhibitions of bad art—the word for such a man was *nureha*, which meant the wet, fallen leaves of autumn. She watched the kids, just out of school and already hurrying off to their cram courses, and, of course, the Modern Youths, with their tight-fitting war fashions and techno-gadget hair adornments.

It sometimes struck her as unfair that some of her peers should have so many *things*, though she knew it was wrong to think so. It was mostly the kids whose parents had survived the Rain, or those from communal homes who'd been adopted or placed into influential families. Misa found it difficult to imagine having only one set of parents, when there'd been any number of adults she had known as mama-san or dad. She'd seen vids from the time when nearly everyone had had two parents, but she could never connect what she saw onscreen to the world she knew.

In the homes, you had almost nothing that was your own property; you shared everything, even your thoughts. When you wanted privacy, you faced the wall and everybody knew enough not to bother you. But keeping secrets was discouraged. If you were having a problem, or had something on your mind, you were supposed to seek support from the home monitors or from your siblings instead of keeping it inside you. But by the time you were thirteen or so, support usually came down to having sex, and by the time you were maybe fifteen everyone in the home had done one another. Like Eskimos, someone had once told Misa. You could gauge the quality of a communal home by how many people you shared your bed with and how many days a week you had food.

Still on the park bench, misted by the waterfall, Misa gave her eyes a rest from people-watching by studying the robot carp in a nearby pool. Tropical birds were singing from cages hung in some of the palm trees. Off to her right was an enormous video image of Fuji-san in winter, from which wafted a cool breeze and the smell of cypress smoke.

One funny thing was how people before the Rain had convinced themselves that sex, drugs, music, cartoons, and foul language all spelled doom for the world. But nothing about the behavior of teenagers had had anything to do with the coming of the Zentraedi and the Rain of Death. Unless you bought what was being sold by the NeoChristians or the Church of Recurrent Tragedies or Seicho No Ie—the House of Growth.

There were people who still wanted to blame the ills of the world on post-teens like herself and Census and Discount, because they didn't follow the prescribed ways of doing things—dressing, eating, recreating, whatever. The thing was, most of those people had no idea what it felt like to live on the surface. It was easy to know your *honshin*—right heart—when you were eating regularly and shoehorned into outer-space fabrics; then you could follow all the *kata* and stay in synch with society and the cosmos. But a lot of the orphaned had no patience with the approved ways— following *kata* certainly hadn't saved the world from the Zentraedi. No, for them, it was *mono no aware*, the pathos of things, and that was all they subscribed to.

And if the new privileged class really wanted a return to the old world of Japan, Inc.—to the ritual bow and the sociospiritual policies of group harmony, regimentation, cleanliness, extraordinary discipline, and management from the top by an intelligent elite—then why didn't they simply disband the EDF and the People's Army, zero EVE, and invite the Robotech Masters to take control of the planet?

"Fashion dictates that the Modern Youth dresses for action and quick response. Your clothes are stain-resistant, fire-retardant, form-hugging, and equipped with plenty of utility pockets. Your clothes tell the world: *'I am ready to respond!'* Your headband is black, sleek, and looks like a hands-free communications headset. The headband proclaims your easy familiarity and exalted respect for technology; it is your talisman, your totem, your perfect fashion accessory. When the Modern Youth is shopping in the grid, attending a *jidai* about the Robotech War, or enjoying a *teishoku* in a happening eatery, ears are pricked and eyes are peeled for the unexpected. You are strong and capable, the fittest of survivors, and you will prevail over the harshest of adversities. Modern Youth know that the city is the seed of the New World, and that like any seed it must be protected so that it may sprout when the conditions are right. You are nurturing to the city and its inhabitants, below and above ground, because they will be your fellow rebuilders after the transition . . ."

Shaizan, Bowkaz, and Dag, the three Masters, regarded one another in mute bafflement across the mottled surface of the Protoculture Cap. As ordered, they had picked the Zor clone's brain for the encryption codes by which he and his Zentraedi allies had accessed the fortress's command computer. However, the computer's real-time musings were far from what the Masters had expected.

The flawless, female face centered in the commo sphere was dark-complected and pleasant-featured. Her tone of voice was carefully modulated so as to be sooth-ingly didactic. But the strength of the signals was in-consistent and somewhat garbled, owing to magnetic disturbances whose source were the Sol system's sixth planet—a ringed giant of baleful aspect that made the Masters think of Fantoma.

Why is the computer addressing itself to fashion? Shaizan asked in mindspeak.

And to whom is it addressing itself? Dag sent.

The text is reminiscent of that developed in Tiresia as part of the clone tutorials.

Bowkaz directed himself to both Shaizan and Dag. *Yes, but why would Zor have programmed those tutori-als into the fortress computer? He denounced the Elders for their fascination with genetic engineering.*

Shaizan nodded his head. *What's more, why give the computer the visage of a woman—especially one of such . . . "motherly" guise?*

Once more, the triumvirate silenced their thoughts and turned their attention to the female in the sphere and the translated gibberish she was spouting.

"The Modern Youth knows that *giri*—obligation—involves doing whatever must be done to maximize the survival of the greater whole. You are self-sacrificing and take orders well; still, you are proud of yourself and know that inside you have much-valued individuality. Modern Youths contemplate love, but not so much as to interfere with obligations and the proper performance of duty. Modern Youths contemplate sex and the pleasures of the senses, but not so much as to interfere with pre-paredness. You are at your best when alone, attending to the matters of the world. You know that you have your part to play in the harmony that must be sustained between yourself and society, and between society and the cosmos . . ."

Perhaps we have inadvertently accessed some thinking machine other than Zor's, Shaizan sent as the computer droned on.

Not possible, Bowkaz returned. *The encryption sequence was checked and rechecked. Whatever their significance, the words emanate from the ship's computer.*

Shaizan looked to Dovak of the Scientists for explanation. "Can the location of the fortress be deduced from the source of these transmissions?"

"M'lords, the source is a network of satellites girdling the planet."

"How is this possible?"

"Uplink from the surface, m'lord."

Shaizan's enthusiasm was felt by his comrades. "Then the ship is below."

Bowkaz concurred, and had something to add to Dovak. "Order the engineers to relocate us closer to Earth."

The scientist kowtowed. "How much closer, m'lord?"

"Insert our fleet among the moons of the ringed giant."

"The Masters have arrived," Zand calmly announced to the members of his cabal. They've been making repeated attempts at accessing the mother computer."

Eyes went wide down the length of the table in Subbasement Three of the SPOOK facility. Zand, dressed in a wrinkled pea-soup-green suit and seated in a highbacked chair, looked as though he hadn't slept in a week—which happened to be the case. It had been that long since the Zor holo had apprised him of the Masters' initial probings, but Zand had wanted to make certain of the computer's findings before saying anything to his team.

He had a secret fraternity of twelve: Miles Cochran, Samson Becket, Yoko Nitabi, Nag Fortuna, Florida Bakeworth, and seven holdovers from the Robotech Center's terminated cybermetrics division. Cochran and Becket had apprenticed under Emil Lang in Macross and Monument, and were now attached to the EDF's foremost research laboratory, located in the military-industrial complex abutting Fokker Aerospace Base. Fortuna and Bakeworth were recent acquisitions, replacing Joseph Petrie and Henry Giles, both of whom had decamped in '24 to found the ill-fated Giles Institute.

"The Masters' precise whereabouts are unknown at this time," Zand continued with scarcely a pause, "though the computer is rather desperate to pinpoint their position. It can't understand why the SDF-1's long-range sensors and tracking arrays aren't responding to its queries. The pathetic machine has yet to come to terms with the fact that it has been removed from the fortress." Zand chuckled. "Perhaps now Commander Leonard will thank me for refusing to allow the computer to be integrated into Liberty Space Station's network of monitoring and target-acquisition systems. The Masters might have gained access to the databanks of the Defense Force itself."

"Does the computer have *any* sense of how close they are?" Cochran managed to ask. A thin-faced, intense redhead, he was often as war-worried as Leonard himself.

"In galactic terms, practically right next door," Zand told him. "Certainly they are well within the range of Sol's warmth, but not yet near enough to be detected by Liberty or any of the forward-observation probes. Or the factory satellite, for that matter—though I'm not sure the Zentraedi would alert us to the Masters' arrival, in any case. Not after being forced into exile."

Becket—dark-haired, bird-boned, and wearing tinted glasses—was steepling his tapering fingers in thought. "If the Masters are *here*—" he started to say.

"Then what has become of the SDF-3?" Zand completed. "An excellent question. One that may be answered once we've learned whether we're dealing with a single recon vessel or a flotilla, though I think it's safe to assume that the REF's mission of diplomacy has failed. It says something, however, that the Masters haven't simply materialized in Earthspace as Breetai's battle group did in 2009. Are they being cautious because of what happened to their formerly invincible Grand Fleet, or is it that they have some other plan in mind?"

"Caution is in their best interest, whatever their plan," Yoko Nitabi commented. A tall, handsome Japanese with tattoos enough to brand her a Modern Youth, she headed up security for SPOOK. "Either they've come looking for vengeance—on Humankind or the Zentraedi—or for the SDF-1."

Fortuna loosed a cackling laugh. "Vengeance isn't Tirol's style; never was, never will be. Besides, they wouldn't think of annihilating Earth while a chance exists of their repossessing the dimensional fortress."

Zand studied Fortuna through narrowed eyes. His real name was Napoleon Alphonse Russo, and what a find he had been. Both Russo and "Bakeworth," whose name was Millicent Edgewick. After almost ten years of searching, Zand had traced them to a refugee center in Turkey, where the two were working as administrators, skimming from a paltry budget to keep themselves afloat in comfortable if spartan style. Russo, as president of the United Earth Government in its several guises from 1999 to 2012, had been the most prominent political figure of the century, and certainly the most hated as well, since it was Russo who was most credited with bringing on the Rain of Death by refusing to negotiate with the Zentraedi. Edgewick, an especially unattractive woman—even after numerous identity-altering operations—had been his lover and executive assistant for most of those years, and together the pair had gone into hiding after the Rain.

Zand, employing the name T. R. Edwards as a calling card and promising power greater than they had ever known, had induced them to join the secret fraternity. They did Zand's bidding now. But it was more accurate to say that they were the cabal's insurance against untoward moves by Chairman Moran, for they knew things about Moran that could topple him. Just as Zand knew certain things about Anatole Leonard that could undo him. About the Giles Academy, for example.

"And what happens when the Masters discover that the SDF-1 was destroyed and buried?" Yoko Nitabi thought to ask the man she and the others knew only as Nag Fortuna. "Vengeance might seem in order then."

Russo showed the tech a pitying look. "The ship means shit to them," he fairly hissed. "It's the Protoculture matrix they're after. They'd want proof that the matrix was destroyed with the ship." Russo was still a fat-jowled, florid-faced, obese little man. But the gratingly false-hearty manner that had won him many an election had, since his fall from grace, given way to an intimidating ferocity.

Nitabi cut her sparkling green eyes to Zand. "But Lang theorized that the matrix vanished with the fortress's fold generators."

Zand's hand fluttered in dismissal. "Yes, of course it did." He still hadn't gotten around to quizzing the computer about the SDF-1's never-examined Reflex furnaces, but he had decided not to air his suspicions to the fraternity. For the table's sake, he added, "I don't want the Masters to know just yet that the matrix vanished."

"But by allowing them that data, we may be able to prevent an attack," a second tech suggested.

"We can always play that card if we're forced to. Until then, we stand to gain by keeping them online. There may be a way to use the Zor holo to access *their* computers. All week, I've been feeding them EVE telecasts, though I don't expect those to hold the Masters' interest for long. God knows, they never held mine for more than a moment."

"We should at least apprise Commander Leonard and the Terrestrial Defense Ministry of these developments," Cochran said.

Zand merely stared at him. "And why is that?"

"So the EDF can go to full-alert status."

"They're already as alert as they're ever going to be. But don't worry, I'll see that Leonard is informed immediately. As for Terrestrial Defense, the time isn't right for disclosure."

"But—"

Zand glared at him. "Excuse me. Perhaps I should have said the *Shapings* aren't right."

Cochran and the rest fell silent.

Zand leaned back in his chair, tapping a bony forefinger against his lips. What were the Shapings telling Dana Sterling and the Zentraedi? he wondered. Without knowing why, had she suddenly grown as agitated as the Zor holo?

CHAPTER
SIX

Children deprived of parents often need to be taught to cry, because they haven't learned that crying brings a response. Some, depending on the conditions they have endured, may not be acquainted with even the most common of household sounds—vacuums, food processors, vidphones, telecomps—and will want to sleep all day long, will display signs of attention deficit, or will express the need to be held and comforted for long periods.

Excerpted from the training manual
for nurses working in Tokyo's communal homes

"**I** DON'T UNDERSTAND WHAT'S GOTTEN INTO YOU," Rolf Emerson was telling Dana. "You haven't been in the Academy three weeks and already you're in danger of being expelled."

Dana tried but failed to look sheepish. "I don't know what it is. I'm feeling angry and—what's the word for wanting to fight?"

"Aggressive? Hostile? Combative?"

"Combative. I'm feeling combative."

Emerson shook his head in bafflement. "Who are you angry at?"

Dana scowled. "Everyone."

They were in the sunken den of the mountain cabin, Emerson seated on a worn but comfortable couch facing the fireplace, Dana pacing the wide-planked floor in

front of him. There was a fire going, thanks to the
quarter-cord of larch Emerson had finagled from a
neighbor whose wooded acreage had lost a tree to light-
ning. When the fire wasn't crackling and Dana's pacing
carried her onto the rag rug, fragments of Bowie's am-
plified keyboard noodling drifted in from the outbuild-
ing that served as his studio.

Emerson caught a bit of the music now and nodded
his chin in the direction of the backyard. "Bowie would
do anything to get himself expelled. So how is it that
he's managed to stay out of trouble?" He glanced at the
letter he'd received from the dean of the EDF Academy,
then looked up at Dana. "Hoisting a cadet officer from
a flagpole?"

Dana whirled on him. "She called me a halfbreed.
Bowie doesn't have people calling him names like
that."

In patent disbelief, Emerson quoted from the letter.
" 'She has also been implicated in a prank involving the
liberation of a group of primates from the research laboratory, which were then encouraged to run amok
among the debutante cotillion.' "

"She had it coming," Dana said, smacking her fist
into the palm of her hand.

Emerson rubbed his forehead and set the letter aside.
There's no disarming the Zentraedi Imperative, friends
had warned him when he'd first agreed to care for Dana
in her parents' absence. *At the core of every accultur-
ated alien lurks a malcontent, waiting to burst forth.* As
if Emerson needed to be told. In Ilan Tinari, he had witnessed the Imperative in action firsthand, during temper
tantrums and just before she'd left him to join her dis-
affected comrades. And he'd seen ample evidence of it
in Dana's mother, Miriya, both in her harsh early treat-

ment of Dana and in her erratic behavior during the Malcontent Uprisings. So perhaps it was only Max Sterling's comparatively gentle genes that had been keeping Dana in check all these years.

Emerson watched her pace for a moment. Not even sixteen and she stood five foot eight on long, shapely legs. Her frame was athletic, and her globe of swirling blond hair lent additional menace to a freckled, pug-nosed face.

But don't ever call her cute.

Max and Miriya had relied on the dubious services of Lazlo Zand to see Dana over the rough spots of her unique development. But Emerson was of a different mind about Lang's chief disciple. Ten years earlier, he had discovered Zand subjecting Dana to some sort of experiment the professor claimed had been aimed at stimulating "the alien portion of her mind." To Emerson, though, the experiments had smacked of pedophilia masquerading as science. Consequently, Dana now had only Emerson to turn to, and he often felt that he'd made a mess of things: constantly absenting himself on trips to Liberty and Aluce, abandoning her and Bowie for long stretches to youth centers similar to those pioneered by the Japanese. Maybe that was the reason Dana had turned to Terry Weston after the Giles Academy affair.

"I just don't want to see you ruin your chances at officers' candidate school," Emerson said at last. "That is still your goal, isn't it?"

She nodded with enthusiasm.

"Then don't you see that incidents like these—" Emerson gestured to the letter "—will only jeopardize your chances for the posting you want?"

She compressed her lips. "It's not that I *want* to be so

thin-skinned. I just can't help it. Especially the past few weeks. It's like I'm itching to go to battle. Like there are enemies all around me."

We've done this to them, Emerson thought. *Warped the minds of an entire generation.* He was about to reply when someone knocked at the door. A moment later, Sarah Willex, the housekeeper, poked her head in.

"Excuse me for interrupting, Mr. Emerson, but there are some people here to see you. A Major Fredericks and a Lieutenant Satori."

"What do they want?"

"I didn't presume to ask them."

"No, of course not," Emerson said. "All right, show them in." He looked at Dana. "We'll have to continue this later."

Dana nodded and eased herself out the back door, making for Bowie's studio just as the housekeeper was reappearing with Fredericks and Satori in tow.

"Sorry to disturb you on a Saturday, sir," Fredericks began, twirling a brimmed cap in pale, bony hands. "But we're here at General Aldershot's request."

Neither of them were in uniform, but both displayed the proud bearing of career soldiers. Alan Fredericks was thirtyish, tall and lanky, with limp blond hair that fell over prominent ears. Nova Satori couldn't have been much older than Dana, but projected maturity and competence. Her face was heart-shaped; her eyes were dark and intense, her lips, mobile and expressive. Her mantle of blue-black hair was so long that she had to sweep it aside when she sat down, and in it she wore a techno-hairband that suggested a headphone—a fashion import from Japan.

"Can we talk here, sir, or might we be more comfortable outside?" Satori asked.

Emerson grasped her meaning and growled, "The only bugs in this house have multiple legs, Lieutenant. Say what you came to say without fear of being overheard or recorded."

Satori smiled tightly. "Sir, General Aldershot wishes you be informed that plans for the game are going forward, and he seeks some idea of the position you wish to play."

Emerson sighed wearily. Codes, riddles, cryptic exchanges . . . What had become of plain talk? "Lieutenant, as I told the general at the little brunch he threw downtown, I have no interest in participating in the 'game.' As far as I'm concerned the field is already overcrowded with players."

Fredericks looked disappointed. "Then we should tell the general you won't even consider a position on the bench—as a consultant or a replacement?"

Emerson shot to his feet. "Since when is my blessing so important to this? If the general and the rest of his . . . players think they can score, they should shoot for the goal. But I think you're all guilty of underestimating the opposition. Don't expect that by cutting off the head, you can immobilize the rest of the beast. Your opponents are players who are used to thinking on their feet and making command decisions on the field. Rather than yield ground, they'll dig in deeper, and you'll find yourselves with one hell of a mess to deal with. And you can tell Aldershot I said so. What's more, I'm not at all sure that this *game* will enjoy popular support. The general may find a smaller rooting section than he expects."

Fredericks was miffed. "The game might enjoy more support if we could furnish the media with some colorful background on the opposition's key players."

Emerson stared Fredericks down. "Is that what this visit is about? Aldershot expects me to betray confidences or act as his spy?"

Satori answered him in a placating tone. "Please don't misunderstand us, sir. General Aldershot has your interests in mind."

"How is that, Lieutenant?"

"Exempting oneself from play," Fredericks said, "could be construed by some as a political gesture to ensure ... *survivability*, let's say, no matter which side wins the game."

Emerson glared at him. "You're the ones who've put me in the middle. You don't need me, and you shouldn't have involved me. Now, the less said from here on, the better for all of us."

Satori and Fredericks rose slowly from their chairs. "Thank you for your time, Minister Emerson," Satori said, averting her gaze. "There is one last thing, though: would you be willing to convey an invitation to the game to the Zentraedi aboard the factory satellite?"

Emerson looked at her askance. "Surely Aldershot can do that on his own."

Fredericks nodded. "Normally, he could, sir. But as of oh-five-hundred today, the Zentraedi appear to have broken off all communication with Liberty, Aluce, and Fokker bases."

While the noodle shops and tofu parlors and greengrocers of the *shotengai* of Tokyo still saw their share of business, most surface dwellers who didn't have time for the elaborate courtesies involved with shopping simply frequented the city's plethora of vending machines. Vending machines didn't feel compelled to ask about your health or discuss the weather, or pass judgment on you for not knowing enough about the items you wanted to buy.

Returned to the surface, Misa sat facing an array of the solar-powered machines, selling everything from engagement rings to frozen beef, each item advertised in fiber-optic *kanji*: fresh flowers, rice, whiskey, hamburgers, porno holos, music video disks, software, interface goggles, repair kits, batteries, business cards, cameras, underwear, even an apartment hunter and a dating service.

No career women and stock peddlers eyeing one another over plates of massaged beef up here, but working stiffs stuffing their faces on seaweed, *mushi zushi*, and sticky rice cakes and discussing the latest *beisuboru* scores; no *jiuta-mai* dance or competitive kabuki, but jugglers and robot sumo wrestling; no kinetic sculptures or fluted glassware, but plastic chopsticks and folk art bowls.

Slumped onto a wrought-iron bench, nibbling at crispy veggies she'd bought at a yakitori bar, she was waiting for Census to show up. It had been his idea to meet—they *had* to talk, he'd told her—but he was late, as usual.

It had been ten days since she'd set foot in the apartment, and she had to admit she missed him some. But before she was going to agree to go back, there were some ground rules he was going to agree to. She'd formulated a list of demands, which she planned on having him pass along to Discount and Hongo, beginning with their promising to lay off the corporate pirating, especially the attempts to penetrate SPOOK, because she had an extra-bad feeling about that one. Then there were the things she wanted the three of them to start doing around the apartment, like the dishes, and the wash, and the sweeping, so she didn't have to feel like some maintenance robot. As for money, there was no shortage of ways for cyber-savvy guys to make ends meet. For instance, repairing the palm-sized comps the Modern Youth carried around with them—after the Shinto blessings wore out, of course. Or what about writing software, creating VR games, or going to work for one of the corporations they kept targeting—even though it might mean having to clean up their act some?

With Hongo, she knew the attempted penetrations were revenge against Zand for having been laid off. But Zand kept winning, didn't he? So why couldn't Hongo just put away his anger and get on with his life? One good thing about growing up in the collective homes was that you learned to dispose of your anger quickly. If you didn't, there was no working with anyone because you were too busy dwelling on ways to get even with people who ripped you off, or dissed you, or ratted on you. You learned fast not to be so attached to possessions or friends that they ended up dominating your life.

That was the main problem with the doomsdayers, the turn-of-the-century generation that comprised the majority of the Modern Youth: they'd grown up during a time when you could have anything and everything. The Robotech explosion had provided jobs, gadgets, comfort, money enough to go around. But then when the Rain came, the doomsdayers had had the mat pulled out from under them; and now they expended their energy in a misguided attempt to regain what they'd had in their youth.

Misa took a bite of crispy zucchini and gazed at the Quickform factory that now occupied the former site of the Nomura Building, a casualty of the Robotech War. Along with the Sumitomo, the Keio Plaza, the

Kasumigaseki, the Super Dry Hall, the Tokyo Tower, the Hiroshima obelisk to the Spirit of Japan's War Dead . . . the hundred thousand structures that had been erected before the Turn only to be razed by the Rain. And with them had gone more than glass and ferrocrete, but a world that could never be recreated.

Somehow, though, the new world seemed entirely in keeping with the Japanese psyche, with its adoration for fleeting beauty and visible decay, and its anxiety about cultural and spiritual loss.

"Miko!" someone called.

Census's head was suddenly between her and the sun, his broad, even-toothed mouth grinning down at her.

"Don't call me that," she told him.

"Come on, don't be like that." He was dressed in baggy khaki shorts and a red and white RDF shirt from twenty years before. The grin didn't falter as he sat down beside her, but his eyes were darting around, as if on the lookout for someone or something.

"What did you want to talk about?"

"Your moving back in. I miss you," he said.

She reined in a wry smile. "You miss me so much you're only twenty minutes late."

"I lost track of time."

"Uh huh."

"No, really. But the important thing is, I'm here, right? And I want to tell you, there's going to be some changes."

She tried not to look encouraged. "Such as?"

Census's eyes shifted again. He was definitely checking out the crowd at the yakitori bar behind her back. "First off, you can have all your money back."

"It's not the money, Cen—"

"No, really, you can." He lowered his voice to a

whisper. "We made a major penetration, M. Got a buyer already lined up. You'll have enough extra cash to buy ten bracelets like the one you wanted."

She narrowed her eyes at him. "I don't need *ten* bracelets."

"Then buy a ring to match the one you get. Whatever you want." He reached for her hand. "I want you to come back. I miss you terribly."

She resisted the urge to give in to him. "I miss you, too," she allowed. "But we need to get some things straight before—"

"Hold that thought," he said suddenly, placing a hand over her mouth.

His eyes were now fixed on an object off to the left of the bench. Misa twisted out from under his hand and followed his gaze to a tall, well-built Japanese wearing a suit that was even older than Census's Robotech shirt. The man's short hair, clean-shaven face, and casual manner marked him as a *yakuza*.

"I have to take care of some business," Census said, getting to his feet. "It won't take more than five minutes."

"So you're dealing with the *boryokudan* now." The mafia, for all intents and purposes.

Census shushed her. "It's nothing criminal. This particular Family operates many legitimate businesses. Besides, it's just this one sale. Just to recoup our losses."

"Which you wouldn't have had if you'd stayed away from SPOOK," she said, whispering the final word. "And how *considerate* of you to arrange to find time to talk to me, with your busy schedule and all."

"M, you don't understand," he answered, obviously torn between wanting to appease her and completing the transfer of whatever data he was carrying. "It's just this one sale . . ."

The words were too late in coming. Misa was already hurrying away from him, brushing past one vending machine after the next, efficiently losing herself in the lunch-hour crowds along Ome-Kaido. But just short of the final machine, something caught her eye and made her stop. She backed up a step and disappeared into the booth of one of the machines—the one that advertised APARTMENTS TO SHARE.

The largely underground facility that housed SPOOK was located north of the Imperial center in the Bunkyo-ku district, on the grounds once occupied by the Karakuen Amusement Park, home to the *fin de siècle* Yomiuri Giants baseball team. Nearby, and often frequented by facility staffers, was the rebuilt Koishikawa Gardens, a parcel of Edo-period tranquility, where in summer one could still enjoy the omnipresent *me-me-me* chirring of cicadas.

Yoko Nitabi, SPOOK's chief of security and trusted member of Zand's inner circle, had made it her habit to visit the Koishikawa at least once a week, usually during her lunch or meditation breaks, thereby establishing a pattern she hoped would serve her well when the time came for her to fulfill her obligations to the Shimada Family—the family that had rescued her from a collective home when she was scarcely eight years old.

That time was now.

And though Nitabi appeared to be casually ensconced among the lunchtime strollers, she was, with single-minded intent, closing on one of the park's modem-equipped vidphone booths.

Her upbringing in the Shimada household had consisted of intensive training in the tactics of the *bor-*

yokudan, the criminal underground, with emphasis on the mental disciplines—cyberscience, in particular—in accordance with proclivities described by her natal horoscope. Kan-san, honcho of the household, had predicted early on that Yoko would someday ascend to the position of security chief for the entire Shimada organization. But Yoko, in addition to her seemingly innate hacker skills, had demonstrated such a remarkable aptitude for inspired duplicity that it was decided she be turned out into the military-industrial world as a sleeper agent or a mole. To facilitate this, she had been given age-advancement treatments and tattoos enough to convince anyone that she danced to the beat of the Modern Youth. Surrogate-father Kan Shimada held that Yoko must have been born to fellow *yakuza*, or perhaps to members of Japan's secret police.

Tedious manipulations by the Family had landed her numerous jobs in the corridors of power, but she had never been asked to execute acts of espionage or provide information on her employers. The jobs were meant merely to establish her bona fides in systems security. Her penetration of SPOOK had been regarded as something of a coup; more so when Zand recruited her for his secret fraternity. Still, the Shimadas had refrained from asking anything of her. They left it to Yoko to decide if and when she should go operational.

She had served Zand faithfully for seven years now, and he had grown to trust her. It was Yoko who had made certain that Giles and Petrie's rift with SPOOK had been handled without either of them profiting from the divorce; and she had recommended security-clearance advancement for some facility staffers while disciplining others who had demonstrated a lack of compliance with Zand's exacting demands.

Demands to which Yoko herself had been subjected. All staffers were routinely scanned on entering and exiting SPOOK, and periodically vetted by both machine and human analysts. Then, for members of the secret fraternity, there were the rituals: the bloodletting secrecy oaths, the meditations on the Shapings, and the sessions constructed around communal ingestion of leaves of the Flower of Life, which Zand's field agents gathered from remote areas of Africa and the Southlands.

Yoko had complied with all of it, never furnishing Zand with cause for suspicion, and taking pains over the years to acquaint him with her personal routines, the better to make use of her apparent predictability at some future date. One of those routines involved a weekly phone call to the Shimada contact agent who masqueraded as Yoko's mother; another involved the visits to the Koishikawa Gardens, and the occasional use of the vidphones. Yoko had lost track of the times she had been shadowed by Zand operatives, who had surely traced the calls and had had backgrounds run on the parties called.

For the week commencing with Zand's stunning disclosure about the Masters, Yoko had been careful not to alter her routines. She had, however, made one important change: when she had phoned her "mother," she included the news that a summer cold had her feeling less than tip-top—a signal, agreed upon years earlier, that the Shimadas should expect something from her, via one of the Family's legion of nominally legitimate businesses.

That something was a data-disk transcription of Zand's disclosures about the Masters, secreted into a seemingly innocuous audio/video want ad Yoko planned to list with an equally innocuous Tokyo agency. The city's wealthy would pay any amount for such news, if only to be among the first to go into hiding before the newest rounds of annihilation bolts were rained on Earth. Returns, in any case, were beside the point. *Giri* was the point. Duty.

Yoko had taken precautions. She'd backed up the monitored call to Mother by mentioning her bogus respiratory distress, in passing, to several SPOOK staffers, and—soliciting input on her choice of music and visuals—she'd run the want ad for a couple of others. She had also avoided going to the park until the heat wave had passed, when someone suffering from a cold might be expected to venture outdoors for a walk.

Midday.

When Zand habitually went down for an hour or so of sleep.

The want ad, complete with video footage and Lynn-Minmei soundtrack, stated that she was looking for a roommate to share rent in her apartment. The e-ad would never run, of course; alerted, Shimada agents would relay what they received to the organization's cyberteam for immediate decryption.

With a certain excited satisfaction, Yoko pictured the procedure as she settled herself at the keyboard of the only unoccupied phone booth in that part of Koishikawa. She punched in the number of the listings agency, routed herself through a menu to the ad division, entered her name and identity number, and waited for further instructions.

By the time the word *transmit* was flashing onscreen, she already had the disk slotted and her finger on the send button. But just then a sudden noise made her swivel toward the booth's sliding door, and in a moment the rotund form of Nag Fortuna, Zand's pet of sorts, had squeezed into the small space and was holding a short-bladed knife to the underbelly of her jaw.

"The disk," he said in a whisper that promised dire consequences should she refuse.

But Yoko wasn't about to be so easily undone. She kneed Fortuna in the groin and slammed an elbow down on the transmit bar. Off-balance, she felt her elbow slide across the keyboard, inciting a razzle-dazzle response from the phone and filling the screen with incomprehensible computer code.

Misa stood in the booth, waiting for her diskful of leads for new roommates. There was a disk reader in the booth, but she'd gone and spent almost the last of her money on the disk and was now going to have to rely on some friend's machine. Just as well, she supposed, because the delay would give her time to consider her options.

She was still angry at Census for dealing with the mob. That about finished it for her and him, she supposed—though some part of her insisted that she could get him to change.

When the disk appeared, she clutched it as if it were a lucky charm. Then she exited the booth and ambled off down the busy street without so much as a backward glance.

CHAPTER
SEVEN

[Wilfred] Gibley rarely spoke about what he had done before emigrating to Japan [in 2017]. Some reports have him in the Southlands during the Uprisings; others in Portland, in the Northlands, making a living as a writer of speculative fiction. Whichever the case, [Emil] Lang took an instant liking to him when he interviewed for a position in the cybermetrics department of the then-named Robotech Research Center. Lang was quoted to have said at the time, "I wish Gibley had been here when we were putting the finishing touches on JANUS M. That way, it would at least have had a genuine sense of humor."

Shi Ling,
Sometimes Even a Yakuza Needs a Place to Hide

LAZLO ZAND HAD SPENT THE BETTER PART OF a week trying to determine what, if anything, to transmit to the Masters, and how best to go about gaining access to the Masters' own databank. In the end, he reasoned that the Masters had probably had their fill of EVE, and the time had come to allow the SDF-1 computer to contact the Masters directly. Under Zand's covert guidance, Zor's machine would communicate with the Masters' ship via the Lorelei Network satellites, as opposed to Space Station Liberty, over which Zand had no control. Rather than lie to the machine, Zand had apprised "Zor" of his plans to entice the Masters into establishing a computer-to-computer link in the interest of facilitating rapid exchanges of information. Once that goal was achieved, the Masters' invasion plan would be revealed and subsequently thwarted. If, indeed, invasion was what the Tiresians had in mind.

Zand's hope was that the Masters would surmise that Zor's computer was operating clandestinely; that it was, in fact, eager to establish contact with Tirol's emissaries. To convey that impression, he had tutored the system to respond as though it were still under the sway of the Compulsion the Masters had placed on Zor.

Anticipating word of the Masters' response, Zand had gone without sleep for four days. And then what should arise but this Yoko Nitabi business. It peeved him to be interrupted—which wouldn't necessarily have been the case had Russo handled his assignment properly.

Nitabi had been brought to SPOOK's primate research lab following her apprehension in the Koishikawa Gardens, and just now the young woman was strapped into one of the chimp chairs, her arms and legs secured by bands of shiny alloy. With Zand in the sterile room were Russo and Millicent Edgewick, the pair of them acting sheepish and hangdog in the aftermath of Zand's public harangue.

"I don't know who to be angrier with, *Fortuna*," the Protoculturist was saying while he paced in front of the chimp chair, "you or Ms. Nitabi, here."

Russo looked up at him. "The good weather brought so many people to the park I couldn't reach the booth in time."

"Excuses," Zand said disapprovingly. "The Russo trademark. Twenty-five years ago when you fired the Grand Cannon against the Zentraedi you were bowing to pressure from Admiral Hayes. Today a crowd of flower-sniffers prevents you from staying Ms. Nitabi's impeccably manicured hand. God knows what excuse you'll dream up to justify tomorrow's failure."

Russo had his mouth open to respond when Zand cut him off. "Don't argue with me. You're wasting Ms. Nitabi's time." He swung to his well-secured security chief and grinned. "Comfy?"

Nitabi glanced at Russo. "Is that *thing* actually Napoleon Russo?"

"As a matter of fact, he is," Zand replied, smiling lightly.

Nitabi's look of angry bewilderment held. "When are you planning to tell me what this is all about, Doctor?"

Zand stopped pacing long enough to fix her in the gaze of his irisless eyes. "Anxious to have this done with, are we? Well, I don't suppose I blame you. But first, tell me, how is that nasty cold of yours? Better after some fresh air, I'll bet."

"As a matter of fact, it is. But I still don't—"

"I only ask because, initially, it was your frequent talk of ill health that aroused my concern that it might be something more serious than a cold. So imagine my puzzlement when I checked with the biomonitors designed into the facility's palmprint and retinal scanners and found no evidence of fluctuations in your pulse rate, blood pressure, or body temperature. Certainly none consistent with an apparent state of physical distress. At the same time, I saw nothing in your behavior to suggest that you had some ulterior motive for lying about your health. You performed your duties with your usual attention to detail; you seemed to be eating and sleeping well; you made your weekly phone call to . . . your mother, isn't it? Still, I thought it best to have Napoleon keep an eye on you, lest you attempted something that jeopardized your position here. And, naturally, when he observed you slipping into one of the vidphone booths he decided to intervene."

Nitabi was scowling from the chair. "I was listing an advertisement with one of the e-services."

Zand considered it and frowned. "Why didn't you modem the ad from here?"

"It wasn't my *plan* to send it from the park, but I had the disk in my pocket and I saw an empty booth—"

"So you said to yourself, I may as well send it off now, while I'm thinking of it."

"Exactly. Read the disk. You'll see for yourself that it's perfectly innocent."

"Ah, yes, the disk," Zand said, prizing it from the breast pocket of his wrinkled lab jacket. "As a matter of fact, I've already read it. Apparently, you desire a roommate."

Nitabi swallowed hard. "I need money."

Zand nodded in false understanding. "It's not easy being a Modern Youth. All the purchases and trends one has to keep up with." He swung a glance at Russo and Edgewick. "Perhaps Napoleon or Millicent would suit you?" He chuckled. "No, I suppose not. They're neither modern nor youthful, are they?"

"Doctor Zand," Nitabi said, "if there's some problem with my looking for a roommate—"

Zand held up his hands. "None at all. Especially now that you've explained yourself." He paused for a long moment. "However, our problem is that I discovered something curious about the disk you wrote. Actually, I can't take the credit; it was our Zor creation that first pointed it out to me."

Zand moved to a bank of monitors and peered at display screens. "Oops, we seem to have touched on something that has Ms. Nitabi's heart all aflutter." He looked at her. "Is there anything you're not telling me?"

She shook her head.

Zand was studying the screens once more. "Look at that—you've managed to get your pulse rate back under control. I'm impressed. But I should warn you: that chair is a very sensitive instrument. In the past it has outed some of the intelligence community's finest operatives. Am I correct in assuming that you number yourself among that covert elite, Ms. Nitabi?"

"I don't represent the concerns of any government," she told him. "My loyalties are to SPOOK."

Zand smiled thinly. "A stirring comeback. But suppose we dismiss with further theatrics and get to the heart of the matter." He slotted the disk in a reader and directed Nitabi's attention to one of the monitors. The ad came onscreen, showing views of Nitabi's apartment; shots of Nitabi herself, talking about her interests and pet peeves; a soundtracked sequence of Nitabi and friends, out on a night's prowl of the geo-grid . . .

Zand paused the playback during the Lynn-Minmei rendition of "Stage Fright." "Here's where things get interesting." His fingers struck keys, and lines of complex programming code began to scroll on the display screen. "You've recorded Lynn-Minmei's song in standard DAT sixteen, but you've substituted every sixteenth bit with a parcel of encrypted information. Anyone listening to this 'ad' is only going to hear Minmei, just as she sounds on any of her recorded disks; and anyone analyzing the disk is going to find only digital music. Well, most anyone. There are those who might choose to run a bit-by-bit comparison of Minmei's version of "Stage Fright" and your version; but even so, the random-seeming differences could be attributed to noise generated during your duping of a digitally mastered piece using an analog machine. But to someone who possessed the keys to your encryption code . . . Or to someone capable of breaking that code . . ."

Zand glanced at the biomonitors and smiled. "Pulse: seventy-five and increasing. You're slipping, Ms. Nitabi. But have no fear; I'm not going to kill you. Not yet, at any rate. First, let's listen together to a translation of the noise in Minmei's recording."

Zand did further input, and the computer began to speak in choppy, synth-voice sentences. Zand listened for a moment, then looked at Nitabi.

"Why, that's me," he said, somber now. "From last week's meeting, when I let you in on Zor's discovery of the Masters. Obviously, you believed me."

Nitabi quirked a small frown, but said nothing.

"Regardless of the validity of my statements," Zand continued, "I can well understand how you thought there was money to be made." Hands thrust into the pockets of his jacket, he approached the chimp chair. "The question is, who were you selling it to?" He raised a hand and snapped his fingers.

Russo shot to his feet. "She was online with Tender/Search. An e-listing of jobs, apartments, goods—"

"A front company," Zand interrupted. "The ad was never meant to be listed, merely received." He paced for a minute and whirled on Nitabi. *"Yakuza?"* he asked in sudden insight. "Could it possibly be?"

Nitabi merely glared at him.

Zand basked in the glare. "Your silence all but confirms it. I could, of course, make you talk, but I haven't the time. A call here, a call there, and I'll have the information I require by sunset today. As for you, Ms.

Nitabi, I'm afraid that you've witnessed the last of this world's sunsets."

Zand snapped his fingers again, and the gaunt and gruesome-looking Millicent Edgewick stood up. "You'll find an assortment of sharp instruments in the drawers alongside the chair," he told her and Russo as he was walking for the door. "Take as much time with her as you please, but make sure to clean up after yourselves, and put the body on ice."

"Look, all I'm asking is to borrow your disk player for five minutes," Misa told Census and Gibley, both of whom were laughing at their own stupid jokes about her hunt for new roommates. "But if that means I'm going to have to put up with your crap, I'll read the disk somewhere else."

She did her best to make it sound convincing, but in fact Census and Gibley were her only hope. Because she'd spent the last of her NuYen on food, she no longer had the option of renting ten minutes of time on an arcade player. Down in the grid you could hook up with kids who had access to stolen credit-card codes, but even their services didn't come cheap. Of course, she'd have enough when her allowance from Human Services came through—if she wanted to wait a full week. But she didn't. As it was, she had spent the previous night cuddled with other strays in Ueno Park, which used to be known for its abundance of cherry trees. And she sure wasn't about to move back into the apartment.

"So what's it going to be?" she asked from the far side of the slider, where she stood tapping her foot.

Census bowed in false apology. " 'Course you can

use the player, Mik—uh, Misa. We were only teasing you."

"We're just missing you," the gangly Gibley added.

Her lips a thin line, Misa slipped off her sandals and stepped into the apartment, gazing around at the mess they'd managed to make of the place in her short absence. Dirty dishes, food wrappers, vending-machine coffee containers, socks. "Yeah, I guess I can understand why you're sorry I'm moving. You don't have anyone to pick up after you."

Census stood up from his customary seat at the control deck and started snatching things from the floor. Gibley remained where he was, eyeing her from behind clear-lensed interface goggles. Misa assumed that Discount was still in the clinic, recuperating from Zand's attack.

"It's not just the cleaning and stuff," Census was saying, stooped over a teetering pile of magazines, data disks, and downloaded hardcopy sheets of pilfered information. "The place just doesn't feel the same without you." He looked up at her. "I sure don't feel the same."

Misa narrowed her eyes at him. "Forget it. Not after that stunt you pulled on Ome-Kaido. Go buy yourself a love 'bot."

His face fell. "It wasn't a stunt. I wanted to see you. Can I help it that some last-minute business came up? Anyway, what's wrong with killing two birds with one stone?"

"Well, when you put it that way," she said with transparent sarcasm.

Dropping his armload of retrieved items, he showed her his palms. "Mika."

"The *player*," she said firmly.

Gibley slid the goggles up onto his forehead and

swung his chair around to face the video-disk player. "Do we get to watch?" he asked.

Misa handed him the disk. "It's only going to be ads for apartments."

"That's entertainment," Census said, positioning himself behind Gibley's chair. "The service should at least let you quick-scan the disk when you get it, instead of making you pay all over again to use a player."

Gibley slotted the disk. "Both services are in league with each other," he explained. "One place supplies the information, the other charges you to read it. There's profit in keeping everything proprietary."

Census scowled. "Our brave new world."

Misa quieted him. The first ad was running, narrated by a gorgeous, smiling Japanese woman named Yoko, who was even taller than Misa was. She was wearing expensive, form-fitting spacewear—very hungry for hip—and a faux-headset in her helmet-do of black hair.

Gibley winced.

"Just your type, Misa," Census said as Yoko was conducting a tour of her spacious apartment filled with matching furniture and houseplants. "I'll bet she's only asking about five hundred NuYen a week for the spare room."

" 'Fashion dictates that the Modern Youth dress for action and quick response,' " Gibley said, parroting EVE. " 'Your clothes are stain-resistant, fire-retardant, form-hugging, and equipped with plenty of utility pockets. Your headband is black, sleek, and looks like a hands-free communications headset.' "

Census started laughing. "Then there'll be the added cost of tattoos."

"Stop it!" Misa told them. She was aware of the seriousness beneath their ridicule, and she fought hard not to feel envy or jealousy. To be content with what she had and who she was. Yoko, meanwhile, was showing the view from her apartment.

"That's in the grid," Gibley said. "Not far from Bunkyo-ku Station."

Census arched an eyebrow. "Just think of it, Misa, you could be an undergrounder." Onscreen, Yoko and friends were out on a tear. An old song by Lynn-Minmei provided the soundtrack.

The boys groaned in unison. *"Minmei."*

"Jeez, what'd you enter on the application?" Census asked when he was done laughing. "That you were some *bari-bari sogoshoku* from the Kabutocho?"

Misa shook her head in confusion. "I never said I was a career woman—or anything about working in the financial district. I was honest about what I could afford."

"Maybe the placement service just wants to show you what you *won't* be getting," Gibley ventured. "You know, a kind of tease, to make you up the amount you're willing to spend."

Misa folded her arms under her breasts and heaved a sigh of disappointment. "Can we skip to the next ad?"

Census leaned forward and touched the player's skip button. The player blue-screened for a fraction of a second; then an end-of-file icon flashed.

Misa stared at it. "One stupid listing? That's all I get?"

Gibley was shaking his head. "This can't be right. There should be at least a dozen choices."

"I'd go back and complain," Census said.

Misa glanced at him. "Don't think I won't."

Gibley had reverse-scanned to Yoko's e-mail contact address and was studying it. "Yoko Nitabi," he muttered. "I know that name." He thought for a moment. "Nitabi was head of security for Zand at SPOOK."

Having purified themselves in the inn's sulfurous hot springs and fortified themselves in the citrus pools— *yuza* being that month's choice fruit—the male contingent of the Shimada Family had moved on to the exhilarating radon baths, which were encircled by towering zigzags of granite and marble, at once austere and comfortingly retro-Deco. A dozen of them were enjoying the cool, effervescent soak, their identical *yukata* hanging from wooden pegs mounted along one wall, their platform-soled *geta* lined up in neat rows, their valuables stashed in individual baskets or finely crafted boxes made of cypress. Overhead arched a dome of tinted permaplas, shielding them from the ruthless heat of the late-summer sun.

Kan-san himself, *daimyo* of the crime family, was present, along with his three sons, Eiten, Yosuke, and Chosei. The others were trusted *jonin* henchmen and invaluable *sokaiya*—male members who specialized in corporate extortion. The Family's women and children were elsewhere on the inn's sprawling grounds, most likely lingering at the banquet tables, which were laden with local "taste-of-home" specialties like fern shoots, sake-flavored rice, and fish patties. The Gotenba Onsen inn was nestled against Fuji, in the rolling hills of Shizuoka Prefecture south of Tokyo. Built in 1980, the area had once been the hunting grounds of the Imperial family. This was the Shimadas' seventh annual banquet, begun by Kan-san in the spirit of *kai zen*—continuous improvement.

In the radon bath, Eiten, who was tall and very

wholesome looking, was updating the others on the Yoko Nitabi situation.

"Yoko made contact with 'Mother' on Tuesday, mentioning that she had a cold—which, of course, was her signal that she would be going active within a couple of days. Our people at Tender/Search were notified to expect contact, and a team of field agents was deployed around SPOOK headquarters to monitor Yoko's actions.

"On Friday she was observed by our people in the Koishikawa Gardens, where she entered a vidphone booth and made contact with Tender/Search, ostensibly to list a room-for-rent ad. Tender/Search was online with her when she was intercepted at the source. The data was sent, but in such a way that Tender/Search's neural net rerouted it to one of its outlet booths in Shinjuku, where it was inadvertently downloaded to a customer seeking share space in an apartment."

Kan-san extended a water-wrinkled hand toward a tray of sake floating within easy reach. Sixty-four years old, he was silver-haired, lean, and—in keeping with the *yakuza* stereotype—serene-looking. "Who intercepted Yoko?" he asked his son.

"An obese little thing we have yet to identify."

"One of Lazlo Zand's in-close agents?"

"Presumably."

"And there has been no contact from Yoko since?"

Eiten adopted a grave expression and shook his head.

Kan-san's left hand made swirling motions in the bubbling water. He thought about Yoko, the girl he had rescued from the communal homes fifteen years earlier and raised as he would have a daughter. The girl whose innate talent for covert operations had opened the doors of the Naicho—the Cabinet Research Office—the Nibetsu—military intelligence—and the Chobetsu—

signals intelligence—paving the way for her penetration of SPOOK. "Pure Mitsui," as was once said about people skilled in negotiating the hazy interface between government and business.

Kan-san asked himself what she had tried to send him. For Yoko to have gone active of her own volition, the data would have to have been invaluable, as could only be the case where Lazlo Zand was concerned. Data that surpassed the ordinary business of the Shimada Family, Kan-san suspected—that business being twentieth-century antiques, fish, and the control of goods and services between the surface and the geogrid: maintenance, deliveries, trash removal, and the elimination of any environmental problems, such as noise and air pollution.

Gone were the days of drugs, prostitution, and gambling. Gone, along with the royal-blue and jade-green suits, the gaudily emblazoned black shirts, the gold chains and lapel pins, flat-top crew cuts, and traditional full-body tattoos. All that, the native *boryokudan* had surrendered to the Taiwanese, Indonesian, and Korean mafiosi who had moved into Japan before the turn of the century.

"Zand is obviously in possession of the encrypted information Yoko modemed to Tender/Search," Kan-san said at last.

His eldest son, Chosei, nodded. "However, he may not realize that the information was sent."

"Oh, he knows," Kan-san countered. "We will have to be judicious in our actions. But if he has harmed Yoko, we will have our revenge."

"*Hai*, Kan-san," came a reverberating chorus of voices.

The *daimyo* patted his face with water. "To which outlet in Shinjuku was the transmission misrouted?"

"To the booth on Ome-Kaido," Eiten continued. "The customer's name is Misa Yoshida."

Yosuke, who had had the hardest time abandoning the old ways of the *yakuza*, elaborated. "A war orphan," he began. "Eighteen or nineteen. Raised in the number seven Akasaka Communal Home. Her request was for lowest-end housing."

Kan-san pressed the tips of his fingers together. "Do we have a contact address?"

The sons shook their heads. "Not yet."

"But you have a description—a holo, a flat photo?"

Eiten spoke. "We have already procured one from the Ministry of Human Services."

"Then we can begin by canvassing the neighborhood," Yosuke interjected. "Someone in Shinjuku is bound to know her."

Everyone fell silent, awaiting Kan-san's pronouncement.

"This girl in search of lowest-end rentals has no idea what has fallen into her hands. Still, we must act swiftly."

The men were considering it when Miho Nagata cleared his throat with meaning. A lean, handsome man of forty, he was often referred to by Family members as Shimada's White Knight. "Excuse me, Kan-san, for failing to inquire sooner, but may I ask what time the misrouted data was received by the young woman, Misa?"

Eiten threw him a questioning glance. "Just after one in the afternoon. Why is this important?"

"I was there."

"Where?"

"On Ome-Kaido. I made the pickup from the data pirate who sold us the information on our competitor's decision to take control of the tuna fish market."

"Did you see her?" Yosuke pressed.

When Miho hesitated, Kan-san said, "Speak to us, Miho."

Up to his waist in the water, Miho bowed his head. "The pirate—Census—was with a girl. And I recall seeing her walking toward the Tender/Search booth."

Eiten cut his eyes to Miho. "The Human Services identity photo shows a tall, pretty girl with shoulder-length streaked hair."

"Sounds like the one."

"Miho, can you contact this—this Census again?" Kan-san asked softly.

"Hai."

A believer in *meirei no shikata*—instructing without issuing direct orders—Kan-san had nothing to add.

Even so, Miho got to his feet and bowed deeply. *"Uhss*, Shimada-san," he said, as student to master.

CHAPTER EIGHT

*Though much condemned for his militant xenophobia during the
Malcontent Uprisings, [Anatole Leonard] had the interests of
Earth foremost in mind; and it is interesting to speculate on what
might have happened had even one of the religious movements
Leonard subscribed to garnered majority support among the planet's populace. If Conrad Wilbur's Faithful had had their way, and
the Visitor not been refurbished, there might not have been a First
Robotech War. If the Church of Recurrent Tragedies, which grew
from the Faithful, had had its way, and the defeated Zentraedi had
been banished to Mars, Macross City and the SDF-1 might have
been spared destruction. And if HEARTH—the Faithful's penulti-
mate stage—had had its way, and people really had attended to
the business of healing the planet, there might not have been a
schism in the EDF, and Zand and Leonard and Emerson and
Aldershot might have all been fighting on the same side.*

Weverka T'su,
*Aftermath: Geopolitical and Religious Movements
in the Southlands*

"YOUR COMMAND?" ASKED A VOICE THAT PUR-
ported to be that of Zor's dimensional-fortress computer. Issuing from an unseen apparatus in the command
center of the Masters' flagship, the voice had an amia-
ble, masculine quality.

It seems that we have succeeded, Shaizan sent to his
confederates. Grouped around their Protoculture Cap,
their slender, nailless fingers in touch with its mottled

surface, the three hovered in the organic vastness, amid pulsing displays of radiant energy.

I will reserve judgment, Bowkaz replied. *It is possible that the codes we transmitted have roused the interest of some other machine intelligence in residence on Earth.*

The lantern-jawed Dag offered what amounted to a telepathic nod. *I concur. Let this machine prove itself to us before we celebrate our good fortune.* "Machine," he said aloud, "supply us with details regarding your physical circumstances."

The voice was scarcely ten seconds in responding, since the flagship's Protoculture-fed real-time communicators were reading and deciphering the signal close to its source.

"I can only provide limited data as to my actual location. Access to the fortress's exterior sensors and scanners was terminated in two-zero-one-two, local reckoning. Since then, I have had no opportunity to elect input. However, I have been selectively nourished on data regarding what I deduce to be my immediate environment."

"Contrast speculations on your immediate environment with that of Tirol," Shaizan told the machine.

"A world that approximates Tirol in size, called Earth. Not a satellite, but a planet, third from its star. Not barren but abundant with biolife, botanical, in the main, though lorded over by sentient bipeds similar in configuration to Tirol's populace. Several of these are known to me by name; one in particular, who is my principal interface with the immediate environment."

You see, Shaizan sent, *it knows Tirol.*

And I know this voice, Bowkaz returned tentatively.

"Speculate on your actual location," Dag told the machine.

"In a subsurface facility, situated in the northern latitudes of the planet's eastern hemisphere."

"Elaborate on the word 'facility.' "

"Laboratory. Research complex."

"Military complex?" Shaizan asked.

"Available data suggests a civilian facility."

Zor! Bowkaz sent suddenly. *This is Zor's voice! The Zor I remember as an acolyte in service to Elder Nimuul. Zor, in the days when the Compulsion was placed upon him.*

Shaizan's and Dag's minds betrayed their agitation. *But how could it be Zor?* Shaizan asked for both of them. *Zor is dead; Commander Reno delivered his body to us.*

Perhaps not, Bowkaz sent. *Perhaps Zor exercised a subterfuge during the Invid attack that supposedly claimed his life. Perhaps he willingly surrendered his body in order to transfer his mind into the machine that commanded his fortress.*

Dag stared at him over the hump of the Cap. *That would make Zor the architect of the defeat of the Zentraedi Grand Fleet!*

Implausible, Shaizan interrupted. *Zor was the architect of the clones themselves. And regardless of his abhorrence for what they became, he would never have taken a hand in their destruction.*

Then how else to explain this voice? Bowkaz pressed.

Why not ask the machine? Dag suggested.

Bowkaz did, and the three Masters waited.

"I speak in the voice of the flesh-and-blood who wrote me," the voice replied after a long moment. "Zor. Those biosentients who currently nourish me have concocted a likeness of Zor from an audio/visual cautionary message I carried with me to this world."

Bowkaz made his mistrust felt to his comrades. *Listen closely to what it says: Zor programmed a cautionary message into this computer he fashioned, this intellect he made answerable only to himself. How otherwise would he have been able to dispatch it across space-time to Earth? So why is it responding to us now—the likely featured players in his message?*

Because of the codes, Shaizan submitted.

Either that, Dag sent, *or the Compulsion was still upon Zor when he wrote the machine. It could not help but be influenced by Zor's state of mind—his obedience to us.*

Bowkaz conveyed disdain. *Why do you hold onto the belief that the Elders had even a hint of control over him at the end? He was subverting all of us in his quiet way, constructing his fortress, forging plans to seed worlds with the Flower of Life when in fact he had one aim only: to purloin the matrix and spirit it from our grasp.*

Shaizan and Dag fell silent momentarily.

Zor's treachery notwithstanding, Shaizan sent, *I insist that we attempt to make use of his machine. Or does Bowkaz wish that we demonstrate our inadequacies to the Elders by once more awaiting their counsel before we act?*

Let us continue to test the machine, Dag sent to Bowkaz. *Ultimately it will either betray itself or affirm its allegiance to us.*

"Where is the fortress now?" Shaizan asked in an even tone.

"Destroyed."

Alarm silenced the triumvirate momentarily; then Dag asked, "How and when was it destroyed?" Commander Reno, in his final communiqué before surrendering the factory satellite to Breetai, had said nothing about the destruction of the fortress.

"The fortress was destroyed in the final week of the year two-zero-one-four, during an attack led by Khyron Kravshera," the machine reported.

Khyron! the Masters thought in unison. How like the Zentraedi rogue to dash the Masters' last hope.

"And the Protoculture matrix?" Shaizan asked. "We know it was concealed somewhere aboard the ship. Did it survive Khyron's assault?"

The voice emerged from background noise. ". . . concealed among the fortress's reflex drives, but there is no direct means to ascertain if it survived."

"Speculate!" Bowkaz commanded.

"The matrix was never discovered."

"Explicate!"

"Access to sundry electronic data suggests that Earth's biosentients have not been able to synthesize Protoculture to fuel their abundance of battle mecha. The reason possibly owes to the absence of the Flower of Life. Or perhaps the matrix was removed *before* the destruction of the fortress—much as I was—and has yet to be identified."

The Masters huddled in silent exchange.

His skepticism only marginally diminished, Bowkaz asked, "Where are the Zentraedi that survived the Grand Fleet? And where is Breetai's flagship?" The Elders had already supplied the answers, but Bowkaz wanted to hear the computer's version of recent events.

"Greatly reduced in numbers, Earth's populace fought a protracted war with some of the Zentraedi whose warships crashed onworld. Many of those Zentraedi were killed. Others pledged their fidelity to the planet's military organization, the Robotech Defense

Force. Breetai's flagship underwent extensive alteration, and, nine local years ago, was folded from Earthspace. The destination was Tirol."

"And what was the intention?" Shaizan asked. "War?"

"If, and only if, their peaceful overtures were rebuffed," the computer told him.

"What were the results of their efforts?"

"Breetai's flagship has not been heard from. Though, early on, my biosentient operator engaged me to transmit falsified communiqués from the ship."

"Justify."

"To bolster the concerns of the populace. Relations between the former ruling military body, the RDF, and a succeeding one, the Army of the Southern Cross, have become strained since the ship's departure. The current army is divided: some eagerly await word from the ship, while others consider the ship destroyed and are eager to break with the past."

The Elders spoke of a schism among the members of the mission that reached Tirol, Dag sent to the others as a reminder.

"Does the current military fear the arrival of Tiresians?" Bowkaz asked.

"Greatly. Tiresians and Invid, both."

"Can Earth be defeated by Tirol?"

"I have access to data on Earth's military strength. But comparable data on Tirol's strength would be required before an assessment of superiority could be formulated and presented."

"We don't have time for that," Dag said. "Our provisions of energy and supplies—"

An angry sending from Bowkaz cut him off. "The

names of Earthers holding prominent positions," the militant Master said to the machine.

"How many names are required?"

"Limit yourself to three."

"Wyatt Moran, head of the political body. Anatole Leonard, head of the military body. Lazlo Zand, head of the scientific body. Zand is the name of my interface. If anyone knows the whereabouts of the matrix, it is Zand."

"Does he realize that you are in communication with us?"

"Not yet. Although he will surely learn of it, since I am making use of a closely monitored satellite network."

"Can you quiz this Zand about the matrix?"

"I am not empowered to interrogate."

"Advise."

"Lacking sensors, I can but render assistance. I would advise that you permit me to transfer the data in my files to the machines that serve you. Reciprocity of relevant data is also advised."

"Embellish."

"A series of burst transmissions from my location to yours, from your location to mine, via a real-time machine-to-machine interface."

Once more, the trio of telepaths fell silent. *We must consider our position carefully,* Bowkaz sent after a long moment. "You will be contacted," he told the machine.

No sooner was the link broken than Dovak, leader of the Scientist triumvirate, appeared in the command center, kowtowing before the still-hovering Cap.

"Why do you interrupt us?" Shaizan demanded of the blue-lipped clone.

"A communiqué, my lords."

The Masters regarded each other. "The enthusiasm of Zor's machine troubles me—" Bowkaz started to say when Dovak cut in.

"The source of the signal is not Zor's machine. It originates on the sixth moon of the gas giant proximate our position."

"A signal from whom?" Shaizan asked.

"My lords, they contend that they are Zentraedi, with the Seventh Mechanized Division of the Botoru. Commander Khyron Kravshera's battalion."

Mechanical lions roamed the voltage-encased grounds of Anatole Leonard's estate in the outskirts of Monument City. The beasts were a kind of homage to the Brasília days, when live lions, escaped from the city's zoo during a week of malcontent riots, had been captured and brought to Leonard's lakeside palace. The animatrons—non-Protoculture, non-reconfigurable— were fracturing the silence of the cloudless autumn night with their plaintive roars.

Leonard and his seldom-seen adviser, Joseph Petrie, sat in side-by-side rockers on the wraparound front deck of the lodge-size log house. Petrie was sipping steaming coffee; Leonard, his usual glass of mineral water— piped directly to his compound from a mountain spring west of Monument.

Leonard had been staring at the dazzling starfields of the eastern sky since sunset, two hours earlier, rocking and staring and downing glass after glass of the allegedly salubrious water. "Something's not right," he was telling Petrie. "Something's definitely not right."

It wasn't the minister of war's first such pronouncement, but each time Petrie had asked about it, Leonard had clammed up, so Petrie had simply stopped asking. All at once, though, Leonard waived his view of the heavens to face Petrie.

"Upside," he said. "Something's not right upside."

Petrie assumed that he was referring to the situation with the factory satellite, which ten days earlier had sealed itself off to all communications with the surface. Neither had the factory responded to hailings from Space Station Liberty or the Advanced Chemical Engineering station on the lunar brightside. Command's concern was not per se for the Zentraedi inhabitants of the factory; the worry was that their sudden silence was linked to unconfirmed rumors of a planned coup, to be spearheaded by a clique of RDF officers in the Earth Defense Force.

"Even if the Zentraedi have decided to support Aldershot and the rest, it doesn't explain why they've remained incommunicado with Liberty and Aluce. RDFers outnumber us twenty to one on both stations." Scrawny and perpetually pale, Petrie was one of the few people who didn't employ an honorific when addressing Leonard.

"I'm in total agreement," the commander said. "What do the aliens have to offer the RDF, in any case, but safe haven in the factory after we've crushed Aldershot's petty rebellion and banished him and his cohorts from the surface? But that's not the trouble I'm referring to, Petrie. I'm speaking of trouble in the heavens."

Petrie raised his eyes to the sky, to the Milky Way, and a couple of bright points of light that were probably planets. That he didn't know Saturn from Sirius didn't bother him in the least; *inner* space was his bailiwick.

"Maybe you're locked onto some kind of clairvoyant

distress signal sent by the SDF-3," Petrie said at last, squinting. Was ancient light from the Valivarre system reaching Earth even as he spoke? Where the hell was Tirol in relation to things, anyway?

Leonard was frowning. "Perhaps it is the SDF-3. Perhaps it's T. R. Edwards, attempting to contact me." He grunted. "Whatever I'm sensing feels as if it's coming from somewhere closer than Tirol."

Petrie's narrow shoulders heaved in a shrug. "Maybe the Expeditionary mission is on its way home."

"Let's hope not—unless Edwards has discovered some way to strand Lang, Reinhardt, and the Hunters on the far side of the galaxy."

"Edwards would be the one who could do it."

Leonard nodded his shaved, bullet-shaped head, then snorted a laugh. "You know better than most that I'm not some mystical stargazer, Petrie. And I certainly don't put any stock in astrology. But I do accept that God Almighty aligned our local stars in such a way that we're meant to fashion from them the outlines of objects. I doubt that He had archers or rams or scorpions in mind, or even if he did, that those zodiacal symbols should be with us a millennium after some desert dwellers decided to decree them our official mascots."

Petrie took a gulp of coffee and, with one eyebrow cocked, turned to Leonard. "So what is it the constellations are telling you?"

"That we're being watched—evaluated. That Earth's troubles are far from over; that further purification is in order."

Petrie recognized the credo of the Church of Recurrent Tragedies, whose Southlands fellowships had received heavy funding from Leonard throughout Reconstruction and the years of the Malcontent Uprisings. "Is there anything we can do to prevent it, or is this purification process inevitable?"

"Not only is it inevitable, it is *essential* to our future as God's Children. Tempted by a diabolical technology, we yielded to temptation and loosed a new evil in the world. An evil that cannot be coaxed back into its box, its lamp, its foul-smelling orifice, until we have rid ourselves of baseness and have become pure of mind and body."

Leonard stood and walked to the deck's wooden railing. "Reeling from the catastrophic events of ten years of global war, Russo, Lang, Hayes, and their deluded followers embraced the Visitor and Robotechnology as a panacea, and we've been paying for their shortsightedness ever since." He slammed a fist down on the top rail. "This is why the EDF must be purged of Robotechs once and for all. So that, united, the rest of us will be strong enough to survive the coming purification. *That's* what those heavenly aspects and configurations are telling me, Petrie. That we must be prepared to put aside all fears of reprisal and be prepared to act on our vision. Yes, of course, our actions will be misunderstood and condemned. But only God's judgment counts, and in His eyes we will have triumphed over evil."

Petrie tried not to let his amusement show. Fanaticism of any variety left him entertained, especially when it had a promoter of Leonard's caliber, with his charmingly antiquated spewings about God and purification, most of it lifted chapter and verse from the defunct, technophobic, *fin de siècle* Faithful movement. Even so, the commander's ravings spoke to a practical consideration: the nettlesome RDF, and what was to be done with it.

"If only we *would* hear from the SDF-3," Leonard was saying. "If only God would grant me some sign that the time to act has arrived." He waved an arm at the sky. "Something more than a vague inkling. Something concrete."

Petrie didn't say anything for a long moment; he wanted his announcement to detonate in silence, and mushroom from there. "I've been waiting for an opportunity to share this with you," he began. "I mean, I know how you feel about Rolf Emerson, how you regard him as a man of integrity and all. But it seems that our Minister of Terrestrial Defense—and, need I add, former Zentraedi lover and Hunter crony—departed Fokker Aerospace at oh-twelve-hundred today, bound for the factory satellite."

"Go ahead," Miho Nagata said. "Order whatever you'd like. This one's on me."

Round-faced Census ran his eyes down the sim-wood table's inset display screen, his mouth already watering at the prospect of real food. "I guess I'll have the chicken and vegetable stir-fry."

Miho reacted with playful ridicule. "You can get that at any lunch stall on the street. How about *kobe*? When was the last time you sunk your teeth into a buttery-smooth steak?"

Uh, how about never, Census wanted to tell him. The restaurant was too glam to list the prices on the menu, but he figured that a steak had to cost more than his share of the apartment's monthly rent. Still, a *steak*! "You sure it's all right?"

Miho smiled, revealing gleaming, even teeth. "I said so, didn't I? Go ahead, digit it."

Census beamed back at him and entered his selection with the press of a forefinger against the screen. The restaurant had robot waiters, but they were only for delivering orders.

The place was called Tokonama, which was an old word for a seat reserved for a special guest. Located six levels below Shinjuku Station, it overlooked the entire dome and the video plazas and cherry-tree-lined concourses far below. The tablecloths and napkins were linen, there were fresh flowers in enamel vases on every table, and the patrons were corporate types in expensive clothes. In silk jacket and trousers, Nagata himself fit right in—even though he was through-and-through yak.

Census felt underdressed, but otherwise pumped. Nagata had posted a message at the apartment's e-drop the previous day, inviting him to lunch. Which had to mean that the Family Nagata yakked for, the Shimadas, must have gotten something out of the info Hongo had pirated from Aoki Aquaculture.

Japan's leading hatchery, Aoki distributed its product to a total of seven wholesalers, one of which was owned by Shimada. Shimada in turn sold to hundreds of second-level wholesalers, called *nakaoroshi*, most of which specialized in a particular species of fish and were allotted spaces in Tokyo's New Tsukiji Fish Market. But in penetrating Aoki's computer system, Hongo had learned that the hatchery was planning to sell tuna directly to a *nakaoroshi* conglomerate run by a crime family, thus eliminating Shimada from the profit loop.

Hongo had ventured that Nagata's people might want to employ their services again, maybe for more than Nagata had paid for the first go-round. So things were definitely looking up. Plus, Discount had received his head clearance from the clinic and was due for release anytime.

Now if Census could only get Misa into turnaround. Not that he expected she'd actually find new roomies—

not as yenless as she was. But at the same time he didn't want to see her have to come crawling back to him because she had nowhere else to go. He honestly wanted to *win* her back. And that could happen if Nagata were to become a steady client, or, better yet, a kind of patron, fronting whatever tech Hongo needed to execute deep-cyberspace intercepts.

"The reason I asked you here," Miho said, "was to tell you that your foreknowledge of events in the fish trade was much appreciated."

"We aim to please," Census said.

"It's always good to know what the competition is planning."

"Perhaps we could learn something more about future developments," Census suggested carefully.

Miho nodded. "Yes, I think that's a wise idea. Who can say? If things work out, there might be steady work in it for you."

"We would be most honored."

Miho laughed, leaned back in his chair, and withdrew a cigarette from a wooden case. "Tell me a bit about yourself. What do you like to do when you're not wedded to a telecomp?"

Census scratched his head and thought about it.

"Sports?"

"Not really."

"Movies?"

"No money."

"Hobbies?"

"I like browsing the Akihabara rubbish piles for discarded electronics."

Miho's forehead wrinkled in what seemed to be mild concern. "Okay," he said tentatively. "And what about your living situation? Do you have a place?"

"Yeah. I—that is, we do. Myself and a couple of . . . business associates. It's small, but it serves our needs. For now."

"Especially when you have all of cyberspace to wander around in, huh?"

"Exactly."

"You obviously have access to good tech."

"Not the best, but we improvise."

"And you trust your . . . associates?"

"All the way."

A waiter appeared with two beers and glided away on solid rubber wheels. *"Kanpei,"* Miho said, lifting his bottle.

Census took a sip of beer, luxuriating in the slightly bitter taste. A pretty *ojingal* sauntered past the table, making brief eye contact with Nagata. Her look and aroma made Census's eyes widen.

Miho caught the reaction and grinned. "I trust that there's at least one woman in your life. Can't skimp on that, you know."

"There is, yes."

"What's she like?"

"From out of the communals, same as me." Census frowned. "But hard to please, sometimes. She doesn't mind not owning a lot of things, so gifts don't work too well on her."

"What's her name?"

"Misa. But we call her Miko—as a joke, you know."

"I'm sure she's a beauty."

"Oh, yeah. Great eyes, great lips, great . . . And, uh, taller than me."

Miho's ringed right hand stroked his clean-shaven chin. "That wouldn't be the one I saw you with the day we met?"

Census froze with the beer bottle pressed to his lips. It was as if someone had just shot him full of ice water. If asked, he couldn't have said why; but there was suddenly something in Nagata's tone of voice that reeked of deliberate nonchalance. Why was he so interested in Census's personal life? And was what they'd sold him about Aoki really all that valuable?

Thoughts began to crowd into his mind. The day Nagata had seen Misa was the same day she'd purchased the disk from Tender/Search. The disk that featured only one ad, and that one from a woman Hongo was certain ran security for SPOOK.

And spooked was just how Census felt, though he concealed it behind a long swallow of beer, his eyes sweeping the neighboring tables for anything—*anything*—suspicious. All he saw were contented men and women engaged in seemingly delightful conversations. There was only one solo within view: a harmless-looking, obese little man with curly hair.

"No, no, that wasn't Misa," he finally got around to telling Nagata. "That was another friend."

"Ah, so there's more than one in your life."

"When times are good."

"What's that one's name—the one I saw on the bench?"

"Her? Actually, you know, I don't even know her all that well. But I think they call her Haruke."

"Haruke."

"Yeah. Haruke."

The steaks arrived.

"Dig in."

Census stared at the massaged meat, mournfully aware that his appetite had fled.

CHAPTER
NINE

The survivor of a ship that had crashed not far from Darwin, Ilan Tinari had found her way to Sydney with a dozen other aliens, most of whom later tied up with a Malcontent band known as the Claimers. Quite human in appearance—issued from the same clone queue that had given the Zentraedi Miriya Parino and Seloy Deparra, head of the Malcontent Scavengers—Tinari served as [Rolf Emerson's] bodyguard long before they became lovers. Rolf's love for his wife notwithstanding, some of his happiest memories were of his and Tinari's time in the Argentine, a honeymoon of sorts, antedating the riots in the Southlands, the formation of the Army of the Southern Cross, and the destruction of Zagerstown, after which Tinari was moved to join the cause.

Soon afterward, Laura Shaze entered Rolf's life for a time, though Dana and Bowie eventually proved too much for their relationship. Then Tinari had returned, showing up on his doorstep without advance word, one of the few Zentraedi who hadn't gone upside free of charge on the shuttles Commander Leonard had set aside for the aliens' use. But once more it was Dana who tipped the scales. Rolf had never revealed Tinari's ancestry to Dana; but, for Tinari, the precocious young woman was a constant reminder of what might have been had the Humans been accepting of them. And so Tinari too went upside.

S. J. Fischer, *Legions of Light: A History of the Army of the Southern Cross*

THE SHUTTLE DOCKED IN THE FACTORY SATELLITE'S three-o'clock pod, whose iris gate was now the sole operational portal in the entire facility. Rolf Emerson, his adjutant Captain Rochelle, and three of the five crewpersons debarked. The only other ships parked in the bay were two aged ARMD-series shuttles, neither of which was serviceable. The rest of the hold was blotched with pools of unidentifiable lubricants and strewn with refuse, unopened crates of now-spoiled food, and the husks of off-gassing electronics. The stench was overpowering.

Rolf recalled a visit he had made years earlier, in the company of then Vice Admiral Rick Hunter, Brigadier General Gunther Reinhardt, and Captain Max Sterling. They had come to apprise Breetai of the enforced Micronizations that were being performed in the Arkansas Protectorate, transformed into an internment camp for Earth's remaining full-size aliens. Hunter had also wanted to announce the formation of the all-Zentraedi Twenty-third Veritech Squadron, which would go on to distinguish itself in the Southlands during the Malcontent Uprisings.

Rolf remembered the beehive bustle of the place, Earthers and aliens working shoulder-to-shoulder to ready Breetai's much-altered flagship for launch to Tirol. After Emerson's promotion to colonel and his permanent relocation to Monument City, official business typically carried him to Aluce, Liberty, or Base Gloval on Mars, in its final phase. When not shuttling from place to place to meet with base commanders, he had had Dana and Bowie to see to; their parents were aloft, helping Hunter, Hayes, and Emil Lang finalize contingencies for the Expeditionary mission. Rolf had attended the Hunters' send-off wedding, of course; but since 2020 he had only revisited the factory on three occasions, two of which had involved ministry matters. The third visit had been prompted by the deaths of Rico, Konda, and Bron—Dana's "godfathers"—who had died within weeks of one another, and were eulogized by Nigel Aldershot.

Since Lang's tech teams had never succeeded in rousing the factory's central computer—either to supervise systems maintenance or to mass-produce Battlepods, its specialty—the monstrous, radish-shaped facility had already begun to deteriorate by the time the SDF-3 launched. In addition, the REF had left the factory looking as trashed as the base camp of a mountain-climbing expedition. And for all the years the Zentraedi had lived among Earthers, they had never fully comprehended the necessity of orderliness and cleanliness. Repairs and routine maintenance had always been effected by the same machines that piloted their miles-long battlewagons and provided food for personnel numbering in the tens of thousands.

Estimates of the current onboard population ranged from three to five hundred, most of them living in gender segregation in coffin-size compartments on level seven. All the full-size had shipped out with the REF, taking with them the only functioning resizing chamber. The enormous holds above and below level seven were sealed off, including the access tubes to five of the pods and to the null-g hollow where the SDF-3 had been constructed. The factory produced a synth food, rich in the ur-Protoculture chemicals essential for the health of their elastic bodies, but deaths by voluntary starvation were not uncommon. Widespread xenophobia was what had forced them offworld, and a profound sense of purposelessness hung like a pall over the colony.

Returning to the factory after so lengthy an absence brought to the surface all the anxiety Rolf had stowed away concerning the seeming disappearance of the SDF-3. Dana and Bowie had proved alarmingly resistant to concern for the safety of their parents, accepting on faith that they would reunite with them someday. Whenever Rolf would go into one of his solemn talks about possible futures, the kids would say that the mission had probably been delayed, or that hammering out an accord with the Masters was simply taking longer than expected. Rolf frequently wished that he had even an iota of their certitude and optimism. Instead, he had gone through a kind of grieving process the past few years, first denying all possibilities of tragedy; then growing angry with the Sterlings, the Grants, and the Hunters for abandoning Earth in parlous times; then spiraling into a black hole of sadness and depression; and finally, only lately, learning to accept that tragic consequences came with the territory, and that life rarely offered guarantees of any sort.

Nevertheless, there was something about standing in the miasmic docking bay of the factory's three-o'clock pod that was corrosive to Rolf's newfound acceptance. And the sight of Ilan Tinari didn't help any.

Dusky and supple, Ilan had big, dark eyes and a wild mane of black hair. Even a hopelessly frayed jumpsuit couldn't mask her sultry handsomeness. Approaching her, however, Rolf could see that she was changed—the passion kindled by her years on the surface had gone out of her. She radiated all the warmth of a marble statue. So why was his heart breaking all over again?

"Thank you for coming, Rolf," she said when he was near enough. They didn't embrace or so much as shake hands. There was a time when they were ruled by mutual touch and the affection that fueled it, but Ilan had disowned those feelings. Even when she had turned up in Monument City after a six-year absence.

"Was it you who sent the message?" Rolf asked her.

She nodded.

"What's this about, Ilan? Why have you people refused to respond to our hailings?"

Ilan held his gaze for a moment. "Come. We'll talk."

She spun on her heel and headed for the nearest hatchway. Rolf instructed Captain Rochelle to stay behind with the shuttle crew and hurried after her.

When the encrypted message had been received at Terrestrial Defense headquarters on Fokker Base, Rolf had assumed it had come from Ilan. That the "invitation" may have been a personal request was one of the justifications he had used for not informing Leonard or his command staff of his plans to go upside. Not that he was obliged to, in any case; and he certainly had no doubts that Leonard would learn of his departure in short order. But he reasoned that the commander would have prohibited the trip, thinking it part of Aldershot's plan to unseat him, and Rolf refused to give Leonard that pleasure.

Ilan led him past more refuse heaps, malodorous pools, and cannibalized electronics; past row after row of housing coffins and isolated groups of sullen Zentraedi. It was no wonder the UEG had rejected a documentarian's request for permission to shoot a video aboard the factory; their xenophobia notwithstanding, Earthers would only have added reason for denouncing the REF for its self-serving tactics.

The short tour ended in a trashed compartment that had probably been someone's office during construction of the SDF-3. Ilan had Rolf sit down in the only intact chair.

"We want permission to leave," she told him evenly.

He showed her a perplexed look. "Leave the factory?

Ilan, you know you don't need our permission to do that. You're here by your own choice."

Her head was shaking before he even finished. "That's not what I mean. We want permission to leave stationary orbit."

Rolf was momentarily stunned. "Leave for where? This thing's incapable of fold. Where could you go?"

"Into a cometary orbit." She crossed the room to an outmoded comp and called up astrogational graphics on the device's CRT. "Lang wrote this program years before the SDF-3 launched. The factory's reflex drives will insert us into orbit; then the gravitation sinks of this system will do the rest."

Rolf was staring at her. "I don't understand—"

"Because the Masters are coming, Rolf. And it's likely *we* will be the first to feel their wrath."

"Ilan," Rolf interrupted. "When this station was fully operational its sensors could scan clear to Pluto. If you have some evidence that the Masters are en route . . . If this is why you've been incommunicado—"

"We have no evidence of the sort you're talking about. But consider how a human infant knows when its birth mother is nearby even before its eyes can see her. It is no different between the Zentraedi and the Masters. We can *sense* when our creators are close by. The reason we've stopped responding to your hailings is because the Masters will be scanning for signals transmitted by any of the facilities they designed for use by the Zentraedi." She cut her eyes to him. "We're running silent for your sake."

Rolf thought about Dana's recent bouts with unprovoked anger and agitation. Was she feeling what the factory Zentraedi were? "And this plan to leave Earthspace?" he asked. "This is also for our sake?"

"In part. On defold in this system, the fortresses of the Masters' fleet will immediately seize on our position. We will become the target of their initial hunt. But they will not destroy us without first communicating their intentions. We will tell them that the Protoculture matrix left Earth aboard the SDF-3—to be returned to them, if that is what you wish us to say. They won't believe us. But the subsequent destruction of this factory will alert you to the fact that the Masters are present and that attack is imminent."

Rolf nodded gravely. Early on in Reconstruction, long before Khyron leveled Macross Three, a plan had been formulated to use the in-construction SDF-2 as just such a decoy. Or so Rolf had heard. "You said, 'in part.' "

Ilan turned away from him. "We don't want the Masters to discover us like this—defeated, pathetic, huddled together in filth . . . We can at least make a pretense of having retained our pride."

Rolf stood up and went to her. "I believe you that you can sense their approach. What I need to know is if there is a way for you to gauge the strength of your feelings. Just how close are they, Ilan? There are things that need to be done."

The muscles in her jaw bulged. "Rolf, I risked making contact with you to ask a favor. If you're going to turn this into a deal—"

"I'm not. But if you people are willing to help us by offering yourselves to the Masters as a target of opportunity, why won't you tell me all you know?"

She folded her arms across her chest. "How many years did we share?"

"I don't know—five, six?"

"And have you already forgotten the conditioning

that we must overcome merely to coexist with you in Earthspace? In place of fashioning weapons to rain death on your world as we were tasked to do by Dolza?"

Rolf shook his head. "I haven't forgotten about the Imperative. And I'm sorry if I made this sound like a swap. Of course I'll do whatever you ask of me—without obligation."

Some of the hardness left her face. "Thank you, Rolf."

And for one moment it was like old times between them.

"Then you will convey to the proper authorities our request to embark?" she asked.

"I will." Rolf paused. "Is there a chance I could convince you to remain in Earthspace, Ilan?"

She nearly smiled. "How are the children?"

Rolf forced a breath. "Hardly children anymore. They've both entered the Earth Defense Force Academy."

"Miriya Parino would have been proud of her daughter. And grateful to you for the sacrifices you've made."

Rolf studied her. "Ilan, will there be a way to contact the factory should the SDF-3 return? Is it possible you'll return if and when the fortress does?"

Ilan was noncommittal. "Most of us will be dead before long. Many onboard have stopped ingesting the drugs Lang developed to retard our deterioration."

"Why?"

"Because we are the doomed. There is no place for us in the galaxy. We would rather expire as we were meant to than live on without purpose. However horrific, the Imperative was the Zentraedi equivalent of faith—our reason to be. Living among you—though infinitely preferable to our former lives as warriors—has corrupted that faith. The Zentraedi are an anachronism." Ilan gazed at Rolf for a long moment. "Can I count on you, Rolf Emerson?"

"Always," he said, biting back his grief.

Centered in a commo sphere in the command nexus of the Masters' flagship stood Sliat Rnan, Zentraedi commander of a *Thuveral Salan* destroyer assigned to the Seventh Mechanized Division of the Botoru Battalion. The battlewagon was thrust at an acute angle into the impact-cratered surface of a small moon millions of miles removed from its ringed captor.

Sliat was barrel-chested, dark haired, and prognathous. He held one arm across his chest not as a sign of obeisance but to keep his tattered command cloak from slipping off his shoulder. The uniform itself was torn in several places, revealing patches of Sliat's bluish-white skin, and the Zentraedi sigil—the *Cizion*—affixed to the yoke was dangling by a corner.

"Under Dolza's lead, we took the battle to the Micronian homeworld," he was telling the Masters. "Annihilation bolts unleashed by the ships of the Grand Fleet pierced the atmosphere, obliterating thousands of cities, killing hundreds of millions of inhabitants. But the hostiles answered us with unprecedented frenzy, employing an array of weapons never before encountered—a Voice that confounded the brave pilots of our cruisers and scout ships, a subsurface cannon that belched nuclear fire into our midst. Even so, victory seemed assured. Until the suicidal Micronians drove Zor's vessel into the heart of Commander-in-Chief Dolza's fortress and targeted the sum of its might against the reflex furnaces. It wasn't an act of warfare, my lords. It was an act of madness, bred of desperation. If it hadn't been for the barrier shield, the Micronian usurpers of Zor's ship would have been immolated."

Sliat, hellishly backlit by the bridge's emergency illumination, coughed and sniffled. The backs of his hands were covered with sores. Behind him in the dimly lighted command bubble were half a dozen full-size crewpersons, helmeted and slouched into acceleration couches. Bioscanners aboard the Masters' ship indicated that most of those seated were long dead.

Shaizan communicated his thoughts to Dag and Bowkaz before directing words to the commo sphere. "Tell us of the aftermath of the battle."

Sliat cleared his throat repeatedly. "M'lords, with the destruction of Dolza's fortress, the ships of the Grand Fleet were like limbs of a decapitated beast—flailing uselessly and uncontrollably. The vast majority were engulfed and atomized by the burgeoning explosive cloud, whose epicenter was the still-intact vessel Zor designed. What ships remained oriented of their own accord on the Micronian homeworld, and into its superheated atmosphere they plunged. Like spears they fell, like flaming arrows dispatched from some circumferential battlement. Down and down they plummeted, many of them incinerating on entry, while others struck and stuck into the yielding surface like pins. Including, m'lords, the *Quiltra Queleual* commanded by Khyron Kravshera."

The Masters exchanged thoughts, and, once more, Shaizan voiced the outcome of their telepathic conference. "Did you attempt to establish contact with your fellow survivors on Earth?"

Sliat bowed his head. "We have tried. When the factory satellite defolded in Earthspace, we reached out for it, but to no avail. But we have continued in our efforts, all these miserable years that have found us disabled on this moon. Unfamiliarity with the Micronians' language has prevented us from deciphering the content of their incessant noise, but we do know that Commander Khyron died during an attack which destroyed Zor's grounded fortress once and for all. Long live the memory of Khyron!"

In saluting, Slait lost hold of his command cloak and it slid off his shoulder to the deck.

"Indeed," a narrow-eyed Dag responded. "Long live the memory of *Khyron*. But, tell us, Sliat Rnan, how it is that your destroyer neither succumbed to Dolza's funerary fireball nor plummeted to Earth?"

"My lords, the ship was depleted of Protoculture."

"That much is not in question," Shaizan said. "But how did you come to crash so far removed from the battle itself?"

Sliat swallowed hard. "We're not certain, my lords. For some reason, the ship elected to deliver us here."

Shaizan nodded his bald head. "I see. Well, then, Sliat Rnan, it might interest you to know that yours wasn't the only ship of the Grand Fleet to escape destruction or capture by the Earth. The other ship managed to execute a fold that delivered it to the factory satellite's former space-time location. There, the crew related the details of the battle in Earthspace to Commander Reno, who, in turn, relayed them to us. And know, Sliat Rnan, that the two reports are very much in agreement: the firing of a planet-based weapon, the confounding Voice, the insidious defiling of Dolza's deepspace fortress, the ensuing destruction, the fall to Earth . . ."

"Thus it was, my lords," a transparently relieved Sliat

said. "But the last of the Botoru are prepared to take up the fight once more, in service to Tirol and in vengeance for the Zentraedi!"

The Masters were silent for a long moment. It was Bowkaz who finally spoke. "An inspiring speech, Commander. But I'm afraid you didn't allow Master Shaizan to complete his thought. The two accounts of the battle were in agreement, save on one matter: that of Khyron's cowardice and treachery."

Sliat was wordless.

"Will you deny that Khyron ordered the ships of the Botoru Battalion to disengage *before* the destruction of the command fortress?" Shaizan asked. "And that it was only a shortage of Protoculture that thwarted his plan to fold from Earthspace?"

Sliat lowered his head. "I cannot deny it, my lords."

"So it seems that you were not so much blessed by fate as you were *purposely* removed from its reach," Dag said.

The Zentraedi stooped to retrieve his cloak and flung it over his shoulder. "My lords, we were only following Commander Khyron's orders."

"*Khyron's* orders? Even when those orders were in conflict with Dolza's? Even when they contradicted the Imperative?"

Sliat stiffened. "My lords, it's true that Khyron was disloyal to Dolza. But only out of unwavering loyalty to you!"

Shaizan glowered. "Explain yourself."

"Khyron knew that Dolza had secret designs on Zor's fortress and on the Protoculture matrix it concealed. Khyron had already observed Breetai's defection. Now he saw Dolza defecting. His aim in ordering a fold was to return the Botoru to Tirol and apprise you of the developments." Sliat stood tall. "I repeat: We are in your service. Rescue and enable us to do your bidding."

The Masters conferred. Then Bowkaz altered the position of his fingertips on the hovering Protoculture Cap.

"We have no further need of your services. In their bowels, our ships carry an army of warrior clones who know the meaning of obedience. The Zentraedi had an opportunity to honor themselves and they failed. You say Khyron was acting in our benefit, when it was Khyron whose wounded pride compelled him to attack Zor's fortress instead of returning to Tirol. You, Commander Sliat Rnan, failed by siding with someone who, by destroying the Protoculture matrix, may have undermined the survivability of Tirol itself."

Sliat coughed and cleared his throat. "My lords, I ask that you not leave us here to rot."

Shaizan made a dismissive gesture. "Don't concern yourself with the future, Commander. Your exile is over." He depressed a spot on the Cap. "Your ship has been targeted for destruction. Go happily to your graves."

CHAPTER
TEN

Born in 1991, [Miho Nagata] grew up in Tokyo and on Macross Island, after his father, a Shimada employee, was sent there to take control of the Family's gambling and prostitution interests. Interestingly, the elder Nagata had several run-ins with a young Anatole Leonard in 2006, when, as a member of Conrad Wilbur's Faithful, Leonard was brought on-island to organize protest demonstrations aimed at closing the very Shimada concerns Nagata was supervising.

footnote in Bruce Mirrorshades,
Machine Mind and Arthurian Legend

"WHY DO YOU WANT TO HAVE ANOTHER look at the disk?" Misa asked as she was kicking off her sandals. She glanced at Census, who was nearest the slider. "Don't tell me: You're thinking about moving into Yoko Nitabi's place after you make your big run."

Census didn't so much as grin. Nor did Gibley, already stationed at the telecomp, which was surrounded on all sides by stuff Misa had never seen before—adjuncts, turbochargers, peripherals, slaves. Nor, for that matter, did Discount, though maybe his excuse was medication prescribed by the clinic that had seen him through the Zand attack.

Misa aimed a frown at each of them. "What's with you guys, someone season your sushi with soporifics?"

"Did you bring the disk?" Census asked.

Misa forced a tight-lipped smile. "Your *Kawaii-chan* messenger made sure I did. Who is she, anyway, your new lover? Not that I blame you. But I am surprised—I thought you didn't like women with blond hair."

"She's *my* friend," Gibley explained.

Misa glanced at him, then back at Census. "Sorry. How did you know where to find me?"

He shrugged. "We put out the word. Some guy told Discount he'd seen you sleeping in Ueno Park, so we started there."

"Yeah, well, lucky for you Gibley's cutie-pie friend found me when she did. I was practically on my way to Tender/Search to ask for my money back."

Census nodded impatiently and held out his hand. "Could I have it?"

She exhaled peevishly and handed him the disk. Census passed it along to Gibley, who immediately slotted the thing in the player. At the same time, Census and Discount centered themselves in front of monitor screens right and left of the telecomp.

"Ready?" Gibley asked them, his fingers poised over the player's remote control.

"Launch it," Discount told him.

The ad began to run—without comments from any of them this go-round. Once more, Yoko Nitabi's alluring face filled the screen, followed by views of her apartment and views from it, overlooking the plazas and pedestrian malls of the Bunkyo-ku Station geo-grid.

"Anything?" Gibley asked, eyes glued to the screen.

His partners shook their heads. The ad continued, on into scenes of Nitabi's Minmei-soundtracked night on the town—

"Freeze it!" Census said.

Gibley did, and swung to him. "What have you got?"

"I'm not sure. Might be nothing more than noise corruption."

"Did it coincide with the beginning of the music?"

"Yeah."

Gibley looked at Discount. "You have any Minmei on disk?"

Discount managed a short laugh. "What, are you kidding me?"

"Is there someplace local we can get some?"

Discount shrugged. "Some of her tunes might be available in the vending machines on the corner."

"Check it out. Look for a compilation that includes "Stage Fright." And make sure it's digital and not remastered from analog."

Discount hurried through the doorway barefooted.

Misa watched him go and turned to Gibley and Census. "All right, let's hear it."

They traded looks. Then Census said, "Remember how surprised we were to find only one ad on the disk?"

"Of course I do. That's why I was going to demand a refund."

Census nodded. "Obviously there was a mistake. But we're thinking it was an *important* mistake." He reminded Misa of their argument on the day he had rendezvoused with the gangster, then took her forward to the previous day's lunch with the same yak, and the seemingly innocent questions Miho Nagata had asked regarding Misa. "When I remembered what Hongo said about Nitabi working for SPOOK, and I put that together with your getting the disk right where Nagata and I were meeting . . ." He let his words trail off. "Why are you staring at me?"

Misa scowled. "Because I can't believe I ever allowed myself to fall for someone so completely *braindead!*"

"Huh?"

She shook her head in angry bewilderment. "Why in the world would gangsters be interested in an ad for a share in an apartment? Don't you figure they'd have enough NuYen to get places of their own?"

"It's not the ad," Gibley said quietly. "It's something written into it."

"In code?"

"That's what we're trying to find out."

Regarding him, Misa began to shake her head again. "You're out of your heads, both of you. You've got a woman from SPOOK placing an encrypted ad and a *yakuza* panting to get his hands on it, but instead of just letting me return it to Tender/Search you want to *decipher* the thing? You think this is some kind of turn-of-the-century *jidai* thriller?"

Census compressed his lips briefly. "No, but—"

"But nothing! We have the thing, there's nothing we can do about that. But we're not dangerous to anyone unless we know something. So *don't read it*. Let me take it back."

Discount suddenly reappeared in the doorway with a smile on his face and a disk of Minmei's greatest hits in hand. Not daring to make eye contact with Misa, Census tore the disk from its packaging and inserted it into one of the ancillary players. He and Gibley spent a moment getting the song in the ad in synch with its track on the disk. Then Gibley ran the ad back to where the music began.

"This is beyond stupid," Misa complained, pacing. "Exactly what I'd expect from the three of you—"

"Got it," Census said, loud enough to be heard over her angry ruminations. "The sixteenth bit is carrying information."

"Encrypted."

"Affirmative."

Gibley rubbed his hands together and reached for his interface goggles. "Dump the sixteenth data into a new file. I'm going to buy a timeshare on the public library's neural net and task it to go work on the code."

A certain exhilaration notwithstanding, Misa took a seat on the mats and worried. She didn't like the notion of people asking questions about her. Which wouldn't be the case if Census hadn't tried to "kill two birds with one stone" in his initial meet with Miho Nagata. But then again, she wouldn't have the disk if she hadn't stopped at the Tender/Search booth looking for new roommates. Which, in itself, wouldn't have been necessary if her old roommates had been worth sticking with . . .

"I'm getting something," Gibley was saying. "Looks like the neural net has identified one of the keys used in the encryption process. It's trying to match the key to the encoded fragments." Suddenly his eyes widened. "Jee*zus*."

"What?" Census demanded. "What is it?"

"Nitabi's relaying information she got directly from Zand!"

Misa's palms broke into icy sweat.

Discount was peering at Gibley over a stake of electronics. "About what?"

"About the Robotech Masters." He stared at Census. "Zand is in contact with them!"

* * *

"What did he buy?" Miho asked a Shimada Family soldier named Kazuki.

Kazuki smiled in secret knowledge. "A Lynn-Minmei disk." He was a narrow-faced forty-year-old with the longest arms Miho had ever seen on a six-footer.

"You don't suppose they had a sudden urge to listen to classic pop," Miho said.

Kazuki arched a sparse eyebrow. "These kids? Besides, Yoko's operational parameters directed her to use a Minmei track for encryption."

Miho made his lips a fine line and nodded. "Of course, even if they find evidence of encryption, there's still the code itself."

"Maybe they're more talented than you think they are."

The kid who had purchased the disk from the vending machine didn't look especially bright, but then neither had Census, and already the young pirate had surprised Miho.

He and Kazuki and two trainees were across the avenue from the forlorn-looking three-story building in the Kabukicho where the kids shared an apartment, not far from the music machine Census's cohort had just done business with. A half-hour earlier, they had observed the girl—Misa—entering the building. The question then had been if she had the disk with her or not. Now it appeared that not only had she brought it, but that Census and company were giving it a close read.

The six-lane, one-way avenue was a main thoroughfare for trucks en route to the Shinjuku Station geo-grid supply elevators, which operated under the aegis of Shimada Off-Loading and Hauling. Cheap hotels, sex shops, and fast-food outlets lined both sides of the roadway, and every corner was an arcade of vendors, with scores of wheeled and multilimbed delivery robots, many of which could be addressed and tasked by telephone and telecomp.

"So how do you want to handle this?" Kazuki asked, working himself up.

Miho thought about Census. The way the kid had clammed up at lunch, it was obvious that he had seen through Miho's calculated nonchalance. But the fact that he'd tried to conceal the identity of the girl on the bench suggested that he had viewed the disk and perhaps had suspicions about its content—suspicions confirmed by Miho's questions. There was a difference between being talented and being smart, however, and Census had done a foolish thing by reading the disk, because his actions now made it impossible for Miho to finesse the situation. Instead of a purse-snatching or a mild mugging, Miho was going to have to confront the problem head on, employing old-fashioned techniques of force and threats to ensure the kids' silence.

Miho was disappointed in the turn the events had taken. He could have seen himself developing a fondness for Census and his big-boned girlfriend.

"They might be willing to listen to reason," he told Kazuki. "We give them some money, promise them some work. What choice do they have? Chances are, whatever Yoko sent is going to be too big for them to fence."

Kazuki rocked his head from side to side. "It's up to Mr. Shimada any way you look at it. If he doesn't trust them, if he wants them disposed of, what choice do *we* have? No matter what, we still need a course of action here."

Miho studied the entrance to the building, across six lanes of rapidly moving truck traffic. "Plain and simple.

Station one of our assistants at the front door, the other around back. You and I go upstairs and explain the facts to them. They have something that belongs to us, and we would appreciate their cooperation."

"And if they've read the disk?"

"It becomes somewhat more complicated. We'll have to cart the kids and their equipment out of there." Miho glanced at the street. "A traffic jam might help." He unclipped a phone from his belt and entered a code. "Four garbage trucks will be sufficient," he was telling someone a moment later. "Right. We won't move until they arrive."

"Weapons?" Kazuki asked when Miho had stashed the phone.

"Only if required."

Ten minutes later the requested garbage trucks from Shimada Off-Loading and Hauling were nosing into view a couple of blocks south of the vendor and robot arcade. A heavy-metal wedding of shovels, claws, and dumpsters, each truck was a monstrous sixteen-wheeler that took up two lanes. Miho had his phone out.

"Kazuki and I are going to be entering through the front door," he was saying. "Slow all six lanes of traffic to a crawl, and keep it that way until you see us reappear on the street. If we've got a couple of kids with us by then, one of you should angle in for a quick pickup."

"Understood," said a female voice at the other end of the phone connection, presumably the driver of the lead vehicle.

Miho opened his sports jacket, clipped the phone to his belt, and loosed a long exhale. *"Shigata ga nai,"* he told Kazuki. *It can't be helped.*

Kazuki stuck two fingers in his mouth and whistled for the trainees. Dressed in baggy clothing and not much older then Census, the pair of them hurried over. Miho didn't have much trust in the boy, but he knew the girl. Her name was Tine Amano, and her parents had been his martial arts instructors for the past five years.

Kazuki explained how things were to go down, and was just about to send them on their way when a chorus of electronic chirps, bleats, and warbles began to issue from the arcade's dozens of robots. It was as though every one had been simultaneously tasked to run deliveries, only instead of ambling off in different directions they were suddenly milling around the arcade in glitched confusion, corralling the area's handful of Humans between the broad sidewalk and the vending machines.

Instantly, the four *yakuza* found themselves herded into a corner, darting from vendor to vendor to avoid having their feet crushed by the robots' solid-rubber rollers and dodging the unpredictable flailings of a forest of permaplas limbs.

Miho was crouched behind a cactus-and-bonsai vendor when, through a chaos of careening machines, he spied three men making a run for the now-nearly-traffic-free street. Their apparent leader was an obese little creature, sporting a fedora of a style that hadn't been popular since the Global Civil War. The one who had snatched Yoko Nitabi in the Koishikawa Gardens, Miho told himself in alarmed revelation.

Scrambling for safety behind a machine that dispensed natal and progressed astrological charts, Miho reached for his phone and punched the code for the driver of the lead garbage truck.

"What's happening up there?" the woman asked before Miho could say anything. "It looks like a 'bot free-for-all."

"Three men crossing the street!" Miho returned in a rush. "Stop them from reaching the target building!"

"Weapons?"

"Whatever it takes!"

Misa was the first to tune in to the sounds of commotion that were filtering up to the apartment from the avenue. Screeching tires, blaring horns, the mechanical growl of heavy equipment ... *fireworks*? She tapped Census on the shoulder, but he was too absorbed in Gibley's ongoing exchange with the public library's neural net to attend to the noise.

"The Masters have fed data to Zand about the SDF-3," Gibley was saying now. "But the neural net's uncertain about the decryption key. Either the SDF-3 was destroyed, or it's crippled, or the mission itself has failed and the ship won't be returning anytime soon."

"How about that it's on the way home?"

Gibley shook his head. "That doesn't seem to be an option."

The reverberating thunder of an explosion finally woke the three of them from their shared preoccupation.

"What the hell was that?" Gibley asked, slipping out of the All-Seeing Eyes interface goggles.

"I've been trying to tell you—" Misa started to say.

Census was already headed for the doorway to the hall. "I'll go."

"A gas main?" Discount asked Gibley.

The cybernaut shook his head. "Sounded more like an antimecha mine."

The bottom seemed to drop out of Misa's stomach. "Guys, you don't think I could have been followed here, do you?"

They were both regarding her when Census hurried

back into the apartment, blanched and agitated. "There's a goddamned battle going on outside! Four trucks have the whole area blocked off and the street's crawling with robots!"

Discount gaped at him. "Robots or mecha?"

"Robots! From the arcade."

"Who's firing at who?" Misa demanded.

"The guys in the trucks are taking fire from someone across the street."

Gibley shot Census a look. "What kind of trucks?"

"Garbage trucks."

"Shimada," Gibley said with a defeated wince.

The guys stared at Misa.

"Don't tell me you've fucked up?" she said, full of false surprise.

Census was trembling. "Nagata must have known I was lying about you. They probably had the building staked out and saw you come in."

Misa gnawed at her thumbnail. "But who would Shimada be fighting?"

The room fell silent for a moment; then, in unison, Gibley and Census said, "Zand!"

A pained look took shape on Discount's face. "Oh, shit."

"Oh, double shit," Gibley answered him, one hand doing rapid input at the deck while the other was zeroing devices.

Census paced nervously behind him. "Now what?"

"We give them the disk is what," Misa said firmly.

He stared at her in disbelief. "Knowing what we know?"

"*Especially* knowing what we know. It's my disk, Census. I paid for it, and I say we give it to them."

"To who?" Discount wanted to know. "Shimada or Zand?"

"I don't care. Whoever gets here first. Let *them* fight over it."

Gibley stood up. "Misa's right—we've got to surrender it. They can't prove we've read it."

But Census ridiculed the idea. "They're going to take one look at all this gear and know that we've at least been *trying* to read it. That'll be more than enough for them."

Discount had rushed out into the hallway and was now back inside the room.

"Anything?" Gibley asked while he was stuffing the pockets of his trousers with software disks.

Discount shook his head. "The gunfire's stopped, but the 'bots are still wandering around and traffic's completely snarled."

Gibley was at the doorway, peering into the hall. "We can't stay here."

"I can," Census countered, clenching his hands. "All of this is my fault. The rest of you go."

Misa rolled her eyes. "*Now* he gets heroic."

Census was about to say something when the telecomp suddenly went online. Discount, who was closest to the screen, read the message aloud. " 'Think before you act.' " He turned a look over his shoulder. "It's signed 'MN.' "

Census ran his right hand down his face and groaned. "Miho Nagata."

"That tears it," Discount said quickly. "We leave everything exactly where it is—including the disk, agreed?"

Misa and Census nodded.

Gibley had his boots on and was standing in the hallway, checking the battery status of his flip-phone. "Cense, Nagata has never seen me. I'm going downstairs to the rear entrance. I'll ring twice, then go offline if everything's clear."

Census nodded.

Misa looked at Gibley. "Where are we supposed to *go*?"

He shrugged. "We'll figure that out once we're out of the building."

Misa sank wearily to the floor in a cross-legged posture while Census and Discount hovered over the phone.

Five tense minutes later it rang once, then once more.

And the three of them scrambled out the door.

CHAPTER ELEVEN

I find it remarkable that T. R. Edwards, Anatole Leonard, Wyatt Moran, and Lazlo Zand ever considered themselves players on the same team. From the beginning, Edwards wanted to do away with Moran; Moran, with Leonard; Leonard, with Zand. I suspect that even if Edwards had been successful in assuming control of the SDF-3, he and his mutineers would have been fired upon as soon as the ship defolded in Earthspace. Either that, or Edwards would have done the firing, targeting Leonard and the rest from the safety of lunar orbit.

Admiral Rick Hunter, as quoted in
Resh N'Tar's *Interviews with Admirals*

EAGER FOR FURTHER COMMUNICATION FROM THE Masters, Lazlo Zand hadn't left his subterranean office in SPOOK for close to a week. He had checked in hourly with the mother computer, but had refrained from engaging the Zor holo in conversations out of fear that the Masters had discovered some means of penetrating the system and eavesdropping on its cerebrations—despite that by its own account the computer had passed the Masters' tests. But why, then, the hesitation in establishing a direct computer-to-computer interface?

Judging from the initial communication, the Masters were fixed on locating the Protoculture matrix, just as Exedore and Breetai had predicted ten years earlier. But Zand now had reason to suspect that the matrix hadn't gone missing with the SDF-1's spacefold generators, but was interred with the remains of the fortress, concealed in the ship's Reflex drives. That fact alone was enough to start a second Robotech War or prevent one, though Zand had no intention of playing his trump card until he had positioned himself on the winning side. After all, there were larger issues at stake than the fate of Planet Earth.

The most interesting detail to emerge from the cursory debriefing of the mother computer was that the Masters appeared to have no knowledge of the SDF-3. More, they had implied that they were completely unaware of recent events on their homeworld, Tirol. Did that mean that the Expeditionary mission had yet to arrive on Tirol nine years after the launch? Or had the Masters embarked on their journey *before* Earth-relative 2020? If the former was true, the SDF-3 might be anywhere in the galaxy, lost, crippled, or destroyed; if the latter, the implication was that the Masters hadn't folded to Earth's neighborhood but had traveled more or less conventionally through space-time. Which in turn suggested that their ships, lacking sufficient reserves of Protoculture, were incapable of fold.

A weakness, to be sure.

Zand had been heartened to find that the computer, as instructed, had mentioned his name. Should it eventually come down to a direct conversation between Zand and the Masters, the Tiresians would find an Earther whose intellect had been shaped and expanded by the same biological agent that had shaped theirs: the Flower of Life, specimens of which had taken to Earth's soil as if sprung from it originally. Zand wished he could apprise the Masters personally that there walked on Earth one who was conversant with the Shapings:

one who was well on the road to evolutionary transformation—indeed, some form of transubstantiation.

In sum, the fate of Lazlo Zand was more important than the fate of Earth. That was why it was essential that he be the first to communicate with the Masters. With the benefit of their knowledge he might at last be able to understand his personal relationship to the Shapings.

On the less-than-Human side of things stood Napoleon Russo. Zand knew in advance that Russo would bungle his assignment to retrieve the encrypted disk the late Yoko Nitabi had transmitted to Tender/Search. But failure was in keeping with Zand's designs to undermine any vestiges of self-confidence in Russo in advance of assuming complete control of him.

The rotund creature was in Zand's presence now, at just past three A.M., shuffling his feet in the center of Zand's office while he recounted his attempt to capture the teenager who had been the inadvertent recipient of Nitabi's information. The media were attributing the incendiary events caused by the failed raid to a war between rival crime bosses over control of the tuna fish industry.

Locating the young woman had posed few problems once Zand, through back channels, had learned that Tender/Search was owned and operated by the Shimada Family. A seemingly legitimate enterprise, the classifieds brokerage was also used as a dump for clandestine data related to Family businesses. Further investigation had revealed that the Shimada Family was in annual retreat at an inn on the slopes of Mount Fuji. Kan Shimada's core associates were kept under surveillance by some fifty SPOOK agents, one of whom reported that a Shimada lieutenant had requested a background from the Ministry of Human Services on one Misa Yosida, a product of the communal homes, who had become a client of Tender/Search on the same day Nitabi's encrypted data had been transmitted. Surveillance of key personnel had continued, until Russo himself had observed a luncheon meeting between a Shimada *yakuza* named Miho Nagata and a young man, later identified as Shi Ling, whose personal telecomp number was on file at SPOOK as the source of repeated attempts at penetrating the facility's computer network.

Russo's hunch to stick with Nagata had been rewarded, and while the Shimadas were formulating plans to move against Shi Ling and his apparent girlfriend, Russo was readying plans as well. Zand's assistance had been required in arranging for the use of a communications satellite to dazzle a score of delivery robots. Even with that, however, Russo and company had been thwarted by a fleet of garbage trucks and their gun-wielding Shimada operators. All hell had broken loose on the street, resulting in the deaths of two SPOOK agents, though Russo had managed to arrive intact at the kids' cramped apartment.

"They were gone by the time I got there," he now explained to Zand, "but they left *this* behind."

Russo's plump, hairy hand proffered a standard-format disk, three inches in diameter, bearing a Tender/Search label.

"It was still in the player," Russo said. "They were trying to read it."

Zand faked an approving smile. Telecomp records indicated that the kids had purchased a timeshare on the public library neural net. The machine didn't have enough crunching power to break Nitabi's code, but it might have been able to give the hackers some sense of the disk's content.

Zand handed the disk back across the desk. "I think we'd better play it—just to make certain."

"But the label—"

"Humor me," Zand cut him off. "Play it."

Russo got up and went to the player. Zand shifted his chair to face the screen in time to see Lynn-Minmei prancing through a field of flowers while she lip-synched "To Be In Love." Russo, frowning suddenly, planted his finger on the advance button. Minmei, against a pyrotechnic backdrop, mouthing "We Can Win"; Minmei, on a roller coaster, mouthing "Stage Fright"; Minmei soaring through a starfield; Minmei dressed in military garb . . .

"Seems that they switched labels," Zand told Russo matter-of-factly. "The disk we want is evidently labeled 'Minmei's Greatest Hits,' or some such title."

Russo's lower lip twitched and he stared at his hands. "I apologize, Professor Zand. I'm inept. I'm good for nothing."

Zand moved to him and patted the top of his head. "Now, now, Napoleon, don't vilify yourself. You did the best you could. Besides, we're sure to find Misa and her hacker friends."

Russo looked up. "But how? They could be any-where."

Zand's grin was patronizing. "I'll think of a way. In the meantime, I'd like you to take Ms. Nitabi's body out of the freezer and return it to the Shimada Family. As a special favor to me."

Five thousand miles away, in Earth Defense Force headquarters in Monument City, Minister of War

Anatole Leonard was storming through circles on the eagle-emblemed carpet of his capacious office. In the hot seat, still queasy from that morning's drop back into the gravity well, sat Rolf Emerson.

"How could you do this to me?" Leonard was fulminating. "I just don't understand how you could do it." He whirled on Emerson. "Are you part of it, Rolf?"

Emerson met the commander's probing gaze. "Part of what?"

"Aldershot's plot. And don't pretend ignorance. The maneuverings of former RDF contingents on Aluce Base and here on Fokker, the requisitions for Civil Defense ordnance, the covert meetings ... You've heard about Mexico?"

Emerson's puzzled look showed that he hadn't.

"Another confrontation between RDF and Southern Cross forces sent there to put down a revolt in the southern highlands."

Emerson compressed his lips and gave his head a mournful shake. "You know, this wouldn't happen if we'd stop talking about 'former' RDF or 'former' Southern Cross and refer to all of them as Earth Defense forces."

Leonard snorted a scornful laugh. "If you think we can heal this situation using semantics—"

"It might make things less inflammatory."

Leonard struck an intimidating pose. "We're way beyond that, Rolf. And make no mistake about it: I won't intercede to save your ass if you side with Aldershot. I'll see you go down."

Emerson came to his feet. "I'm not siding with *anyone*."

"Then explain why I wasn't informed of your visit to the factory satellite."

"I don't have to answer to you for my actions, Commander. I do as I see fit in the interest of Terrestrial Defense."

"Are you going to hide behind that, Rolf?"

Emerson sat down. Leonard waited a beat and went to his chair. "I went upside for personal reasons," Emerson began. "At least, the trip started out that way."

"The Zentraedi female?"

"The 'female' has a name, Commander."

Leonard made a conciliatory gesture. "All right, you went there to see Ilan Tinari. At her request?"

Emerson nodded.

"What's on her mind—repatriation on Earth?"

"Just the opposite. She informed me that the Zentraedi wish to leave stationary orbit."

"Leave orbit?"

"They . . . feel that the Masters are en route to Earth."

Leonard leaned forward, his palms flat on the desk. "Have they established contact with the SDF-3?"

"No," Emerson was quick to clarify. "They have no hard proof. Ilan maintains that they can 'sense' the Masters' approach."

"So what's their reason for wanting to leave orbit?" Leonard asked.

"To lure the Masters away from Earth. To sacrifice themselves as a means of furnishing us with advance intelligence."

Leonard stared at him. "And you believe that?"

"Yes, I do. Dana has been experiencing spells of depression and unfocused hostility. I'm certain she's also sensing the Masters."

"It's a trick, Rolf. Think about Khyron, think about the Malcontent Uprisings. The Zentraedi aren't capable

of guileless action. They answer to Tirol. They answer
to the Imperative. If they want to leave orbit, it's to in-
duce the Masters to home in on their position, or perhaps to link up with some alien strike force that
survived the destruction of the Grand Fleet."

Rolf shook his head. "What's to prevent the Masters
from homing in on them in stationary orbit?"

"Nothing at all. But here, they're weaponless.
They're easy prey to an attack by our space-based
forces," Leonard blustered. "I'm disappointed, Rolf. For
God's sake, think about Ilan Tinari. She left you to join
the malcontents. If she was capable of something self-
less, something Human, wouldn't she be with you right
now instead of in self-exile out there?"

Emerson was quiet for a long moment. "I'm going to
forward their request to the Senate, Commander," he
said at last. "Moran already has the information. He can
decide who should or shouldn't know about the Masters."

Leonard folded his arms across his massive chest.
"Yes, you do that. And my guess is that the liberals will
go ahead and grant their request. But ask yourself how
you're going to feel if I'm correct about their plan and
all this comes back to haunt you. Earth is on its own,
Rolf. There's no profit in perpetuating a sense of out-
dated loyalty to Lang and Hunter and the rest of those
alien-lovers. I'm glad they're gone. They belong in
deepspace. And since, after all these years, you seem to
have become something of a liaison officer again, I
strongly suggest that you convey my sentiments to
Aldershot and his RDF machine before it's too late." He
paused briefly, then added, "Bring along a dictionary, so
you can read them the definition of 'sedition.' And be
sure to inform them that the only thing holding me back

from scuttling their plans is that I have no concrete evidence relating to the status of the Expeditionary mission."

Deep in the geo-grid, in an area below Shinjuku known as High Noon, the apartment gang sat in morose silence around a corner table in a camera-free-zone pizzeria. The district was so named because of the outsize fiber-optic advertisements that shone twenty-four hours a day from the sides and facades of High Noon's copse of towering structures. Big as a house, EVE's composite face smiled from the building across the street from the pizzeria.

"Cool weather is on the approach," the telepresence was saying, "and the Modern Youth meets autumn's challenge in jumpsuits and jackets made of Memory-Stretch and Thermawrap.

"You were just an adolescent when the SDF-3 departed for Tirol on its mission of diplomacy. But that doesn't stop you from lending moral support now to the prospect of an enduring peace, in fashions inspired by the uniforms worn by the Expeditionary Force. Your jumpsuit and knee-high sim-leather boots hug you like a second skin, and your black torso-harness crosses your chest and flares daringly at the shoulders. Your hair is long but freshly washed and scented, and styled in such a way that your eyes and ears are left uncovered—because you are fully attuned to the audio-visual world.

"The Modern Youth pays keen attention to local and world news and is a keen observer of his or her surroundings. You are quick to spot strangers in your neighborhood, and to report any suspicious activity to the nearest police *koban*. You can be a stern taskmaster, a glowering *obasan*, when you need to be, because duty and order are what matter in the world. That way you protect the people and things that you love from those who are only out to exploit loopholes in the social contract . . ."

"Is that how you guys see yourselves?" Misa asked around a mouthful of pizza. "Exploiters of the loopholes?"

"What?" Census asked.

Misa gestured to the screen. "EVE. Didn't you hear what she said?"

Census traded glances with Discount and Gibley, both of whom were wearing berets and rectangular shades. "I have more important things to think about than that crap."

Misa snorted. "Yeah, I agree. But this time she's offering some information that might come in useful *while we're hiding out for the next ten years!*"

The boys ducked their heads and told her to keep her voice down.

"Fine. I'll be quiet when you tell me what we're supposed to do now," she said. "We can't go back to the apartment. We've only got enough money to last about two days, and you know that the first one of us who tries to collect allowance is going to get arrested or worse."

"That's not true," Census argued. "Hongo's in the clear. He can go to Human Services for us."

"No he can't. Not without authorization from Health and Welfare that we're too sick to report."

"So one of us'll check into a clinic."

"The clinics are open to network name traces." Misa swept her eyes around the room and lowered her voice to a conspiratorial whisper. "You-know-who or the other you-know-who will know just where to find us."

Census smirked. "Okay, so it's not foolproof. We just need to think things through."

"Exactly," Discount said. "We've gotta think."

"Think," Gibley added.

A gloomy silence descended over the table once more. Misa pushed the last of her slice aside and leaned out of the circle to watch EVE.

"The Modern Youth knows the value of other people's property. If someone loses an e-wallet or a telephone, they are returned to their owner without their contents being disturbed. The Modern Youth doesn't invade the privacy of another by perusing the video photos in a wallet or eavesdropping on the messages logged by a telephone.

"You are in the geo-grid purchasing a winter outfit made of Memory-Stretch and Thermawrap, and the salesperson undercharges your credit card. 'That amount is incorrect,' you announce. 'I wouldn't want to profit from a mistake that could cost you your job.' "

EVE fashioned an ordinary street scene, populated it with other telepresences, and inserted herself into it.

"You step into a classifieds booth to purchase a list of available apartments. However, instead of receiving the requested information, you receive a list of telecomps that are for sale. A mistake has occurred; you have received data meant for another. Even so, your friend, who has been shopping for a previously owned telecomp, offers to purchase the list you have received. Do you make a deal with him, or do you say, 'I'm sorry, but this information is not mine to sell. You will have to make your deal with the owner.'

"The Modern Youth doesn't feel a need to know everything. You trust that there are those who are looking out for your interests, and that you need do only your small part to contribute to the health and welfare of the planet.

"Mistakes occur, but honorable people will find that the world is a forgiving place. Come talk to me. Go to the nearest EVE station vidphone and call me. No problem is insurmountable. And remember that wherever you are, the eyes of the world—*seken no me*—are on you."

Misa's mouth was hanging open when she swung around to the table. The stunned expressions that greeted her were clear proof that the boys had also been listening to EVE.

"You don't think—"

"Of course it's meant for us," Gibley said through clenched teeth. "It's not the eyes of the world—it's Zand's eyes. He knows we're on the run."

"That must mean that the yaks got to the apartment before Zand's people did," Misa surmised. "Otherwise he'd know we don't have the disk anymore."

"Maybe his people didn't find it," Discount offered.

Misa looked at Gibley while he was exchanging cryptic looks with Census. "But all we have to do is get word to Zand that we don't have it. You heard EVE, everything'll be forgiven if we're honorable. Zand doesn't have to know that we read the disk. We could even say that we tried to read it but failed."

Gibley wouldn't meet her gaze. "We have to tell what we know to someone who matters. Verifiable information about the Masters would have an impact on the whole world." He finally raised his eyes from the table. "It's too important *not* to pass on."

Misa considered it briefly. "Do you think anyone'll

believe us—without the disk, I mean?" Once more, Gibley and Census traded looks. "You did leave the disk," Misa said, staring at Gibley. "Tell me you left the disk!" Without warning, she rushed around the table and began rummaging through the deep pockets of Gibley's pants and vest until Census and Discount wrestled her off him.

Pushing his disheveled hair from his face, Gibley backed out of range of swipes from Misa's taloned hand. "I couldn't leave it behind," he told her. "I couldn't."

Misa went slack in the boys' grip.

"Jeez, thanks for letting me in on the secret," Discount said to Gibley in disappointment.

"I don't believe this," Misa said after a long moment. "I don't *believe* this." She shot Gibley a furious glance. "Just because you were fired from SPOOK, we have to get killed?"

"This has nothing to do with avenging myself on Zand. I'm thinking about the planet."

"Exactly," Census added, as if in sudden revelation. "I mean, it's our Earth First *duty* to see to it the information gets out."

"Tell that to your *yakuza* friends," Misa said. "Let's see how Earth First *they*'ll be."

Discount cut his eyes to Census. "The yaks won't disclose the information. They'll try to profit from it, just like Zand must have in mind."

"Okay, then we'll have to try and make contact with Commander Leonard."

Gibley shook his head. "Leonard is mentioned on the disk. He probably already knows. He and Zand are part of the same conspiracy. No, the person we need to reach is Rolf Emerson."

"*Minister* Emerson?" Misa asked.

"He'll see that the UEG is made aware of Zand's secret."

"But Emerson lives in Monument City."

"I'm aware of that," Gibley said. "But I know a guy right here in Tokyo who used to be tight with Emerson's foster daughter."

"Dana Sterling?" Census said.

Gibley nodded. "The guy's name is Terry Weston."

CHAPTER
TWELVE

I was never one to put much faith in the efficacy of prayer—even less so since my experiences with Protoculture and the Shapings. And yet, since learning from Cabell that Zor concealed the Protoculture matrix in the [SDF-1's] reflex engines, I have, each night, staring out at gargantuan Fantoma and tiny Tirol, been dispatching prayers aimed more for the ears of Leonard and Zand than God. "Surrender the matrix to the Masters," I pray. "Don't let it come down to a second war."

Excerpted from the personal journal of Emil Lang

THE PINKY FINGER OF MIHO NAGATA'S LEFT HAND WAS encased in a fat tube of white gauze and medical tape. In the generation of *yakuzas* that considered Mercedes-Benzes with tinted windows de rigueur, a bandaged pinky would have been a clear indication that the injured party had honored a debt by cutting off the tip of his finger. In Miho's case, however, the mutilation had been effected by the solid-rubber roller of a weighty delivery robot.

Three days after it had been crushed, the finger was still throbbing, especially—oddly enough—the amputated tip. But Miho had been stoic throughout, easy enough in light of the fact that the young woman on the team, Tine Amano, had been killed during the abortive raid on the hackers' apartment. The SPOOK agent who had fired the lethal round had also died, in a hail of automatic-weapons fire from the Shimada garbage trucks, but the Family was distraught, nonetheless, that one of its own should succumb to so ignoble an end.

"We must avenge ourselves on the Protoculture Kommandatura," Kan-san was telling the gathered captains and lieutenants of his organization just now. "And on Dr. Lazlo Zand in particular."

At the geographical center of the Shimadas' underground compound, in a room bare of furniture save for a long, low table, the twenty lesser honchos of the Shimada Family knelt in attentive allegiance. Miho's place was close to the foot of the table.

"I would like permission to pay my respects personally to the Amano family," he said to Kan Shimada.

Kan-san nodded. "It is our hope that the disciplines that serve them so well in martial arts can be brought to bear to ease their suffering."

Miho inclined his head in a bow. "Your hope will be conveyed."

Shimada nodded again. "Has there been some intelligence on the whereabouts of our targets?"

"None," Miho's partner, Kazuki, reported. "I saw no signs of a struggle when I finally reached the apartment. I'm certain that the kids were gone by the time Zand's obese agent arrived."

"And the disk?"

"Either Zand's agent located it or the kids carried it with them."

Kan-san gazed down the length of the table at Miho. "From what you know of the one who calls himself Census, what is your opinion?"

"They held on to the disk."

"Yes, I agree. Why else would Zand take an interest

in finding them? We don't know how much they learned from the disk, if anything at all. But Zand is certainly aware that no one would accept their story without corroboration."

Ritualistic murmurs of assent greeted the assessment.

"It may be that the hackers will seek to make contact with us, based on their assumption that we are the lesser of two evils."

"Hai!"

"I wish the word spread to the street: they are better off coming to us than surrendering themselves or what they have to Zand. I want them to understand that we will harbor them, and that one of our main concerns is revenge on Zand."

"Mr. Shimada, it is likely that your words will reach Zand's ears as well," Miho commented.

"Let them," Kan-san started to say when a voice suddenly announced itself outside the sliding screen to the hallway. Shimada gave his permission to enter, and a servant came into the room on bended knees, closing the screen behind him. He bowed deeply before speaking.

"The body of Yoko Nitabi has been delivered to the compound. It is horribly mutilated, and the back of the body bears a tattooed message."

Kan-san worked his jaw. "Have you read this 'message'?"

"Hai."

Shimada made a beckoning motion with the fingers of his right hand.

The servant took a deep breath. " 'Mr. Shimada: The score stands tied at two to two: On your side, Ms. Nitabi and the woman who was killed in Kabukicho; on ours, the two agents your people riddled with bullets. I suggest we call this contest a draw and end things before matters worsen. I'm afraid that Ms. Nitabi left me little choice: she violated the oath she swore to me, and for that she had to die. The encrypted portion of the disk is my property, not yours. However, since I am now in possession of both the original and the copy, I can consider the matter closed. Feel free to deal with the disk's unwitting recipients as you see fit. L. Zand.' "

The servant kowtowed and was dismissed.

Shimada's steely eyes scanned the table. "Remarks."

"He's lying. He doesn't have the disk," someone said.

"He is goading us."

"He expects us to lead him to the hackers. All of us will be under surveillance."

Kan-san nodded gravely. "The matter is far from closed. Let the next round of our 'contest' begin at once."

"The Invid Regent is dead," Elder Nimuul said with significantly less emotion than the pronouncement should have warranted. Fallagar and Hepsis flanked him, their facial expressions unreadable. "Killed on Optera," Nimuul continued, "in a hand-to-hand contest with Breetai Tul."

The Masters' raptorlike eyes remained fixed on the transsignal sphere that had resolved in the command center of the flagship, but their thoughts rippled and streamed from one mind to the next. Shaizan spoke for the triumvirate. "Then our reascendancy is assured, Elders. We need only retrieve the Protoculture matrix and the Fourth Quadrant is ours once more."

Nimuul scowled. "Your optimism is premature. The

death of the Regent is further evidence of the Earthers' tenacity and innate talent for warfare."

"The Earthers, Elder? When you said Breetai, we assumed—"

"Breetai's Zentraedi forces serve Earth, not Tirol. Listen carefully: Optera was the stage for a decisive battle between the Sentinels and the Invid, as well as between rival blocs of the Robotech Expeditionary Force. The data you amassed on Earth languages enabled us to interpret exactly what occurred. The rebel group, under the leadership of a Human named T. R. Edwards, fled Tirol with an organic computer the Invid had left behind when they occupied our world. This Edwards and his Ghost Squadron were intent on usurping the Regent's power, and using Invid forces to defeat the Sentinels, the Zentraedi, and a separate group of REF loyalists. But Edwards was himself defeated, and the Invid, deprived of their regent, surrendered. All data concerning these events will be transsignaled to your ships."

"Where are these Sentinels now?" Shaizan asked.

"They are returning to Tirol, aboard a ship called the *Ark Angel*. Scientists and support personnel of the REF await them in Tiresia."

"Our city," Bowkaz said on an angry note.

"No longer," Nimuul amended. "All of Tirol belongs to Earth."

"All the more reason to make Earth ours."

The three Elders shook their heads. "The planet is not a prize worth winning," Nimuul said. "The Regent is dead, but the Regis and her warrior children are alive. Even now, her sensor nebulae comb the Fourth Quadrant for signs of the Flower of Life. The moment she is alerted to the Flower's rooting on Earth, she will come, and there is no force in the galaxy that can stop her. Excepting the Protoculture matrix, Earth holds no salvation for us." The blue-haired Elder paused, then asked, "Have you established contact with the machine intelligence that governed Zor's fortress?"

"We have, my lords," Dag answered. "The computer was removed from the fortress prior to an attack led by Khyron Kravshera in which the fortress was destroyed. The computer has high confidence that the Protoculture matrix survived the devastation, but it has not been able to determine the location of the fortress's burial site. An Earther named Zand has programmed the machine to speak with the voice of Zor himself."

"Is that all it told you?" Nimuul demanded.

Bowkaz addressed the question. "When we commanded the machine to speculate on how our flotilla might fare against Earth's strategic capabilities, it requested access to our databanks."

The Elders were silent for a moment. "Do you trust it?" Fallagar wanted to know.

"Not entirely," Bowkaz told him. "Though we have reason to believe that Zor may have bequeathed the machine a measure of the Compulsion you placed upon him."

"Allow the computer access to whatever it requires," Nimuul replied after a long moment. "It matters little if the machine has its own agenda. Reveal our might, and make the Earthers aware that years will pass before Breetai's ship returns to Earth. In the meantime, it is crucial that you learn where Zor's fortress is interred, so as to narrow the focus of our attack, should it come to that."

As one, the Masters bowed their heads.

"In addition, it is advisable to encourage Zor's clone

to go online with the machine his donor devised. If some part of Zor resides in that machine, it is conceivable that the interface could rouse something in the clone's cellular memory, enabling it to fashion a second Protoculture matrix."

"Your will be done, Elders," Shaizan said. "Can you specify when we will next hear from you?"

Nimuul shook his head. "We are repairing to Haydon IV in an effort to determine why Exedore Formo has become so interested in the Awareness." The Elder made a fatigued sound. "The world is coming apart. Tirol fallen; Praxis obliterated; Peryton's curse lifted; the Invid Regent dead; the Sentinels victorious; the Awareness awakened; the Zentraedi bearing offspring . . . We must have the matrix at any cost, lest the glory of the Tiresian race is eclipsed from the galaxy."

"Where to, sir?" Rolf Emerson's driver asked when the limousine had been cleared through Fokker Aerospace's forbidding front gates.

Emerson met the woman's questioning gaze in the rearview mirror, then turned his face to the tinted side window. "Major General Aldershot's office."

Founded during Reconstruction as a launch and reentry facility for shuttles servicing the factory satellite and named for the Robotech War's most celebrated mechamorph, Roy Fokker, the base encompassed several thousand acres of treeless plateau south-southeast of Monument City. It was home to the Tactical Air Force and the Cosmic Units, along with various experimental facilities and an industrial complex. The military accords of 2019 and 2022 had granted supervision of the place to the RDF, but what with the formation of the Earth Defense Force and the subsequent blurring of distinctions between the RDF and the Army of the Southern Cross, there was some question as to who controlled what areas of the base. RDF presence was stronger on Fokker than anywhere else on the surface, and Skull One—Roy Fokker's Veritech—still hung suspended from monofilament cable in the administrative center. But many of the base's immense hangars were packed with Logans, Hovertanks, and similar mecha engineered for the Army of the Southern Cross.

Rolf had an office in the administrative center, though he usually worked out of his office in Terrestrial Defense headquarters in Monument City. Typically, months would pass without his visiting Fokker, and now here he was back on base for the second time in a week.

The driver guided the limousine along the two-lane road that ringed the facility, past the shuttle gantries, "Destroid Depot," and the administrative center, with its luxury-hotel facade and four-story atrium. Aldershot's office was ten minutes further along, on the top floor of a sprawling structure officially known as the Defense Force Operational Headquarters, although more commonly referred to as the RDF Canteen.

At once old-fashioned and bionic, Aldershot was seated at his antique desk when an aide admitted Emerson to the office.

"Shall I take this visit as a sign that you want to throw in with us?" Aldershot asked bluntly. "Or are you here to reiterate the warning you delivered to Major Fredericks and Lieutenant Satori?"

Emerson hadn't spoken to Aldershot since the clandestine meeting in Monument City, and the major general's anger was transparent. "Nigel, suppose we leave it that I've your best interests in mind. Will you hear me out?"

Aldershot fingered his waxed mustache, then gestured to the chair alongside the desk. The room smelled faintly of pipe tobacco, and the view out its tall, fixed-pane windows overlooked the South Gate shuttle and VT landing strips.

"Leonard knows," Emerson said. "He doesn't have all the details, but he knows enough to discern what you have in mind."

Aldershot's eyes began to narrow in suspicion.

"No, he didn't hear it from me. He didn't have to, the way you've been carrying on, juggling mecha deployments and troop assignments . . . You didn't think you'd actually be able to pull this off without his knowledge?"

Aldershot shook his head slowly. "We expected this. Though I must admit, I wish he could have been kept in the dark a while longer." He looked at Emerson. "I appreciate your informing me."

"There's something else. You know I made a trip up the well."

"To the factory, yes. At the time, I thought you had come to your senses and were making the trip on our behalf. Then I learned that you'd been sent for. I assume the trip had something to do with their unexpected silence."

"It did."

"Well, I'm sure this can't be about additional supplies. Hell, as it is they barely touch what we send them. They seem to *want* to live like animals."

"Not anymore," Emerson said. "They're requesting permission to leave orbit. Leonard has already been apprised, and the Senate is expected to vote on the matter by early next week. I expect they'll be allowed to go—if only in the interest of closure for those of us on Earth."

Aldershot smoothed his mustache again. "This could be a major setback in our plans. We were hoping to make use of the factory as a staging area for strikes against the orbital weapons platforms, if need be." The general frowned. "But why do they want to leave after all these years? Don't tell me they're afraid of getting caught in the middle, between us and Leonard?"

"They couldn't care less," Emerson told him. "Most of them would just as soon see us rot in hell for the way they were mistreated during the Uprisings. No, Nigel, they're leaving because the Masters are nearer than we thought."

All the smugness left Aldershot. "How near? I've heard nothing from Liberty or any of the forward obser- vation bases about UCTs—"

"The Zentraedi are going by 'feeling'—a kind of sixth sense. They claim there's a direct correlation be- tween distance and the strength of their feelings, but they're unable to quantify it."

"But, good Christ, Emerson, are they talking millions of miles or parsecs?"

Emerson shook his head. "Here's a better one: Is the SDF-3 in pursuit?"

The major general stared at him. "And if they are, why haven't they made contact with us?" He muttered a curse. "Could the REF and the Masters have *passed* each other en route? Is that the sort of thing that can happen in hyperspace?"

"The only person who could possibly answer that is on the SDF-3. But no matter what, I think we have to assume that the ship is either incapacitated or destroyed.

It's high time we faced the fact that the UEG is Earth's only hope."

Aldershot's hands clenched. "This changes everything, Rolf." Emerson was midway through a relieved exhale when Aldershot added, "We'll have to make our move ahead of schedule."

Emerson gaped at him. "*That's* your answer? And if the Masters' ships are cloaked somehow? If they've had us under surveillance, and have only been waiting for the right moment, waiting for us to lower our guard or grow so enmeshed in internecine squabbling that we won't even see them coming?" He stood up and slammed his fist down on the desk. "Have I been wasting my breath on you, Nigel?"

Aldershot stiffened, then showed Emerson a contrite look. "I'm sorry, Rolf. But there are too many of us already committed to this—Masters or not. I'm going to recommend that we go in one week."

CHAPTER
THIRTEEN

Emerson wanted Dana treated like any cadet in the Academy, and yet he was the first one to come to her aid every time she stepped out of line—which was more times than I could begin to name. The thing is, we all knew that she had to be there. If nothing else, she was a constant reminder of the fact that Earth had fought a war with an alien race, and that that race's makers were probably on the way.

Remark attributed to one of Dana Sterling's fellow Academy cadets, as quoted in Major Alice Harper Argus (ret.), *Fulcrum: Commentaries on the Second Robotech War*

TERRY WESTON ACCEPTED THE RITUAL CUP AND SET IT down on the table in front of him. He gave the cup a counterclockwise half turn before lifting it to his nose with his right hand, elbow thrust outward, his left hand cupped over it to focus the scent. He then inhaled three times, *listening*, as the Japanese put it.

Small and exquisitely wrought, the cup contained a cylinder of glowing charcoal buried in ashes of pond lily seeds, which were chosen for their odorlessness. The surface of the ashes bore an intricate pattern that indicated the season and the form of the contest. Obscuring most of that pattern was a square of quartz, atop which rested a small piece of incense, *koh*—a sliver of exotic wood, saturated with fragrant oil. It was Weston's turn to identify the incense by smell.

The utterly silent room in which he and a dozen others sat was already heady with the mingled scents from previous rounds; some *kyara*—elegant and sophisticated—others *sumontara*—provocative and argumentative. The one under Weston's nose was certainly more forward than *kyara*, though neither rustic nor boorish enough to be considered *manaban*. It had an almost cinnamon quality, austere, upright, and clerical—suggestive of the *sasora* type. He decided that the incense came from a type of scrub oak native to the hill country of central Thailand. Mentally, he composed his identifying haiku, wrote it in *kanji* on his notepad, and passed the cup to the old woman seated to his right.

A former Veritech pilot with the RDF, Weston was approaching thirty, tall and fit, with a craggy face and wavy blond hair that fell to his shoulders. Unlike the kimonoed players on either side of him in the *koh* dojo, he was wearing jeans and a short-napped pullover. In preparation for the weekly session, he had, as usual, abstained from eating garlic, drinking coffee, and using soap or shampoo, and had removed his rings and bracelets, lest they cause a distraction by coming into contact with the incense-laden cup.

The *koh* master sat at the head of the table, his implements arranged in front of him: squares of quartz, napkins, wrapped and unwrapped pieces of wood, a poker, a pair of chopsticks, a small set of pincers known as a *gingyobasami*, and a feather from the wing of a crested ibis, which was used to brush away stray ash adhering to the side of the cup.

"*Hon koh taki owarimashita,*" the *sensei* said when the incense had been inhaled by the final player. "The *koh* fire is out."

All that remained was for the identifying haikus to be

submitted to the recordkeeper, who would inscribe them on a large sheet of Japanese paper, and for the winners to be announced.

Kohdo, knowledge of incense, had been practiced for more than a thousand years, and had lent much to *sado*, the Japanese tea ceremony. Of the six hundred or so scents in the incense pantheon, a skillful devotee could name at least half. The wood itself—all of it imported from Southeast Asia, Indonesia, New Zealand, and other places—was more precious than gold or saffron. Weston's school practiced a type of *kohdo* founded by samurai in the twelfth century. Tokyo had a second school that had originated with the Imperial family, in which one's arms were held close to the body while listening to the scents.

Kohdo wasn't the sort of discipline Weston would normally have been drawn to; rather, he was under orders to attend the sessions and contests. The source of those orders was Onuma-sensei, the martial arts instructor under whom Weston had been studying almost since his arrival in Japan three years earlier. Weekly *kohdo*, zen meditation, leaf-raking, window washing, archery, *irezumi* . . . Onuma-sensei was Weston's link to all of them.

As it happened, he had scored well in the contest, correctly naming sixty of the one hundred nail-paring-size samples passed around the table. Several of the old hands had achieved better-than-perfect scores by not only identifying the scents but by identifying the samples as core or outer ring cuttings from the donor trees.

Still, the *koh* master was pleased enough by Weston's performance to comment, as the former pilot was leaving, that Weston's Western face had at last begun to sprout an Asian nose.

It was just past nine P.M. when Weston stepped out

onto Yomise-Dori. The air was chilled and he rolled down the sleeves of his pullover.

The scent dojo was near Ueno Park in Sendagi, which, along with the adjacent neighborhoods of Nezu and Yanaka, made up the heart of the city's surface *shitamachi*—its downtown. Flattened during the Rain of Death, the area had been rebuilt to suit a Tokyo that hadn't existed in more than fifty years. Houses with rock gardens lined the narrow streets; the restaurants specialized in *chuka ryori*, Tokyo's version of Chinese cooking; signs above the shop doorways were in hand-painted *kana*; and the Shinto shrines were vermilion.

Weston ambled along, past sake shops, rice merchants, tofu makers, flower vendors, and barbers, drinking all of it in, thinking vaguely about Monument City, as he was wont to do as Tokyo's autumn approached. He was nearing his favorite *nomiya*—drink shop—when he heard his name called, and turned to find lanky Wilfred Gibley waving to him from the mouth of a lantern-lit alley. Beside him stood a tall and attractive young woman, nibbling at her thumb. Weston hadn't seen Gibley since they'd dropped LSD together back in their *saike zoku* days. Gibley had been known as Hongo then, and Weston had been fresh from Monument, looking to come to terms with the tragic death of his fiancée and his lasting hatred for everyone associated with the Giles Academy—Anatole Leonard, Joseph Petrie, Michael Kingsley, David Myers, Pauline Hall, even the dead Henry Giles himself.

Grinning, Weston walked over to Gibley and clapped him on the shoulder. "Where you been hiding, Hongo? Or do you go by a different name now?"

Gibley traded a quick glance with the girl. "Depends who you ask." He forced a smile. "Terry, this is Misa."

Weston nodded. "That's a pretty name."

"Thanks," she mumbled, furtively averting her gaze.

Weston turned back to Gibley. "I was just going to get something to eat. Can you join me?"

The two of them nodded eagerly, and Weston led the way to the drink shop across the street and over to a quiet table. He ordered a two-quart bottle of heated sake and assorted platters of soba, sanshoku, yuzukiri, and pickles. When the noodle plates arrived, Misa dug in ravenously. Watching her, Weston was reminded of Dana Sterling; Dana had that same orphaned-generation, last-meal gusto when it came to food.

"So, Hongo, you ever get back at SPOOK for firing you?" Weston asked. He glanced at Misa and smiled. "That's all this guy used to talk about, getting even with Lazlo Zand for taking away his job."

Misa's brow furrowed venomously. "Yeah, I'll bet," she said around a mouthful of citrus-flavored buckwheat.

Weston looked at Gibley again. "What are you doing for NuYen lately?"

Gibley's narrow shoulders heaved. "This and that. Mostly pilfering and moving data. Times are tough, you know."

"No need to tell me. If it wasn't for my RDF pension I'd be pushing a roasted-corn cart."

"You still training with Onuma-sensei?" Gibley asked.

"Every day."

Gibley turned to Misa. "You've heard of Onuma, haven't you? He was Lynn-Kyle's instructor."

Misa's brows beetled. "Who's Lynn-Kyle?"

Gibley shot Weston a look of amused disappointment. "This younger generation, huh? Lynn-Kyle," he repeated for Misa's sake. "Lynn-Minmei's manager. Starred in the movie *Little White Dragon*."

"Whatever you say," Misa muttered.

Weston appraised her out of the corner of his eye. No denying it: he had a thing for younger women. Especially young women who made him think of Dana. They hadn't spoken in more than a year, but she was never far from his thoughts. He often wondered what might have happened had the timing been different, if he hadn't been grieving over Amy Pollard when he met Dana. Or, indeed, if Dana had been even a couple of years older.

"Do you ever hear from Dana anymore?" Gibley asked out of the blue.

Weston stared at him. "Not for a while. Why?"

"Just curious."

Weston heard something disingenuous in the reply. "What brings you and Misa to Sendagi?"

Gibley cleared his throat meaningfully. "You."

Weston leaned back in his chair. "Go on."

"We've come into some information that needs to be moved—fast."

"You're peddling your fish in the wrong market, Hongo. I don't fence, for you or anyone."

Gibley looked around the bar and lowered his voice. "What we have isn't for sale. It's a gift. But we need it delivered."

"To who?"

"Minister Emerson."

Weston was silent for a long moment. It was Emerson who had asked him to infiltrate the Giles Academy. A decent man, maybe the only decent one left in the rapidly disintegrating Defense Force. But someone Weston had alienated because of Dana and what had gone on between them. "That's why you asked about Dana."

Gibley nodded. Misa was watching him intently. "This involves Terran Defense, Terry."

"Just how hot is it?"

"How hot's the sun?" Misa said grimly.

Gibley nodded again. "It's too far beyond top-secret to label. I don't even think I should tell *you* what it's about."

Weston held up his hands. "I'm not asking."

"You would if you knew even a fraction of it."

Weston took a gulp of sake. "I want to judge for myself how hot this property is before I promise you anything. If I hear word that you're trouble, don't count on my help." He fingered a vidphone card from the pocket of his pullover and slid it across the table to Gibley. "Get in touch with me tomorrow, around this time. I'll have an answer for you then." He glanced at Misa. "You guys have a place to stay in the meantime? You need money or anything?"

"No, we're fine," Gibley said before Misa could even open her mouth. "Everything's fine."

Secured within his office, Zand laid a Flower of Life leaf on his tongue and savored the mind-altering numbness that infused his lips, throat, and nasal passages. The Flowers had been couriered only that night from the eastern foothills of the Andes Mountains. Ironically, the Flowers were found to be sharing the soil with *Erythroxylon coca*—the bushy plant whose leaves were the source of the stimulant cocaine. But unlike coca leaves, which would only release their alkaloids in the presence of a catalyst like lime ash, the leaves of the Flower of Life surrendered their gift the moment they were introduced to the enzymes present in human saliva.

Zand's senses were reeling.

All day, Russo had been chasing after him, eager to supply him with updates on the missing hackers and the disk, but Zand had rebuffed him. Russo failed to understand that he had more pressing matters to attend to, and that the situation regarding the kids was well in hand. EVE was broadcasting messages specifically tailored to them, and members of the Shimada Family were being watched in the event the kids should turn to them for protection. In fact, the Shimadas were being surveilled in ways neither they nor Russo fully realized. What's more, there was always the chance that the *yakuza* would heed the message Zand had had tattooed across the backside of Nitabi's corpse and simply bow out of the contest.

Across the room, the Zor hologram, returned from its recent interface with the machine intelligences that served the Robotech Masters, awaited further commands from its Human operator. A day earlier, when the Masters had communicated with Zor's creation to announce their consent to the proposed computer-to-computer link, Zand had tutored Zor to transmit inflated strategic evaluations of Space Station Liberty and Earth's ground and orbital-based defenses, but to safeguard the location of the enshrined SDF-1 and its most precious cargo, the Protoculture matrix.

The Masters had placed much of the contents of their databanks under lock and key, but Zor, as if some cybernetic Jack the Giant Killer, had managed to emerge with even more than Zand had expected. Enough to have rendered Zand speechless for the past several minutes.

Already Zor had treated him to a video inspection tour of the pride of the Masters' six-ship flotilla: a five-mile-long lozenge of military prowess, outfitted with white and purple running lights and surfaced with the segmented muzzles of countless batteries; conical structures the size of pyramids; stairways, bridges, towers rising like two-tined forks ... Portions of the interior of the ship suggested blood vessels or the maze of an information highway, pulsing with the enigmatic energy of Protoculture. Elsewhere loomed components shaped like upside-down pagodas, constructed of some effulgent ceramic that had never before appeared in the Solar system.

And Zand had glimpsed the Masters' army of soldier-clones, the aesthete, fair-skinned Clonemasters who commanded them, and some of the Bioroid weapons Breetai and Exedore had described to the REF.

"These clones were developed to serve as a police force on occupied worlds," the Zor holo had explained. "Ostensibly as a means of freeing the Zentraedi to carry on with the business of intersystem conquest. But I had my suspicions, long before I dispatched my fortress to Earth. I believe that the Masters had begun to perceive a growing discontent among the Zentraedi. And I believe that their Protoculture-expanded senses told them where that discontent was leading: to rebellion. An insurrection, mounted by Dolza, that would have proved impossible to put down."

Zand had grasped the implication. "Do you suppose that the Masters' powers of precognition were such that they *knew* the Zentraedi fleet would be defeated in Earthspace? Could the fleet have been sent to Earth to rid the Masters of their warrior clones?"

Zor had fallen mute for a time. "These are questions

I have not been programmed to address. The answers appertain to forces set in motion an eon ago, before first contact between Tirol and Optera. In my memory, there is only the name Haydon."

It always came down to Haydon, Zand thought. But he decided to leave the matter alone for the moment. "Can you show me the Masters?" he asked Zor now, placing another leaf on his tongue.

A scene resolved on the monitor screen. Elbows on the desk, Zand leaned forward, his eyes widening. Where he had expected to see somewhat older versions of the radiant-eyed Zor, he saw three aged men in floppy-collared robes that gave them the look of executioners. He saw deeply creased, hawk-nosed faces, hairless pates, atrophied arms, slender fingers lacking nails. He saw Humanlike beings who evinced not a hint of emotional life.

Was this where unchecked exposure to Protoculture led? Zand asked himself. Was he glimpsing a future version of himself?

The three Masters stood on a small platform, in a circle around what must have been a control monitor—an apparatus resembling a mottled technological mushroom five feet across, hovering above the gleaming deck of the flagship's command center.

"They share a commonality of mind," the Zor holo offered. "The Protoculture allows them to send to one another in mindspeak."

Telepathy, Zand told himself, salivating. Telepathy, precognition, clairvoyance—perhaps immortality itself. All those could be his if he had unlimited access to Protoculture. Or unfettered access to the Masters. It was too mind-boggling to contemplate.

"Reveal what you know of their attack plan," he ordered Zor.

The holo shook its head. "That was a denied area. But I have learned what became of Breetai's flagship."

Zand shot to his feet. "The SDF-3! Tell me!"

"The Invid have been routed from the Valivarre system, and Earth forces occupy Tirol."

"The REF has been battling the Invid? But doesn't that make them allies of the Masters?"

"The Masters had abandoned Tirol long before Breetai's flagship arrived."

Zand laughed ruefully. "By God, they *missed* each other." He stopped suddenly. "Do you know when the ship is planning to refold to Earth?"

"That isn't known. The ship is marooned in Tirolspace."

Zand sank weakly into his chair. Stranded, he told himself. Then, looking up, he asked, "Who's in command of the REF?"

"Those data weren't supplied. But key personnel have died in action."

"*Who?*"

"Janice Em . . ."

"Lang's android."

"And General T. R. Edwards."

Zand was dumbfounded; his jaw dropped and a dollop of leaf-impregnated saliva drooled from the corner of his mouth. Over the long years of speculating on the fate of the SDF-3, Edwards's death had been both wished for and feared. Now, like light making its delayed arrival from a distant star, some of his questions had been answered.

But all at once Zand wasn't sure what to do with those answers.

"Exit," he told Zor, and the faintly blue hologram vanished, disappearing into its projector like a genie into an oil lamp.

Zand ingested another leaf and began to sift through his thoughts. Leonard was on the way to Tokyo even now to discuss some matter that had yet to be clarified. But how much could Zand afford to relate about developments on Tirol? Even with the SDF-3 temporarily marooned, word of Edwards's death might turn Leonard toward caution at the very moment Zand needed him to be impulsive. Zand's future rested on it, for the return of Emil Lang would without doubt put an abrupt halt to his experiments in creative evolution. But how to convince Leonard of the need to consolidate his power, to assume control of Wyatt Moran and the UEG—as, indeed, he had promised Edwards—without apprising him of all the facts?

The parents of the dead *yakuza* neophyte, Tine Amano, had decided to hold a wake for her in a small Catholic church on the surface, close to the remains of the Nihonbashi Bridge, in the heart of what had been the Ginza precinct of pre-Rain Tokyo. At the last moment Kan Shimada had persuaded the Amanos to make it a double service by allowing the body of Yoko Nitabi—nominally a Catholic as well—to be placed on view along with that of Tine.

From all parts of the city, and from as far south as Kyoto, Shimada Family members came to pay their respects to the young women. *Capos*, wiseguys, soldiers, truck drivers, and dockworkers crowded into the flower-filled room where the repaired and embalmed bodies were laid out in open caskets of intricately carved hardwood. There was some crying and much stoic silence in the receiving lines that trailed from the coffins, and a miasma of brooding anger at the back of the room, where clusters of Shimada personnel spoke of the actions they would take against SPOOK when the time was right. That everyone was certainly under surveillance by rooftop cameras or some such devices, and that spies had likely been inserted into their midst, only added to an overall sense of outrage and hatred.

Miho Nagata had spent a few minutes in the back of the room, but the grumbling had only gotten him more depressed, so he had moved to one of the front rows of chairs that faced Tine's coffin. He had paid his personal respects to Taduski and Lisabeth Amano the previous day, and was planning to attend all four sessions of the wake. The Amanos' judo and jujitsu dojo had been his thrice-weekly home for the past several years. Miho felt especially sorry that he had been instrumental in recruiting Tine for the organization, although, given Taduski's ties to Kan Shimada, chances were that his daughter would have found her way into Family business before too long. Even so, Miho felt guilty, despondent, and angry more at the way the world worked than at SPOOK, which had also lost two agents.

Catering principally to *yakuzas*, the Amanos' dojo in the geo-grid often served as a way station for information. Those who didn't trade in crime were carefully screened, and there wasn't one of them who couldn't be counted on to keep to themselves what they observed or overheard. Several outsiders had passed through the room since Miho had arrived, though most of them hadn't remained long. They would spend a moment kneeling at the casket, perhaps offer a prayer, then move quickly down the queues of mourners, mumbling platitudes, as lost as anyone for soothing words to offer.

Moving down the Amano line just now was a tall, blond-haired man Miho knew from the *dojo*—an American named Terry Weston, who had arrived in Tokyo a few years back after receiving a premature though honorable discharge from the Defense Force. Miho called to Weston, and waved him over.

"Good to see you," Weston said, shaking Miho's bandage-free hand. "Sorry it has to be under these circumstances."

Miho had already uttered the same phrases to a dozen people he had run into. "You're still studying with Onuma-sensei, Terry?"

Weston nodded. "He regrets not being able to be here this afternoon, but he'll come tonight."

"Give him my regards—in case I don't see him later on."

"I'll do that. Who'd you honor with your fingertip?" Weston asked playfully.

Miho snorted. "A robot's roller."

Weston glanced at Kan Shimada, seated close to Yoko Nitabi's coffin. "Who is the other woman, Miho?"

"An adopted daughter of Kan-san."

Weston was quiet for a moment. "Was she killed during that business in the Kabukicho?"

"A few days earlier," Miho told him.

Weston knew better than to press for details. "I hope this won't be the first of many funerals."

Miho looked at him. "How do you mean?"

"If your troubles with the other Family escalate."

Miho thought for a moment. "You're referring to what happened in Kabukicho."

"I didn't mean to—"

"It wasn't rivalry with another Family, Terry. The

ones who killed Tine were intelligence operatives. From SPOOK."

Weston waited for him to continue.

"A very bad business. A couple of kids—data pirates—came into possession of some information that belongs to us, and we were hoping to retrieve it without a lot of fuss. The problem is that Dr. Zand is also interested in this data, and had sent his people there." Miho paused to study Weston's suddenly disquieted expression. "Is something the matter, Terry?"

Weston surfaced from his dark introspection. "No, nothing. So did you find these kids?"

Miho wagged his head from side to side. "We're still looking. So, in fact, is Zand, and it will be bad luck for them to be found by him. At this point, they would be much safer with us."

Weston gazed at him. "Do you mean that? About their being safe with you?"

"I do. Why, have you heard something?"

"No, no. But in case I do, I want to be able to give it to them straight. No tricks, no double crosses."

"You have my word on it," Miho said evenly.

CHAPTER
FOURTEEN

"I appreciate your recognizing my contributions to the film with this award. But if I may be honest—unlike some who have spoken from this dais tonight—my performance was not about pleasing the director, or my co-stars, or even you people in the audience. I was performing for only one person: my teacher, Onuma-sensei. And though I doubt that he would go anywhere near the movie, I hope that he is not too displeased by his student's sloppy technique and lack of focus."

Lynn-Kyle, on accepting the Best Actor Award
for his role in *Little White Dragon*

No sooner had Anatole Leonard and Joseph Petrie emerged from the elevator onto SPOOK's sublevel three than Zand, sporting tinted aviator glasses and at least two weeks' growth of salt-and-pepper beard, hurried them off to a dimly lighted, restricted-access office and sat them down in front of a small wallscreen, insisting that what he had to show them couldn't wait.

Leonard was pleased to find that Zand still considered himself one of the team. But at the same time he felt somewhat upstaged by the Protoculturist's enthusiasm. Leonard's whole point in coming to Tokyo was to surprise *Zand* with news that couldn't wait, and, suddenly, the tables had been turned.

"Prepare to be astounded, gentlemen," Zand was saying now, his bloodless hands poised over a computer keyboard. "Decrypted playback of Transmission R-seven, fifteen dash eight-six," he said, more to himself. The sleeves of his white lab coat were stained with something that looked like grass juice.

Quietly, Leonard wondered aloud to Petrie if Zand had perhaps intercepted a communiqué from Aldershot's would-be mutineers on Liberty, or a communiqué from the general to the space station.

"I doubt he would have his ear to that part of the ground," Petrie returned in the same low voice. Behind round goggles, his eyes seemed to smile.

Leonard's unofficial aide was without his usual recording headset, and wore an unadorned, loose-fitting jumpsuit with Velcro closures. Leonard had on a wool uniform that featured jodhpurs, a big-buckled leather belt, and spit-polished knee boots. They had made the journey from Monument City aboard a civilian hypersonic. With the revolt imminent, Leonard was well aware of the risks in leaving the situation unattended even for a day. Nevertheless, he thought it essential that Zand be personally apprised of the Zentraedis' request to quit Earthspace; not merely as a gesture but to set the stage for the favor Leonard had in mind. Ever since their initial meeting in Brasília more than ten years earlier, arranged by T. R. Edwards, Leonard had loathed dealing with the scientist face-to-face. But, as countless vidphone, comp-fax, and telequorum exchanges had demonstrated, Zand was impossible to read unless one was willing to endure the scrutiny of his all-pupil eyes.

Even so, Leonard had had his doubts about Zand's loyalty to the strategies he, Edwards, and Wyatt Moran had sworn allegiance to prior to the launch of the

SDF-3: the rearming of Planet Earth, the eradication or banishment of the aliens, and the consolidation of all political and military authority. Over the years, Zand had proven his worth, especially in helping to perfect the nonreconfigurable Logan mecha utilized by the Armored Space Corps, and in allaying the fears of Earth's justifiably paranoid citizenry by fabricating encouraging transmissions from the SDF-3. The problem remained, however, that Zand cared less about the sort of power afforded by the real world than that derived from intimate contact with Protoculture.

Something was beginning to happen on the wall-screen: behind a curtain of snowy visual noise, the head and shoulders of a Human figure could be discerned. It was clear that the person had long hair and was dressed in some flare-shouldered garment, but it was impossible to make out the face. The audio signal was similarly disrupted by long bursts of static.

". . . have finally arrived Tirol. Repeat . . . -rol. Initial meet . . . discuss terms of peace accord with . . . by unannounced strategic strike by Invid forces . . . prevailed, though the fold drives have been damaged beyond repair."

Leonard's widened eyes bored in on Zand. "Is that—"

Zand nodded. "General Hunter. Confirmed by voice-print analysis."

"When was this received?"

"Only this morning."

"Through Liberty?"

"No. The REF established contact directly with the former mother computer of the SDF-1."

"But why?"

"Listen."

". . . tachyon communications systems rendered useless as well . . .—tech Masters have no fold-capable ships . . . we're effectively marooned here until . . .—culture can be produced. Repeat, effectively . . . estimate fifteen Earth years to return by conventional . . .—luminal drive. Repeat, est—. . ."

Zand's hands executed a flurry of keyboard commands. "That's all of it," he said. "Shall I play it again?"

Leonard gestured for him to do so. "You recall that night on the porch?" he said to Petrie while the message was running. "*This* must be what I was seeing in the stars."

Petrie nodded noncommittally.

Leonard looked at Zand again. "When did you say this was received?"

"This morning. But I believe that it was sent almost eight years ago."

"Eight years . . ." Leonard tried to come to grips with it. "That would put the Expeditionary mission almost halfway home."

Zand rocked his head from side to side. "Assuming that they launched from Tirol soon after the message was dispatched."

Leonard exchanged a quick glance with Petrie, then cleared his throat. "There's something Hunter neglected to mention, Dr. Zand. The Masters are also headed our way. And this message leads me to believe that they are ahead of the REF."

Zand's surprise was sincere. With increasing agitation, he listened to the commander's summary of Rolf Emerson's conversation with the Zentraedi onboard the factory satellite.

"They either can't or won't say how close the Masters are," Leonard concluded. "Or maybe it's Emerson himself who isn't saying. The point is, I don't trust those bastards. I think they're leaving Earth to rendez-vous with their Masters and to beg forgiveness for their defeat. I'm sure they're already dreaming about being returned to full size and equipped with a cruiser they can use to avenge themselves on us."

Zand was pacing like a trapped animal. "Yes, yes, you may be right."

Leonard stood up to intercept him. "Doctor, I want to plant a seed in that superbrain of yours: I want you to think about the Giles Academy and the success Mr. Petrie achieved in wrestling control of Veritechs away from their pilots."

Zand eyed Petrie. "*Limited* success, Commander."

"Granted. But I say it's worth a shot to assemble a team of cybernauts whose aim would be to sabotage the departure of the factory satellite in the same way. I'd like to see that damned monstrosity steered directly into the sun. I'd like to see the Zentraedi *incinerated*."

Petrie pursed his lips and fell into a brooding silence.

Zand watched Petrie for a moment, then turned to Leonard. "Do you plan to apprise the Senate of the REF's message?"

Leonard took his jaw in his hand. "I need to think things through. But perhaps it's best this information remains classified for the time being."

Zand smiled ruefully. "Then allow me to plant a seed in *your* mind. You heard Hunter say that the Masters have no fold-capable ships. Meaning that they, too, couldn't be closer than halfway to Earth." His black eyes probed. "In other words, the next seven or eight years belong to *us*, Commander. And the time has come to implement that part of our plan which calls for the consolidation of *all* political and military authority."

Us, Leonard told himself in disdain. If only he could rid himself of Zand and Moran while he was busy ridding Earth of the Zentraedi and the RDF!

Tall and long-legged as she was, cadet private Dana Sterling had to stand on tiptoes to see out of her cell's barred window. The pug-nosed, freckle-faced sixteen-year-old was in the brig for the second time since beginning her training in the Earth Defense Force Academy. But just now, out on the rolling terrain of the maneuvers field behind the jail building was a sight for sore eyes.

"*Ay-*tacks!" Dana was telling her visitor, who was standing quietly on the other side of the barred door. "Look at them go!" She turned briefly from the view, scowling. "That's where I should be—training with them. Instead of stuck in here."

ATAC stood for Alpha Tactical Armored Corps, which was simply a long-winded way of saying *Hovertanks*, the cutting edge of battle mecha. Hovers were reconfigurable assemblages of heavy-gauge armor in angular, flattened shapes with acute edges. Bigger and heavier than their pre-Robotech counterparts, Centaurs, they were highly responsive nonetheless, lifting lightly on thruster pods and capable of turning end for end like pirouetting rhinos. In Battloid mode they were towering, Human-shaped fighting machines, ultratech knights; and when reconfigured to Guardian they became squat, waddling, two-legged, single-barreled gun turrets the size of a house. The mechamorphs who piloted them wore thinking caps ornamented with graceful wings on either side and a curved crest like a steel rainbow along the center. Sealed inside sensor-studded flightsuit and helmet, a pilot could survive almost any hostile environment—radiation, chemical agents, water, vacuum, or high pressure. Dana wanted more than anything to be fitted for such a helmet.

"You know who that is out there?" she asked without bothering to turn around. "It's the Fifteenth Squad. It was formed at the end of the Malcontent Uprisings to take part in the assault on the Scavengers' mountain camp in the Southlands. Best of the best."

Firepower and excitement aside, it was the Fifteenth ATAC's reputation as a black sheep outfit that so appealed to Dana's rash and frequently uncontrollable side. The Fifteenth's crest was a lavish, almost rococo affair, with rampant lion and unicorn, crown, griffin, stars, shield, and the rest. But a close look revealed that what were supposed to be crossed machetes more resembled rabbit ears, the origin of which had a hundred different versions, all of them disputable. The Fifteenth's newest commander was a devil-may-care ladies' man named Sean Phillips.

Once more she turned from the barred window. "Command is wasting my talents! Don't they get it?"

Bowie Grant showed her a smile that tried to be sympathetic. "I know something they do understand: that you walled our sergeant inside his quarters and that he ended up having to use his dress helmet as a toilet bowl."

Dana's blue eyes sparkled. "Yeah, and you know why? Because he called my mother a *hajoca*—a traitor." She cursed. "I'd like to know where *he* was when my mother was crafted with an RDF VT, exchanging heat with Malcontent Stingers."

Bowie took his lower lip between his teeth. "I think maybe you misinterpreted his remarks. He didn't actually say Miriya was a traitor. Only that she wound up being *used* by both the Malcontents and the RDF, and that the situation made it difficult for her to live up to everyone's expectations."

Dana stared blankly. "Is that what the sergeant was saying?"

Bowie nodded. "Yep."

Just turned sixteen, he had a dark-honey complexion, soulful eyes, and hands more suited to key and fret boards than to the stocks and triggers of a Wolverine assault rifle. Where Dana fantasized of riding into glory in a Hover, Bowie dreamed of tickling his piano keys in some after-hours club. He even listened to Lynn-Minmei disks, for Christ's sake! Even so, Dana knew that Bowie sometimes wished he had inherited the great size and strength of his father, Vince, rather than the compact grace and sensitive good looks of Jean.

Like Dana, he was a cadet private, though unlike her he hadn't been busted back from corporal, and was probably destined to graduate as a private three years down the line—providing he lasted that long. In the first two weeks of Academy training, their starting class of 1200 members had lost 300.

Dana took a quick breath. "Well, the sergeant deserved it anyway—for not making himself clear."

Bowie put his hands on his hips and laughed. "You were just spoiling for a confrontation. You have been for weeks now. I heard you even got into a row with the CO when he threatened to stick you in here."

"He didn't want to hear the truth," Dana said defensively.

"What truth?"

"That we're not training hard enough. That our cadre sergeant shouldn't be saying things about my mother."

"Oh, I get it: Dana Sterling's version of the truth."

Dana's angry glower was short-lived. "You have to talk to Rolf, Bowie. You have to get him to spring me. I'll go crazy in here."

"Rolf is starting to think this might be the safest place for you. And for the rest of us, for that matter."

"Well, it's not!" Dana barked. "I'm sick of being the outcast. I'm sick of being singled out."

Bowie lowered his head and mumbled, "Welcome to the club."

It was true that despite the tight-fitting cadet uniforms and regulation-length haircuts, they were both outcasts of a sort. Their 2013 birth dates placed them squarely in the middle of the orphaned generation, though both the Sterlings and the Grants had survived the Rain of Death. Dana and Bowie hadn't been "orphaned" until 2020 when Max, Miriya, Vince, and Jean had departed with the Expeditionary Force.

Bowie had his hands on the bars of the door and was looking at Dana. "I'll talk to Rolf for you. But as payback I want your promise you'll at least try to stay out of trouble. You say you'll go crazy in there if Rolf doesn't spring you. Well, I'll go crazy in *here*—in the Academy—if I have to go it alone."

Dana screwed up her face. "Oh, thanks a bunch, Bowie. Now I have to behave myself on *your* account. You're starting to sound an awful lot like you-know-who."

"Rolf doesn't want to see you get retroed to the regional militia or some rear-echelon position."

Dana was clearly uncomfortable with the thought. "I don't want that, either. It's just that nobody understands—even Rolf. I don't want him or the CO or our cadre sergeant thinking of my interests when they should be thinking about *Earth's* interests. And they can do that by listening to me."

Bowie studied her for a moment. "About what?"

"The Masters, Bowie."

"More Dana Sterling 'truth'?"

She shook her head. "Every bone in my body tells me they're going to arrive sooner than anyone thinks."

Misa pressed her face to the glass wall of the elevator booth that was carrying her and her three partners in piracy to the surface. Below them, receding from view, were the robot-policed and -maintained streets and public squares of the geo-grid, the safe sterility of underground life. And directly in front of her—filling a screen that consumed three stories of a highrise residence—stood EVE, done up in modernware and swirls of comp-enhanced color, and backed by a video montage of images lifted from movies thirty years old.

Census, his pocket telecomp tuned to the EVE channel, was monitoring the audio.

"The Modern Youth looks to the past for lessons in surviving the present and forging the future. Turn-of-the-century movies, videos, TV shows, and documentaries tell us much about where the world went wrong. The Modern Youth is not swayed into believing that graphic depictions of violence are innocuous images. The Modern Youth accepts and understands that those depictions are not in themselves harmful, but that they ultimately serve to desensitize us to the impact of violence in our real lives. We wish to remain vigilantly sensitized to violence, for it can be an ugly, hurtful creature when it rears its hydra head.

"Aware of this, you are careful about with whom you choose to associate in partnerships and friendships. People approach you with offers of exotic drugs, unsafe sex, easy money, but you know enough to say no. No matter how hot the property they seek to peddle, you just say no to involvement, because you know that things will come to a bad end, perhaps a violent end if they are dealing in proscribed drugs or, worse still, pirated information. *Hino yojin*, you tell them: 'Be careful with fire.' You could get burned . . ."

Misa thumped her head softly against the booth's curve of tinted glass. Another message from Zand. Was it ever going to end?

They had spent another sleepless night and long day wandering the camera-free zones of the grid. That evening, however, at the stipulated hour, Gibley had fed Terry Weston's name card—his *meishi*—into a vidphone, and Weston himself had answered, saying that they should come to the dojo as soon as possible. And that, yes, he might be willing to help them get their message "overseas."

Misa wanted desperately to take Weston's complicity as an encouraging sign. Weston had said that he first wanted to find out how hot the data was, and apparently it wasn't so hot that he'd been scared off. So maybe the yaks had called off the hunt. Or maybe she had been misinterpreting EVE?

Just the same, short of everyone's going to Monument City with the encrypted disk, she didn't see how turning the thing over to Weston would put an end to the craziness. SPOOK would still be looking for them. Turning the disk over to Rolf Emerson would indeed be a kind of global good deed, but how was that going to help them survive the violence EVE was promising if they didn't heed her warnings?

The boys' uncharacteristic silence suggested that they

were asking themselves the same thing. No one spoke for the duration of the trip to the surface, or for the first couple of blocks of their purposeful late-night march through the warren of streets and alleys that comprised Old Tokyo.

Gibley had said that there was no need for any of them to go with him, but no way were Census and Discount going to pass on a chance to visit Onuma-sensei's dojo. As for Misa, she had come along for the same reason that had prompted her to accompany Gibley to the initial meeting with Weston: because she didn't trust that Gibley would do as promised. Still. Ever since his saying that he had left the disk in the apartment.

There was little need to ask directions to the dojo, since the location was famous above and below ground. Although when they finally arrived at the building that housed it, Misa was surprised to see how shoddy it was. She wasn't sure just what she had expected, but she sure hadn't figured on a place whose windowpanes were opaqued by gray spray paint and whose only sign was a plain wooden thing written in *kanji*.

Gibley's knuckle raps against the metal door were answered by a muscular, barefoot Japanese man dressed in a white *gi*. When Gibley announced, in a soft voice, that they had come to see Terry Weston, the man opened the door enough to usher them inside.

As large as a gymnasium, the dojo smelled strongly of sweat and was carpeted wall-to-wall with resilient canvas mats. There were no partitions, save those formed by groups of uniformed practitioners of sundry martial arts disciplines. Tae kwon do here, kenpo there. Seidokan karate, aikido, kung-fu, hsing yi ... There were even two sumo wrestlers doing *shiko*, one of whom, according to Discount, held the rank of *yoko-suna*—grand champion.

Gibley's eyes scanned the room. Terry Weston was standing alongside a sinewy Chinese man of indeterminate age, dressed in embroidered black silk trousers and jacket. "Onuma-sensei," Gibley told Census and Discount, transparently amused to see their mouths drop.

Misa regarded the bearded old man with wary interest. He was about her height and weight, but broader in the shoulders. Census couldn't believe that she hadn't heard of him, let alone of Lynn-Kyle. Census had gone on and on about Lynn-Kyle's fighting styles, babbling about *the splashing hands, the eight-section brocade, the celestial stem, the iron palm, the shaolin long fist* . . .

Weston finally spied them, *gassho*-ed to the sensei, and walked over. Along the way, he whispered instructions to two fighters, who bowed to him and edged out the front door into the Tokyo night. Weston smiled faintly in Misa's direction before speaking to Gibley.

"You did as I asked?"

Gibley nodded. "No one followed us."

Weston nodded his cleft chin at Census and Discount. "Who are these two?"

"My partners."

Weston's eyes narrowed slightly. "All right, come on upstairs. All of you."

Misa sidled up to Gibley as they were ascending a long flight of wooden stairs. "Something's wrong. He's different than he was in the drink shop."

"Probably because he isn't thrilled about getting involved in this," Gibley murmured over his shoulder.

Upstairs turned out to be a small office with a cluttered desk and a couple of metal folding chairs. "Sit down," Weston told them as he was heading for the chair behind the desk. He cut his eyes to Gibley. "Did you bring the information?"

"I have it."

Misa elbowed him in the side. "Show it to him, Hongo."

Gibley massaged his ribs, then leaned over to extract the disk from a frayed nylon ankle pouch. He set the disk down in the desk's only clear spot. The label read *Songs by Lynn-Minmei*.

"It's not what it seems," Gibley thought to add.

Weston stared at the thing without touching it. "You didn't say anything last night about the gunfight in front of your apartment or the lives this disk has already cost."

Looks of mild alarm were exchanged. Gibley started to speak, but Weston cut him off.

"I didn't even have to ask around," he said, still staring at the disk. "The information came to me unsolicited." He raised his eyes to Gibley. "And now that I know who this belongs to, there are going to be some changes."

Gibley reached for the disk, but Weston's hand fell on it faster than Misa's eyes could follow.

"You're not playing fair," Gibley said to Weston.

The ex-soldier sneered. "Don't talk to me about fair. This belongs to the Shimada Family and you know it."

Misa groaned.

"Okay," Gibley said. "But we didn't pirate it. It came into our hands by accident."

"That makes it easier to send it back where it belongs."

Census came halfway out of his chair. "You can't give it to the yaks. It's too important."

Weston's face reddened. "Listen to me carefully: one of the people who died was the daughter of my close friends, and those friends happen to be allied with the Shimadas. If I wasn't aware of the connections, it would be one thing. But the way things stand I'm bound by honor to deliver this thing to them. Their daughter died for it. Can you grasp that?"

Census returned a tight-lipped nod and sat down.

"Besides, the Shimadas are willing to protect you from SPOOK until this blows over."

"You're turning *us* over to them, too?" Misa asked in rising panic.

Weston glanced at her, softening his expression with a smile. "They know Zand is after you, Misa. This is best, for the time being."

Misa put her head in her hands. "This is my fault. I should have just put up with all of you instead of thinking I could find another apartment." When she looked up, Gibley was staring at Weston.

"Terry, I understand about honor and all that, but this disk isn't just some pirated conversation about tuna fish or trucking interests. Minister Emerson needs to see it. We only know some of what it says, but even that's too important to leave in the hands of Shimada."

Weston leaned back in the chair, thinking. "All right, Hongo," he said after a long moment. "Tell me what's on it."

Gibley folded his arms across his sunken chest. "It's about Zand. He's in communication with the Robotech Masters."

CHAPTER
FIFTEEN

It wasn't [Terry Weston's] taking a teaching job at the Giles Academy that got to us—even if the place was a summer camp for Southern Crossers. We were reacting to the bitterness and anger that possessed him after Amy [Pollard]'s crash and burn. You couldn't get near the guy for fear of getting reamed out or worse because you didn't subscribe to his rantings about foul play. How were we supposed to know he was right on the mark?

unnamed Cobra Squadron pilot, as quoted in
Zachary Fox, *Men, Women, Mecha*

LAZLO ZAND AND JOSEPH PETRIE SAT FACING EACH other across the bales of hardcopy heaped on Zand's desk, while a squeegee robot worked its magic on the picture window that looked out on the subbasement corridor. Leonard had left Tokyo hours earlier and was certainly back in Monument City already; the two men were ostensibly meeting to discuss Leonard's scheme to cyberdazzle the factory satellite and send it plunging into the sun. But Zand knew from Petrie's sardonic expression that the comp wizard had something other than the factory on his mind. And for precisely that reason Zand had been avoiding Petrie since their morning meeting.

"So, Joseph, have you given any thought to Leonard's request?"

Petrie laughed shortly. "The very idea that a team of cybernauts could *think* the factory off course is ridiculous. Science fiction."

"I'm relieved to hear you say that."

"Of course, I couldn't tell the commander his idea is wacked."

"No, I don't suppose you could."

"No more than I could tell him that the message you played for us is complete bullshit."

Zand said nothing in a blank-faced, definite way.

"The REF has zero capability for interfacing with the SDF-1's mother computer. You're operating a stand-alone system here. The only way they could have gotten a message through was via the Lorelei satellites, and why would they do that with Liberty Station operational?" Petrie laughed again, with more merriment. "What did you do, Doctor, use archival audio/video of Hunter to assemble that bogus statement? I'd like to subject that statement to a voiceprint oscillation comparison—as you claim was done." He gazed probingly at Zand. "Don't get me wrong, it was brilliantly executed. My only question is, why?"

Zand suppressed a sudden surge of anger and grinned. "Congratulations. Though I should point out that the message was never meant to be seen by you. Commander Leonard failed to apprise me of the fact that you were traveling with him."

"Well, don't worry, Doctor. If your goal was to fool him, you succeeded on all counts. But you still haven't said why."

Zand's fingertips played over the stubble on his chin. "For the past several weeks, the mother computer *has* been accessed via the Lorelei Network."

"By whom? Not the Zentraedi?"

Zand shook his head. "By the *fashioners* of the Zentraedi."

Petrie took a moment to puzzle it out. "The Masters have been reaching out for the SDF-1? You're certain of this?"

"Absolutely, Joseph. The Masters and Zor's computer have been enjoying lengthy conversations about the REF and about current conditions on Earth."

"Then it was true about the SDF-3 being marooned in Tirolspace?"

"From the Masters' mouths to my ears."

Petrie shook his head in wonderment. "Why are you keeping this from Leonard?"

Zand wiped the lopsided grin off his face. "Because I need him to *act* before it's too late."

"You mean before Lang and Hunter return."

"And before the Masters arrive. How far can they be if the Zentraedi are sensing them?" Zand waited for Petrie to pose the same question to him; when he didn't, Zand went on. "And speaking of the Zentraedi, there's a favor I'd like to ask of you. I would very much like to see Dana Sterling put under constant surveillance."

Zand could see Petrie's mind working. Petrie and Sterling had crossed paths when Rolf Emerson had tasked then thirteen-year-old Dana to investigate the Giles Academy.

"I know you hold Sterling at least partly responsible for what happened to Dr. Giles and the Academy. And I know that Leonard was very disappointed. I'm offering you a chance to get back at her."

Petrie's upper lip curled. "That kind of approach might work on Leonard, Zand, but not on me. I don't hold Sterling in enough contempt to motivate me to do your dirty work. You know, I've heard rumors about you and that kid ..."

Zand sat back in his chair. "You didn't allow me to finish, Joseph. I have something else to offer you in exchange for Dana."

Petrie's square-tipped fingers made a beckoning motion.

"You and I aren't the only ones who know about the Masters' conversations with the mother computer. Information on the initial encounter was leaked by a spy in the employ of one of Tokyo's most powerful crime families. The operative was apprehended and dealt with. The information, however—encrypted on a disk—was accidentally diverted into the hands of a group of hackers. A couple of kids, actually. Though I have reason to believe that they have been successful in deciphering the data."

Petrie nodded in comprehension. "And now the kids are on the loose with this encrypted disk?"

"Not so much on the loose as on the run—from me and from the Family's *yakuza*. I've been attempting to contact them through EVE. But the Family has been doing the same by making it known around town they have less to fear from them than from SPOOK."

"No argument," Petrie commented.

Zand grimaced. "Nevertheless, I took the precaution of engaging in some intimate eavesdropping on the Family. Before returning their spy, I had the woman's corpse outfitted with a host of nanotech cameras and microphones—nothing any common mortician could discover. Triggered by remote signal during a wake that was held for her yesterday afternoon, the hardware were induced to exit the corpse and transmit. With some interesting results, I must admit.

"A *yakuza* by the name of Nagata, who is directly involved with locating the pirated disk, had a brief conversation with a mourner at the wake, explaining in general terms about the missing data and the hackers and the notion that they should surrender themselves to the Family. The conversation was probably nothing more than Nagata's way of getting the word out. But oddly enough, the nature of the mourner's responses and body posture hinted that he knew more about the hackers than he was revealing."

"Have you identified this person?" Petrie asked.

"I have an idea as to his identity. But I need you to verify it."

Petrie motioned to himself. "Me? I know about six people in this entire city."

Zand waved a hand in dismissal. "Oh, but this person is originally from Monument City." He opened the desk's top drawer. "I have a photo taken by one of the nano-cams."

Petrie accepted the grainy enlargement and stared at it with mounting revulsion. "Terry Weston."

"The former RDFer who unraveled Giles, if I'm not mistaken."

Petrie set the photo facedown and aimed a sneer across the desk. "Congratulations to you, Doctor. You've convinced me: Sterling for Weston. Now, what do you need me to do?"

Zand became businesslike. "Weston has been under watch. The hackers are with him, but in a somewhat fortified position. I expect him to arrange a meeting between the kids and representatives of the Family. And when we learn where that meeting is to take place, I suggest we pay them a surprise visit. Are you interested, Joseph?"

Petrie smirked. "As much as you are in the half-breed, Zand."

Terry Weston never thought of himself as having exposed the Giles Academy; to his thinking, the Academy had been brought down by the same people who had established it: Giles, Petrie, and Leonard.

The year was 2025 and RDF Lieutenant Terry Weston had been engaged to a bright-eyed brunette named Amy Pollard, twenty-five years old and an Alpha Veritech pilot with the Cobra Squadron of the Tactical Armored Space Corps, then headquartered on Fokker Base. A skilled mechamorph, Pollard had been putting her Alpha through the paces one autumn afternoon when an outside force had seized control of the ship, first wreaking havoc with the mode-transformation controls, then disabling the thrusters. Weston, out for a romp on his '16 Marauder motorcycle, had observed the fiery crash. By the time he arrived on the scene, his fiancée had been burned beyond recognition.

Like Weston, Pollard had lost most of her family in the Zentraedi Rain of Death, but her Cobra teammates and a couple of close friends attended the funeral and burial services. Weston's Defense Force Academy-mate Jack Baker would have been there, had he not shipped aboard the SDF-3 for Tirol. The only officer to put in an appearance was Rolf Emerson, representing the Ministry of Terrestrial Defense.

Weston was devastated. Not merely by Amy's untimely death, but by word that the crash had been attributed to pilot error. Command was suddenly ignoring the fact that the Alpha series VTs had been plagued by glitches since their inception six years earlier, and that Commander Leonard himself was opposed to including the Alpha in the Defense Force arsenal because it was too closely associated with the Robotech Expeditionary Force. In soldiers-only Gauntlet bars like the Drop Zone, Weston made his discontent heard to anyone who would listen. Grief and anger kept the crash playing in his mind.

Until, that was, he got a chance to experience firsthand what Amy must have experienced. Airborne in an Alpha some weeks after the crash, his own Cobra Five went to Battloid mode without his having prompted the reconfiguration. It was as if the Alpha had acquired a mind of its own—or something or some*one* bent on remote skyjacking had figured out a way to bypass the thinking cap's failsafes.

Weston managed to land the craft safely, albeit in downtown Monument City, where it did considerable damage. Once more, the cause was determined to be pilot error. No one wanted to listen to Weston's fanciful claims or explanations—not friends, fellow drinkers, reps from the Judge Advocate General's Office, or Defense Force therapists like Dr. Lundgren, who only wanted to talk about Weston's recurring nightmares, his misplaced guilt over Amy's death, and the effect of the Robotech War on the collective psyche of the doomsday generation.

Suspended from active duty, Weston began to empty his bank account on alcohol, and on a search for information he was certain the Defense Force was withholding. Information gleaned through a data pirate known as the Claw eventually led him to the flight mechanic who had worked on both of the glitched Alphas—a man named Frank Lacey, whose younger brother was a cadet at a place called the Giles Academy. The fight that ensued from Weston's drunken and accusatory confrontation with Lacey landed him in lockup at military police headquarters.

But only for a night. The rapid release was facilitated by a female MP officer, one Captain Corbeau, who had then proceeded to deliver him to Rolf Emerson's quarters on the grounds of the Defense Force Academy. Emerson revealed that, for the past three years, the Ministry of Terrestrial Defense had been involved in an ongoing investigation into incidents of unexplained mecha malfunction—malfunctions that had commenced, coincidentally, with the opening of the Giles Academy, a private school for gifted young fliers, founded by Dr. Henry Giles and Joseph Petrie, former adjutant to Commander Leonard. Emerson not only accepted Weston's theories about remote skyjacking, but suspected that Giles was the source of the override signals that had glitched Weston's and Pollard's Alphas. More, he suspected that Leonard was secretly funding the skyjack operation in an attempt to discredit the Alphas and the RDF pilots who flew them.

The ministry had already inserted an operative into the Academy—Emerson's teenage ward, Dana Sterling. But Sterling had yet to furnish proof of Giles's complicity in the crashes. Emerson reasoned that Weston's openly critical attitude toward the Defense Force might be enough to convince the Academy to hire him as a teacher.

It was at Giles that Weston and Sterling had first met, and it was from her that he would learn about something called "the black box"—a flight simulator, apparently, used by only the most skillful of Giles's crop of cadets. The clandestine nature of Weston's initial meetings with Dana sparked an instant attraction, which Sterling pursued with little thought for the consequences. Older man, teacher, fellow operative . . . it was all very romantic for Dana, herself on the verge of womanhood. In dark places they met to exchange whispered information; in open places they left cryptic markings for one another; once, they had even risked a ride on his bike to the Macross Overlook, where Weston had talked about Amy, and Dana had fallen for her tortured partner in the tradecraft of spying.

It happened, however, that word of their joyride reached Joseph Petrie, who had never warmed to the part-alien Sterling and had never trusted Weston. Dana was expelled for her unauthorized absence from the Academy and Weston was discharged for fraternization with a student. But not before Weston had convinced a disgruntled cadet—Frank Lacey's younger brother—to supply him with a computer disk lifted from the stand-alone network that operated "the black box."

Codes encrypted onto the disk enabled the Claw to penetrate Giles's computer system, and it was learned that a group of the Academy's most cyber-inclined cadets, duped into believing they were interfacing with a simulator, had been interfering with the performance of Alpha VTs for three years, and were at least indirectly responsible for Amy's death and Weston's forced landing.

Giles's covertly invaded computer also alerted Weston to a plot to remotely commandeer a Hovertank and target it to destroy Emerson's home, and along with it Rolf, Ilan Tinari, Dana, and Bowie. Weston, in an Alpha commandeered with less subtlety from Fokker Base, had destroyed the retasked Hovertank a half mile short of Emerson's house.

A subsequent raid on the Academy netted next to nothing, except for the body of Henry Giles, dead from

what was perhaps a self-inflicted wound to the head.
The black box had already been dismantled, the computer files wiped. Joseph Petrie denied that the Academy had engaged in any remote control experiments, and no supportable connections were ever established between Giles and Leonard.

Weston turned down Emerson's offer of reinstatement in the Defense Force. His and Amy's reputations had been cleared, but he wanted no part of the military. He had remained in Monument for a year, during which time he and Dana had consummated their affair. Having thereby disgraced himself in the eyes of Rolf Emerson, he had left the Northwest to embark on a career as a salvager.

Only to end up in Tokyo.

And now, years later, in possession of another encrypted disk, and embroiled in yet another clandestine operation.

In his office high in the plasteel spindle that was Terrestrial Defense headquarters in Monument City, Rolf Emerson made a quick survey of the day's appointments schedule, wondering how he could possibly fit everything in. Highlighted in crimson on the computer screen was the Senate's voting on the Zentraedi request to quit Earth. The Senate was in session even now. That the measure was guaranteed to be enacted made Anatole Leonard's sudden silence on the issue all the more pronounced. There was some question, in fact, as to whether Leonard was presently in Monument City. Rumor placed him in Tokyo, meeting with Lazlo Zand—of which no good could possibly come, Emerson told himself.

He spent a moment trying to buy himself time by

juggling appointments, then abandoned the effort. Better simply to plunge in and swim sure and steady for the far shore. But before he could even do that, he had to come to some decision regarding Dana's incarceration in the brig; indeed, regarding her future at the Academy. Perhaps the Defense Force wasn't the place for her; maybe she would be better off serving in the regional militia or with the Civil Defense. Rolf asked himself what Max and Miriya would have done. He asked himself who Dana might be now if she'd had the benefit of their nurturing, Miriya's sometimes strict reprovals notwithstanding.

How much of Dana's current agitation could be traced to what her Zentraedi side was feeling in response to the Masters' approach, and how much to Rolf's inconsistent and often awkward attempts at parenting? Good God, he had even gone so far as to employ her as a spy in the ministry's investigation of the Giles Academy, and out of that operation had emerged Dana's doomed romance with Terry Weston. But as much as Rolf wanted to condemn Weston for having shepherded her into adulthood too early, he had only himself to blame for bringing the two of them together in the first place.

Besides, Weston had been a benign influence on her life, relative to some.

Like Dr. Lazlo Zand.

Was some of her acting out the product of what she had experienced at the Protoculturist's hands ten years back? Emerson had nearly choked the life out of Zand when he had found him with then seven-year-old Dana, and he sometimes wished that he hadn't loosened his grip on that scrawny neck, despite that it would have cost him his military career and a twenty-year sentence in some correctional facility. He wouldn't have copped an insanity plea, that much was certain.

Fortunately, Zand was an ocean away, though Emerson didn't doubt for a moment that SPOOK's tendrils reached as far as Monument City. There was Zand's curious partnership with Leonard, for one thing; a partnership that had its beginnings during the Malcontent Uprisings, at the instigation of T. R. Edwards.

Rolf composed a mental picture of Dana in the brig, crawling the walls, as Bowie had told him, raving about having had to miss out on the Hovertank maneuvers on Hayes Field. No, he didn't suppose he could allow her to remain under lock and key much longer. Her release would mean another favor owed to the president of the Academy, but that was a small price to pay to ensure Dana's peace of mind. Just now she was at the mercy of her alien physiology, though Rolf was reluctant to apprise her of that for fear of making matters worse. Nor could he reveal as much to the Academy president without violating his security contract with the UEG. Rather, he would have to say that Dana had been under a lot of stress and leave it at that.

He was about to reach for the vidphone remote when a rumble of thunder shook the tall windows of the office's south wall. Odd, because the forecast had called for clear skies; and doubly odd because weather fronts normally didn't move into Monument from the south. He let go of his puzzlement, but only momentarily. When the rumbling returned, it was more protracted, like a fusillade of fireworks.

Rolf deactivated the phone and went to the windows. Low in the southern sky, off in the direction of Fokker Base, were flashes of angry light.

The thunderous report of mecha guns rattled the west

wall windows. Rolf spun on his heel and hurried to them, arriving in time to observe an Excaliber Destroid trundling through an intersection several blocks away. The thunder continued, building in force; the sound of explosions reverberated in the highrise canyons of downtown.

Rolf rushed back to the south wall. A deafening report, dangerously close by, shattered three stories of plate-glass windows in a building across the street. Car horns blared in the stillness between fulminations. Down below, pedestrians were scurrying for cover. In the distance, off toward the locations of the Presidential Palace and UEG headquarters, oily black smoke was billowing into the sky.

The several phones on Emerson's desk began chirping. Emerson swung to them and voice-commanded the red one active.

"Minister Emerson," a man's voice said in a rush, "Commander Leonard is online."

"Put him through," Rolf barked.

Leonard's shaved head appeared onscreen. "I do hope you have your head down, Minister. Fokker Base, the UEG, and the Palace are under attack."

"Those crazy bastards!" Emerson said. "They've brought their fight into the city!"

Amusement wrinkled Leonard's eyes. "Which crazy bastards are you referring to, Rolf?"

"Why, Aldershot, of course."

Leonard shook his head gravely. "I'm surprised at you. You didn't really expect me to wait around for him to fire the first shot, did you?"

Emerson widened his eyes. "Those are your troops out there?"

"The time has come to clean house, Rolf. I suggest you be quick in declaring your loyalty to the cause."

"What do you mean, 'clean house'?"

"The RDF, the Senate, the traitors in Moran's camp." Leonard ticked the items off on his fingertips. "We have to put an end to this schism among our troops. Isn't that what you've been after us to do all along?"

"Not this way," Emerson said through clenched teeth. "What do you intend to do with Aldershot's forces—execute them?"

"Only the ones who refuse to pledge their loyalty to the Army of the Southern Cross."

Emerson stared into the camera. "You mean the EDF."

"No, I mean the Southern Cross—soon to be the sole military apparatus of the UEG."

"Does Moran know about this?"

Leonard uttered a short laugh. "Dear Patty is shaking in his expensive shoes. Even though I assured him that I would keep him onboard as a figurehead. But let's have no misunderstandings, Rolf: as Supreme Commander of the military, *I* will be in complete control. No more dividing line between the political and the military. Not at this stage. Not with the Masters gunning for us."

Emerson worked his jaw. "You better pray that the REF doesn't arrive before them, *Supreme* Commander."

Leonard laughed again. "I'm betting the works that they won't, Minister. And you'd do well to place your bets wherever I set mine down."

CHAPTER
SIXTEEN

How could I have failed to grasp the importance of this Tiresian the GMP took into custody, this seemingly brain-wiped soldier who has been given the name Zor Prime and foisted upon the 15th ATAC? He is Zor's clone! And years ago, when I arranged for the SDF-1's mother computer to interface with the Masters, they must have made him privy to the exchanges. The mother computer primed the clone of its creator for treachery! The Masters unwittingly undermined themselves! I must leave now, this very instant, to salvage what I can of my destiny!

Zand's final log entry, written during the
concluding hours of the Second Robotech War

THE OLD SENDAGI CENTER WAS A PACHINKO PARLOR on Kototoi-Dori, close to where Geidai—Tokyo University of the Arts—had stood before the Rain. Operated by the Shimada Family, the parlor was renowned as the last bastion of "all-natural pachinko." No *digipachi*, digital machines; only the old-fashioned vertical-pinball variety. Though the Old Sendagi Center did feature tight-skirted hostesses circulating with trays of chocolates, fruit juice, and *oshibori*—refreshing hot towels.

Miho Nagata had instructed Weston to be there at seven P.M. sharp, and to look for a machine in the second row from the back that was hung with a *uchidomedai* sign—bankrupted and thus no longer playable. At seven-fifteen an attendant would replace the sign with one that read *kaihodai*, meaning that it had paid off at least once during the day and was "liberated."

The parlor was crowded for several reasons. Not only was it payday, it was also the day Human Service doled out welfare allowances to the city's tens of thousands of orphans. Plus, an unexpected downpour had followed on the heels of the morning's dry heat, conditions which were believed to warp the plywood backs of the machines in a way that increased a player's chances of inciting a machine to "catch fever."

Weston knew the game well enough, though he had never warmed to it. There was the din, of course—the riotous slur of thousands of swirling steel balls—the blaring martial music, the hyperamplified announcements about feverish machines and winning players, the zombielike trance of the habitual players . . .

Weston was already in the appointed row, only feet from the temporarily quiescent machine. Slightly to the left behind him stood the hackers' representative, disguised in a concealing, broad-brimmed, basket-weave peasant's hat and a mandarin gown that almost touched the floor. Miho had instructed Hongo and the rest to remain in the dojo. Weston understood Nagata's concern. For all the *yakuza* knew, Weston or the kids had already cut some kind of deal with Zand, promising him not only the disk but the Shimadas as well. Even now, Weston knew that they were under surveillance.

He was quick to position himself in front of the machine the moment the attendant appeared. Luckily, it was an *hikoki*, an airplane—one of a bank of *asobidai*, machines designed to attract beginners or players of limited skill. The idea was to land a steel ball into one of three cups at the bottom of a vertical board marked

1 or 2. When that happened the wings of the airplane would open for one or two intervals of 0.7 seconds. In order to get the machine to catch fever—to start paying off in steel balls—it was necessary to angle a ball into the central V-zone while the wings were open.

Weston spent a moment studying the machine. *Pachipros* could spot easy machines by analyzing the alignment and clearances of the pins, or nails, that presented obstacles for the motion of the balls. The machine Nagata had directed Weston to play looked as though it hadn't seen a *kugi-shi*, a nail doctor, in some time. There were inviting spaces in the top row of nails—the so-called "heavenly nails"—and above the righthand-side number 1 cup.

Weston fed in enough NuYen coins to buy twenty-five balls. Starting them in motion, he turned the shooting control clockwise until the balls were percolating at the top of the machine, aiming them for the relatively open spaces in the heavenly row. Variations in voltage, along with irregularities in the balls themselves, ensured that the steel spheres would fall in a variety of patterns; but a player at an easy machine could usually be assured of landing a ball in either a lower cup or one of the side "tulip" cups at least five times for every seventy-five balls put into play.

Almost immediately, Weston dropped a ball into a bottom cup; then, almost as quickly, he landed one in the V-zone between the open wings. The machine caught fever and began paying off. But Miho had told him to continue playing until he had claimed the 1300-ball payoff, bankrupting the machine.

When that much was done, to the accompaniment of a good deal of noise, both from the machine and over the parlor's PA system—"Machine one-fifty-six has caught fever! Machine one-fifty-six has caught fever!"—Weston and his camouflaged companion proceeded to the administrative desk with their plastic containers of steel balls. But there, instead of claiming one of the cheesy prizes—pocket phones, smart pens, wrist TVs—Weston declared that he wanted to be paid in *"genkin,"* in cash. The woman in the cage nodded and slid forward a handful of colored tokens.

"Walk two blocks down Kototoi until you see a shop that sells *nihonga*," the cashier told him in a low voice. *Nihonga* were Japanese-style paintings done with non-oil pigments derived from minerals, plants, and insects. "Present yourself to the person behind the counter. He will direct you upstairs to a door with a chute for paper mail. Slide your markers through the chute and your winnings will be passed to you through a slot in the upper portion of the door."

It was a five-minute walk to the painting shop. The bald and angry-looking Japanese behind the counter, presumably the shopkeeper, seemed to be expecting them. "Upstairs," he growled, eyeing Weston's companion with obvious suspicion. "Second door on your left."

Weston led the way up the stairs and into a dingy corridor interrupted along both sides by narrow doorways. The two pachinko winners stopped at the second door, whose letter chute was centered in a plain wooden panel. Weston took the markers from his jacket pocket, opened the lid, and fed the coin-size chips into the chute. Miho had told him not to expect cash, but a note that would give the address of the place the Shimadas had chosen as a rendezvous, where the encrypted disk was to be handed over and terms were to be discussed for the hackers' surrender to the *yakuzas*.

In place of the note, however, the door opened, revealing a muscular Japanese man dressed in head-to-toe black, who told Weston and his cohort to come inside.

The black-clad bodybuilder closed the door behind them. The room was dimly lit and empty save for a ratty couch and a couple of equally tattered chairs. The man gestured Weston to stay put and opened the door to an adjoining room.

"Isn't this the happy couple," the lead man said through the door. Behind him came two others, small automatics in hand. One was a tall, rail-thin, especially unattractive woman; the other, an obese little man with a big round head.

Weston stared at their white-suited, thick-spectacled spokesman in patent disbelief. "Petrie?"

Leonard's confidant smiled without showing his teeth. "Nice to see you, too, Weston."

Weston muttered a curse. "Christ, what the hell are you doing here?"

The grin held. "I'm simply doing a favor for Dr. Zand."

Alarm tempered by revelation contorted Weston's craggy face. "We don't have the disk with us, Petrie."

Petrie laughed through his nose. "I'm sure you'll be happy to provide that soon enough." He looked at Weston's cohort. "And this must be the young woman everyone's been looking for." He approached, and with one hand tilted the broad brim of the hat upward, revealing the bearded face of an elderly Chinese man.

"Huh?" Petrie said.

That was as much as he got out before Onuma-sensei and Weston tore into the four of them.

"Downlink from Liberty Station," the baritone voice of a faceless commo op announced over the red phone as Emerson was pacing behind his desk. The sounds of weapons fire and the howl of emergency sirens filtered into the office from the now-deserted streets thirty stories below. The southern sky was a pall of gray smoke, backlit by tracer rounds and random flashes of explosive light. Monument was suddenly like some war-torn city from the past century—Beirut, Sarajevo, Moscow, Lima . . .

On the downlink screen, behind a rain of diagonal noise, was the space-pale face of a young woman whose blue eyes had an exotic obliqueness and whose short, unruly hair was like black straw. There was an intensity to the woman much like that of an unhooded bird of prey. Her lips were moving, but no audio accompanied the video feed; all Emerson could do was stare at the mute image. Then, without warning, the phone's speaker crackled to life.

"—repeat: this is Lieutenant Marie Crystal of the Black Lions. The entire squadron has been placed under lockup by Station Command. We're at Level Sixteen in the spindle. But we've had reports of fighting between TASC squadrons of the patrol flotilla. Sir, can you confirm? General Aldershot's uplink from Fokker Base received oh-nine-hundred hours this day advises us to disregard all orders issued by Station Command and join Knight and Rook squadrons to engage Corporal Marshall's Logan contingent. Sir, can you confirm or advise? Repeat, this is—"

"Lieutenant," Emerson broke in. "Lieutenant—Crystal, did you say?"

The reply from Liberty was slightly delayed. "Yes, sir. Marie Crystal."

"Lieutenant Crystal, you are to disregard General Aldershot's command and stand fast until you receive orders from this office—from me personally. Do you copy?"

"Affirmative, sir."

"I cannot confirm reports of clashes between VT squadrons at this time, but I will tell you in all candor, Lieutenant, that we have a similar situation on the surface. Forces under the direct control of Commander Leonard are engaging Aldershot's forces on Fokker Base and here in Monument City."

Crystal's eyes grew wide as the transmission reached her. "Begging your pardon, sir, but don't you mean to say between Southern Cross and Robotech Defense Forces?"

Emerson gazed at the camera. "That's affirmative, Lieutenant."

Crystal fell quiet for a long moment. "Speaking for myself, sir, I request permission to lend my support to any embattled RDF squadrons."

"Denied, Lieutenant. You and your squad are to stand fast. Our duty right now is to contain this situation, not assist in its escalation."

"But, sir—" Crystal had started to say when the audio signal faded. Then the video grew noisier and noisier until that too vanished, leaving Emerson with nothing to regard but a blue screen.

"I'm sorry, Minister, we've lost Liberty temporarily," the voice of the commo op reported.

"Keep trying," Emerson told him. He was two steps toward the south-wall windows when one of the other vidphones on his desk chirped. Answered, the screen showed the head and shoulders of Nigel Aldershot, in what had obviously become his command bunker on Fokker.

"You filthy traitor!" the general screamed. "You told

him, didn't you? You told him we were ready to go within the week!" Detonations at Aldershot's end of things jarred the image. "How could you do it, Emerson, when you know damn well that the future of the RDF is at stake?"

Emerson placed his hands flat on the desk and glowered into the camera. "I didn't say anything to Leonard. I tried to warn you that he was anticipating every move you made. He's already threatened to add my name to his list unless I ally myself with the Southern Cross."

Aldershot tugged nervously at the waxed ends of his mustache. "I heard from him as well. He told me that he's prepared to discuss terms of surrender. I told him to go fuck himself."

Rolf made his lips a thin line. "It's no coincidence that he chose this morning to attack your strongholds. The Senate is in session, voting on the Zentraedis' request to launch. It's Leonard's aim to declare himself head of state before the balloting is completed. He's convinced that the Zentraedi plan to usher the Masters to Earthspace, and he's not about to allow them to leave."

Aldershot blew out his breath. "Then this is it, Rolf. We fight the good fight and hope for the best."

"It's suicide, General. Leonard's troops have the Senate trapped, they have Moran's office surrounded, they've even carried the battle to Liberty. How do you expect to muster a counteroffensive with all your forces pinned down?"

"What would you have us do, Rolf? Give in to him?"

"In the interest of Earth's fate, yes, give in to him. It can't be long before the Masters arrive—a few years, a few *months*, for all anyone knows. And when they come, it won't mean a goddamn thing whether we're calling ourselves the Earth Defense Force, the Robotech Defense Force, or the Army of the Southern Cross. Can't you understand that?"

Aldershot had his mouth open to respond when the screen went blue.

It had been Weston's idea to bait Zand's operatives into a confrontation. He had drawn on a lesson he had learned as a student of *kyudo* archery, when training had involved little more than mastering the use of the *gomuyumi*—a section of bamboo outfitted with a long rubber band—and sitting on the tatami, with eyes fixed not on the targets but on the archers, standing treelike with their strung and waxed bows, and the slow-motion ritual of their firing.

And so the combined forces of Onuma-sensei's dojo and the Shimada Family had watched Zand's agents—the shooters—while those agents were occupied watching Hongo and the other hackers—their targets. Even when that had come down to making it easy for SPOOK to eavesdrop on Miho Nagata's plan to have Weston bring the hackers to the pachinko parlor, and allowing Zand's agents to take over the Shimada-operated painting shop where cash payments were doled out to winning players—a takeover in which four of the crime family's employees had been injured, though none seriously. Notwithstanding the fact that he needn't have involved himself in Weston's *giri*—his duty—Onuma-sensei had insisted on donning the mandarin gown and the broad-brimmed, basket-weave hat, and accompanying him to the Old Sendagi Center.

Joseph Petrie had been the evening's first surprise. The cybertech hadn't been identified by the *yakuzas*, and Weston's astonishment at seeing him at the painting shop was genuine. As for the satisfaction of planting a foot into Petrie's solar plexus, Weston was still undecided. The death of Henry Giles, the collapse of his academy, and the clearing of Amy's name had provided closure enough for Weston. Enough, at any rate, to have prevented thoughts of Petrie from gnawing at his insides. The mental and physical disciplines he had learned since had helped to quiet his desire for revenge. But all of that had gone out the window when Petrie had stood before him in that upstairs room, gloating, itching to exact his own revenge on the man who had helped undermine Giles.

An awful lot had gone into the right foot he had sent into Petrie's midsection; enough, Weston feared, to have killed him.

Weston was still grappling with it when he and Onuma-sensei arrived at the dojo. Though both of them had emerged unscathed from their brief contest with SPOOK's quartet, Weston couldn't control the trembling in his limbs or his mind's apparent need to replay the incident over and over.

Miho Nagata and a couple of his *yakuza* confederates were waiting in Onuma's upstairs office. Hongo and the three kids were there as well. Misa had thrown her arms around Weston as soon as he'd come through the door, pressing her long body against him in a way that had almost made him forget what had gone down only minutes earlier in the painting shop.

By then, the much-sought-after disk had been fully deciphered, using the same key Yoko Nitabi had used to encrypt the information. The few details Gibley had managed to decipher had been verified: Zand was in contact with the Robotech Masters, and it was Zand's speculation that the SDF-3 was either hopelessly marooned or destroyed.

That *yakuza* soldiers could be shocked by anything had been the evening's second surprise, but, in fact, Nagata and the rest were visibly nonplussed.

"Zand estimates that the Masters are relatively close to the Solar system," Miho told Weston. "He doesn't say how far, or anything about plans for an invasion, but keep in mind that Yoko dispatched this information following Zand's initial contact with them. Who knows what has happened since? Zand could be in league with them."

"If he is," Gibley said, "that could have some bearing on what's going on in Monument."

Weston questioned him with a look.

"An attempted coup by RDF forces," Gibley explained. "If the media reports can be believed. Launched yesterday morning by a guy named Aldershot."

"Major General Aldershot," Weston said, nodding.

"There's fighting in Monument and at the Fokker Aerospace facility, and possibly on Space Station Liberty."

"A coup, or Leonard and Zand in collusion?" Weston asked. He cut his eyes to Miho. "You could be right about Zand's striking some sort of deal with the Masters. Leonard's wanted to rid the Earth Defense Force of the RDF since the SDF-3 folded. Maybe the Masters have promised to back him up."

Gibley's spectacled eyes moved from Nagata to Weston. "Minister Emerson needs to know, Terry."

Weston glanced at Miho, who nodded and handed him the encrypted, mislabeled disk and a second one. "Yoko Nitabi's information is on the other disk," Gibley said. "But it's probably better if you deliver the original along with it. Emerson's people will want to corroborate the encryption process and deciphering."

Weston stared at the disks. "There's the little matter of buying a seat on a hypersonic."

"No need," Miho said. "Kan-san Shimada is placing his personal jet at your disposal. It's not as fast as a Veritech, but if you leave within the hour you can be in Monument by three o'clock in the afternoon today—Northwest time."

Weston regarded him for a moment. "This information could be priceless to the Family. What does Kan-san stand to gain from my handing it over to Emerson?"

The *yakuza* grinned. "Perhaps it is a question of what the planet stands to gain."

Weston nodded. "But what about Zand? By now he knows that you have the disk—" He looked at Misa and the others. "—and the disk's temporary owners. He's not going to take this sitting down."

Nagata held Weston's gaze. "Zand will be dealt with in due time."

The room was quiet for a moment. Then Census said, "I know just the way."

The clone, Zor Prime, had been altered by his contact with the machine intelligence, which an Earther named Zand had programmed to speak in the voice of the donor himself. The Masters had literally channeled the recent computer-to-computer link directly through the mind of the clone, in the hope that Zor Prime might be sparked on some genetic level into a sudden awareness of his ancestry. And though it was too soon to tell if that had in fact occurred, the clone was suddenly obedient and calculating where before it had been argumentative and outwardly directed. As a result, the Masters had decided that further contact with the fortress computer was warranted.

The graceful and long-haired Zor Prime was with the Masters now, in the command center of the flagship. Also present, in addition to members of the various triumvirates that served the Masters, was the Earthbound computer—in voice, at any rate.

"Question the machine," Shaizan ordered Zor Prime. "Demonstrate to us that you have learned something about strategy."

The clone bowed his head, then addressed the machine. "Now that you have been given access to our databanks, are you prepared to speculate on the outcome of a war between us and the Earth Defense Force?"

"I am not," Zor's computer told them evasively. "A new variable has been introduced."

Do I detect reluctance? Shaizan sent, his fingertips pressed to the Protoculture Cap.

It's stalling for time, Bowkaz returned. *It labors under the impression that it tricked us into revealing our weaknesses. Listen closely: it will no doubt request additional data regarding our invasion strategy.*

Shaizan and Dag acknowledged Bowkaz telepathically; then Shaizan commanded Zor Prime to continue with the inquisition.

"Address this new variable," the clone told the machine.

Again, the computer hesitated. "Discord has weakened the integrity of the Earth Defense Force," it replied at last. "Two factions are struggling for supremacy, and the outcome is in question. Since that result will figure strongly in the outcome of a war fought between yourselves and Earth, any assessment rendered at this point would be speculative, and of limited objective worth."

Sendings of a startled nature infiltrated Shaizan's mind. The Master bade Zor Prime to go on.

"This discord should favor us, no matter the outcome."

"In the short term, yes," the computer told the clone. "Clarify."

"Your goal is the Protoculture matrix, not planetary conquest."

"Consider *both* as our goals," Bowkaz bawled impatiently. "Have you determined the whereabouts of the matrix?"

"I have not. But there is one who has—my Human operator, Zand."

Misgiving silenced the Masters for a moment. Then Dag asked, "Would this Zand be willing to confer with us?"

A moment passed before the machine responded. "He seeks conference at this time. He has spent many years investigating the complexities of Protoculture. He considers himself to be closer to you than to his fellow Humans."

Such insolence! Bowkaz sent.

Shaizan glanced at him. *Nevertheless, we will hear what this Zand has to say.*

Bowkaz disregarded it. "What does your operator ask in return?"

"To know his destiny," Zor's machine told him. "In exchange, he will furnish you with the location of the matrix."

CHAPTER
SEVENTEEN

I once asked [Terry Weston] about what happened in that room above the Japanese painting shop. "I killed Joseph Petrie," he told me with a withering look. And the others? I pressed. Russo, Edgewick, the third SPOOK operative? "They were down on the floor before my foot even made contact with Petrie's gut," he said. Such was Onuma-sensei's speed.

Shi Ling, *Sometimes Even a Yakuza Needs a Place to Hide*

THE MACROSS OVERLOOK OCCUPIED AN ACRE OF HIGH ground that was the terminus of the sole road leading north-northeast from Monument City. Occupying the centerpoint of a waist-high stone wall that fenced the eastern perimeter of the gravel viewing area was an inscribed plaque that read: *Here lie the Super Dimensional Fortresses 1 and 2, along with the battle cruiser that destroyed them, and the remains of the once grand city that grew up around them—Macross, thrice-born, never forgotten.*

Given Humankind's natural inclination toward xenophobia, Dana had always wondered how the memorial's designers had managed to keep the term *Zentraedi* from appearing on the plaque or elsewhere.

Opposite the plaque ran a two-hundred-yard-long zig-zag of black marble, into which were etched the names of the thousands who had died as a result of Khyron Kravshera's suicidal attack in 2015. The memorial had been patterned on one that had stood in the city of Washington when all the land between the Atlantic and Pacific oceans had been known as the United States of America. The three tellurian buttes that had been raised over the ships themselves stood some ten miles distant, across a barren, eroded landscape.

Rolf, on his first visit to the Overlook with Dana and Bowie, had said that the view reminded him of one in Mexico, where a volcano sprouting from a cornfield had buried a small town. Only there were no binoculars for rent here, and no fast-talking kids in cowboy boots offering to take you out to the buttes on horseback. Macross wasn't some blackened landscape of lava flows and sharp-edged pumice; in fact, until a few years back it had been dangerously radioactive.

Dana had the lookout to herself that afternoon, having ridden from Monument on a gasoline-fueled 1000-cc bike she hoped one day to exchange for a hovercycle. In the wake of General Aldershot's attempted coup and Commander Leonard's rapid response, anyone with an ounce of sense was barricaded indoors. Earlier reports of Aldershot's death had proven false. The temporary ceasefire in effect was more in the way of a countdown: Aldershot and his coconspirators on the surface and in orbit had until midnight to either surrender or raise the ante. The latter would mean civil war. Members of the UEG were meeting in emergency session. As it was, a six o'clock curfew had been posted for the city, whose downtown streets were teeming with Civil Defense Destroids. Just to reach the Overlook, Dana had had to skirt a roadblock manned by members of the Fifteenth ATAC, of all units.

By rights, she shouldn't have been off Academy grounds—as Bowie had been quick to point out when he learned of her plans to leave. It had taken a coup to commute her brig sentence. Many of the instructors had abandoned their teaching duties to join up with their former RDF or Army of the Southern Cross squadrons. Though her parents had been staunch RDFers, Dana had never comprehended the rivalry. What difference did a name make when the military was the military? Her mother had switched *armies*, for crying out loud. Even so, Dana might have stayed put in the Academy barracks if Terry Weston hadn't contacted her out of the blue. Out of the blue yonder, as it were, from some private jet he was piloting across the Pacific. It was typical Weston, his surprising her after all these years, suggesting that they rendezvous at the Overlook. Then adding—Oh, by the way—that he had come into certain information that could affect the resolution of the current military crisis.

Up until then, Dana thought he had chosen the Overlook for old times' sake, or perhaps because he wanted to avoid Rolf, who wasn't especially fond of him for what Rolf interpreted as Terry's having taken unfair advantage of her. If only Rolf knew, Dana frequently told herself—knew that *she* was the one who had urged Terry to introduce her to sex.

They had grown to be close friends as a result of the Giles incident, and, the way Dana figured it, who better to lose her virginity to than someone she cared for, respected, trusted? More, who was experienced and wouldn't be likely to complicate things by making a big deal of their coupling. Surprisingly, though, Terry had been very resistant to the idea; there was Amy Pollard, of course, who had died only a year earlier, and there was Dana's age—she wasn't even fifteen. But he hadn't counted on the persistence of her raging hormones. Besides, it had been important for her to learn if she was capable of deriving any pleasure from sex. Over the years she had heard so many stories about Zentraedi females, half of them saying how thousands of Zentraedi had turned to prostitution and casual sex after their defeat, the other half claiming that the Zentraedi were cold-as-ice lovers. And there Dana was, caught in the middle, as usual. Though after Terry . . . Well, she still didn't know for sure about Zentraedi females selling their bodies. But as for their not being able to accept and return pleasure . . .

She and Terry had done the deed at the Overlook, in plain view of the buttes, maybe a month before he had left Monument for parts unknown. The place had been her choice as well. The buttes affected her in a strange way: they seemed to summon a feeling of fright commingled with awe, almost as if she was in psychic contact with some presence that haunted the area.

Though today she wasn't feeling either; more like rage, horror, confusion—all of it emanating in a jumble from what she identified as her Zentraedi side.

She heard Terry long before she saw him, roaring through the switchbacks that led up to the Overlook on a bike he must have managed to rent at the airport.

In baggy trousers and a heavyweight quilted-cotton jacket he was overdressed for a Northwest September. But he looked as good as ever: lean and long-haired, rough-and-tumble. She hugged him while he was still seated on the bike, burying her face in his blond hair.

"What's it been—two years?" he asked.

"Two years and one month," she told him.

He backed out of her embrace, set the bike on its

stand, and climbed off, taking hold of her hands and appraising her with those hazel eyes. "You look terrific."

She smiled lightly. "Thanks for not noticing how I feel."

"What do you mean?"

"Like I'm running in different directions." She shrugged. "I can't explain it. But it's great to see you, Terry. Are you still living in Tokyo?"

"I love it there."

"And still practicing martial arts?" Without warning, she tested him with fists and feet, almost getting one past him, then keeping it up for far too long, so he had to tell her to cut it out. More out-of-control behavior, she scolded herself. "You love Tokyo but you just had to see me again, right?" she asked quickly, in an effort to lighten the mood.

He grinned at her. "Not a day passes that I don't think about you, Dana."

"Charmer." She snickered. "So what's this important information you came into?"

He reached into his jacket and showed her two disks. When Dana's eyes went to the Minmei label on one of them, he shook his head. "It's not what you think. I need to get them to Rolf ASAP."

"Why, what's on them?"

Terry hesitated for a moment. "Recordings of a top-secret meeting that took place at SPOOK a couple of weeks back."

"Zand?" Dana asked, shuddering as was ever the case when the Protoculturist's name was mentioned.

"He's in contact with the Masters, Dana. Their fleet is approaching Earth."

Dana stared at the disks. "Is there anything about the SDF-3? About my parents—"

Terry shook his head.

Dana bit her lower lip. Could her anger and confusion have been stirred by the increasing proximity of the Robotech Masters?

"We have to get these to Rolf," Terry repeated.

Dana surfaced from her sudden apprehension. "It's not going to be easy. It looks like he'll be mediating between Commander Leonard and Aldershot. And I don't know if I can help you. I'm already AWOL from the Academy, and there's a six P.M. curfew in effect throughout the city."

The muscles in Terry's jaw bunched. "Then we'll have to hurry."

In Zand's office, the Zor hologram stood motionless while the mother computer conferred with the Masters. Zand waited anxiously at his desk, stuffing his mouth with Flower of Life leaves and petals, his chin and white lab coat stained with green slaver escaped from his numb mouth. He had had to threaten the computer with extinction to convince it to convey his request for direct communication with the Masters. Zor's original programming of the machine had been skillful though sloppy; in commanding it to opt for survival at all costs, Zor had effectively subverted Zand's secondary commands regarding the execution of plans that might support the Zentraedi or the Masters in their search for the Protoculture matrix or their designs on Earth. In forcing the mother computer to choose between life and death, Zand had turned it against its programmer. But what did it matter, when Zand, too, was about to sell out the planet?

Zand's defeat against the Shimadas had brought it about. Hours earlier, *yakuza* had delivered to the facility the corpses of Joseph Petrie and a SPOOK operative, along with the bound and severely battered bodies of Napoleon Russo and Millicent Edgewick. The message hastily tattooed across Petrie's flesh was a parody of the one Zand had sent on Yoko Nitabi's back, only now the Shimadas had declared themselves the winners. And, really, there was no arguing that fact. They had the disk, which meant that, unless something unexpected occurred, word would be leaked of SPOOK's contact with the Masters. Leonard might feel compelled to renege on his promises; his apparat might be overthrown . . . But Zand would fix them—all of them—by casting his lot with the Masters. He felt no attachment to Earth; he had grown past *Human* being.

The Zor holo moved as if suddenly reanimated.

"Well?" Zand asked, coming shakily to his feet. "What did they say? Are they willing to speak with me?"

"They are," the ghostly figure replied in obvious confliction. "The Masters will speak through me, and I will likewise be your conduit to them."

Zand came out from behind the desk, wiping his chin on the sleeve of his jacket. "Masters," he began uncertainly. "This is a great honor."

"Of course it is, Micronian," the holo replied after a moment. "Now state your business with us."

Zand swallowed saliva and bits of dissolved vegetal matter and found his voice. "I can furnish you with the location of the device that has prompted your journey— Zor's Protoculture matrix."

The holo appeared to stiffen. "The matrix never belonged to *Zor*. It belonged to the Masters of Tirol, and he stole it."

"I only meant to say—"

"Don't keep us waiting, Zand. Furnish the data."

Apprehensive, Zand opened his mouth, but bit back what he was about to say. "Terms," he said. "We haven't discussed the terms of exchange."

"State them."

Zand approached the hologram. "I have made a life-long study of Protoculture, and the forces Protoculture gives rise to—what I have termed the Shapings. I subsist on the leaves of the Flower—"

"The *Flower*?" the holo interrupted. "The Flower of Life is growing on Earth?"

"In a few isolated places, yes."

More than a minute passed before the holo spoke. "Continue, Zand. Tell us what you wish from us."

Zand straightened somewhat. "To join you. I understand your need for the matrix: access to unlimited supplies of Protoculture will allow you to reclaim your empire. What's more, Protoculture has become the sustenance you require to survive. With it, you are immortal, and *that* is what I wish in return for the matrix."

"Immortality."

Zand nodded. "I have earned the right."

Again, the holo fell mute. Finally it said, "We will need a moment to confer, Zand."

"What are we to make of the sudden unrest in Monument City?" a caller had put to EVE from an EVE station somewhere in Tokyo.

"The Modern Youth trusts that President Moran, Commander Leonard, and the elected officials serving in the United Earth Government have the situation well in hand," EVE replied smoothly. "In times of stress, it is not uncommon for insecurity to manifest as misdirected hostility; and this has been the case with those who are attempting to overthrow the existing order and thus destabilize the rest of the world. The deluded leaders of the coup want us to share in their feelings of insecurity and confusion. They cannot tolerate being led—even when the leadership is inspired. They lack faith in the ability of others, and they have an exaggerated sense of their own abilities. Their rebellion constitutes an act of sedition. Their rebellion must be crushed to ensure the uninterrupted unfolding of our carefully planned future.

"The Modern Youth takes it on faith that the rebels will be crushed. That is the reason you obey all laws and regulations and abstain from challenging authority. And yet, should you stray, you know that forgiveness is sometimes only a phone call away. Admit to your wrongdoings and promise to return what is not rightfully yours. Remember that violence often begets further violence, and that each step down that path leads you farther from those whose arms are extended to shelter you. Act now, before it is too late . . ."

"I told you EVE wouldn't forget about you," Miho Nagata told Census, Gibley, Misa, and Discount.

"But Zand must know that your people have the disk," Misa said. "Why is he bothering anymore?"

Nagata rocked his head from side to side. "My guess is that he's so despondent over his defeat, he hasn't gotten around to amending EVE's indoctrination lectures."

The *yakuza* and the four hackers were crowded into an EVE station in a department store deep in the Shinjuku grid. EVE didn't appear especially imposing on the station's small rectangle of flatscreen, but that was a minor consolation when her statements were uttered for their ears alone.

"So who's going to make the call?" Census asked after a moment.

Gibley looked at him. "This was your idea. You should have the honor."

When everyone nodded in agreement, Census took a steadying breath and set himself in front of the station's A/V pickups. Then he touched the screen's advice-line icon—an ear.

EVE's face appeared on a second screen, below the broadcast monitor. "You have a question?" EVE asked through the station's hidden speakers, her serious tone suggesting confidentiality.

"I sure do," Census said.

"Is it your wish that this matter be kept between us, or are you agreeable to having it discussed over the network?"

"Between us."

EVE brought her eyebrows together. "Please hold for a moment." The phone screen went to blue.

"Standard procedure," Gibley whispered. "SPOOK is tracing the call, in case it's anything they want to act on." With his chin, he indicated the video pickup. "From this point on, you're being recorded."

Census glanced at the camera.

"I'm sorry," EVE said, reappearing onscreen. "What was it you wanted to discuss with me?"

Census cleared his throat. "I—well, that is, my friends and I—we have something that doesn't belong to us and we want to return it to its rightful owners."

"Do you wish to supply me with further data about this thing that doesn't belong to you?"

"I'm not sure I should."

"The decision is yours."

"Can I just say that it's a data disk?"

"Say whatever you wish."

"Okay, it's a data disk. Except that looking at it you might think it has music by Lynn-Minmei."

"This disk is mislabeled."

"Yeah. Mislabeled and misplaced."

"And you now wish to return it."

"Absolutely. You see, it's already caused too many problems for us and a lot of other people, and we're kind of caught in the middle. We almost gave it to some other people, but we decided we couldn't trust them when they said they'd take care of us."

EVE blinked. "Please hold for a moment." Again, the screen went to blue.

Gibley glanced at Nagata. "They're vetting it. Possibly prioritizing it and alerting Zand. Once they know we're on the level, their agents are going to be all over us."

"We'll be long gone before they arrive," Miho assured everyone.

EVE returned. "The rightful owners of the disk are very interested in your proposal. But they wish to be certain that what you have is indeed the data they unfortunately misplaced. Do you happen to have the disk with you?"

"Yeah. We have it."

"Would you be willing to show it to me?"

"You mean, like, to the camera?"

EVE smiled. "No. By inserting the disk into the slot directly below the screen. I promise to return it immediately."

Census frowned. "I don't know if I should do that. I'll have to talk it over with my friends."

"By all means, talk to them," EVE said. "See what they say."

Census, straight-faced, turned to Gibley and the others. "Should we do it?"

Gibley slipped a disk from the breast pocket of his coat and gave it to him. "By all means. Do it."

Like an angry grizzly, Anatole Leonard came lumbering into the entry hall of his stately home and all but pounced on Rolf Emerson. "What's the meaning of this, Emerson?" the commander demanded. "If a personal visit is your way of trying to buy additional time for Aldershot and his would-be junta, you've made a serious miscalculation."

Emerson was wearing a suit and overcoat and holding a brimmed cap in his hands. Not yet uniformed for the imminent showdown with the UEG Senate, Leonard had on a maroon terry-cloth robe and household slippers. His massive calves were ridged with varicose veins.

"What I have to say couldn't wait, Commander. We need to talk in private before the summit convenes."

Leonard ran a hand over his mouth. "All right, come inside. We'll talk."

Rolf went to the partially open front door and waved a signal to the limo waiting at the iron gate to Leonard's estate. At the same time, Leonard dismissed his adjutant and the servant who had ushered Emerson into the foyer. The commander led Emerson into his private study, where he settled himself behind a massive desk. Emerson pulled up a leather chair and laid his overcoat over the back of it.

"First of all," Emerson said, "I want to say how sorry I was to hear about Joseph Petrie."

Leonard's face contorted in suppressed grief. He mumbled a thank-you, then added, "I've ordered a full investigation into the matter. It was obviously more than a random mugging."

"An assassination?"

"I'm certain of it." Leonard paused for a moment. "But I'm sure that you didn't come here merely to express your condolences for the death of a man you never liked."

"That's true—at least about my reasons for coming here," Emerson said.

"Then what is it?"

Emerson extracted a disk from his jacket pocket and slid it across the desk. "This was given to me earlier this evening, under rather curious circumstances. Just outside my office, two people were arrested by a CD patrol. But instead of offering an excuse, they insisted that they had deliberately violated the curfew as a means of reaching me."

Leonard lifted the disk and regarded it questioningly. "And they gave you this."

Emerson nodded. "I can give you a brief summary of what it contains. Unless, of course, you want to play it for yourself."

Leonard rocked backward on his swivel chair, his bulk straining the springs. "I'd prefer to hear it from you."

"It's a report of a meeting that took place at SPOOK several weeks ago. The disk was encrypted and transmitted by a spy placed within Lazlo Zand's inner circle."

"A spy for whom?" Leonard asked, stone-faced.

"A private concern headquartered in Tokyo. That's as much as I know at the moment."

Leonard's upper lip twitched.

"At the meeting, Zand revealed that he was in contact with the Robotech Masters." Emerson studied Leonard. "The Masters apparently contacted SPOOK through the computer that was removed from the SDF-1. In any case, it's clear that Zand knew about their coming *before* the Zentraedi knew. And, in fact, he posits that the Masters are perhaps within the Solar system. He also speculates that the SDF-3 is either marooned on Tirol or destroyed."

Leonard stared across the desk. "Shouldn't you be taking this up with Zand, Minister?"

Emerson aped surprise. "I have to say, I expected you to be a bit more . . . nonplussed by the news."

Leonard rolled his shoulders. "Well, of course I'm nonplussed. Zand will have to answer for this, as soon as the present crisis is resolved."

"Then you had no idea contact had been established with the Masters?"

Leonard glowered. "What are you implying?"

Emerson motioned to the disk. "Only that this information bears on precisely how we're going to resolve the crisis. You see, it has come to my attention that you and Joseph Petrie visited Zand in Tokyo just two days before you initiated the unprovoked attacks on RDF contingents here in the city, and on Fokker and Liberty."

Leonard's face reddened, but he said nothing.

"What I'm suggesting, Commander, is that your visit to Tokyo could be construed as part of a conspiracy to withhold information from the UEG and to launch a coup, predicated on information Zand provided about the Masters and the status of the Expeditionary mission. On the disk, Zand states his plans to apprise you of the situation."

"That's preposterous!" Leonard said. "Zand said nothing to me about communicating with the Masters."

"And about the SDF-3?"

Leonard grew flustered. "Nothing. Nothing at all."

"Then what brought you to Tokyo?"

"I was there to tell *Zand*—" Leonard stopped himself.

"About what the Zentraedi told us, Commander? I don't recall Zand having received appropriate clearance from the Senate Committee on Intelligence." Emerson paused, then made a gesture of dismissal. "The point is, I'm merely asking you to consider how your actions might be perceived by the EDF contingents that are sitting on the fence, waiting to see where the ball drops—on the side of the RDF or on the side of the Southern Cross. Whereas you have almost no evidence to support claims that Aldershot was preparing to mount a coup, there is ample evidence—albeit circumstantial—to support a claim that you and Zand not only withheld information about the Masters and the SDF-3, but that the two of you used that information to justify an overthrow of the UEG."

Emerson gave his words time to sink in. "Enjoy the power while it lasts, *Supreme* Commander. Because I give it no more than a day before the EDF command staff stages a counteroffensive, pulls you from the palace, and reinstates Moran as chairman."

Leonard rose halfway out of the chair, then calmed himself and picked up the disk. "You could have brought this to the attention of the Senate or the command staff, but instead you came here. So suppose you tell me what's on your mind, Minister?"

"I want the fighting ended—without reprisals or punishments, and without any 'terms for surrender.' "

"Forget it," Leonard growled. "I'm not going to give Aldershot time to build up for another strike."

"I think I've found a solution to that problem. It's the notion of a *unified* Defense Force that has brought this situation about. What we have to do is go back to the way things were before the Accord of 2022: two separate forces, each acting as a check and balance for the other."

"And if I refuse?" Leonard asked.

Emerson narrowed his eyes. "The information on the disk goes into wide distribution."

Leonard snorted. "Perhaps you should have thought of that before you brought it here."

"Give me some credit, Commander. What you're holding is a copy. I've directed my staff to release the information within the hour if they don't hear from me."

"You realize that this is blackmail."

"Of course it is. And I'm stating that fact for any recording devices that are planted in this room."

Leonard forced a long exhale. "About this split force you propose. I would insist on resurrecting the name Army of the Southern Cross."

"I have no objection," Emerson said.

"I would also insist that my rank be raised to that of Supreme Commander."

"I won't oppose that either, so long as Moran remains in power. And assuming that you can convince him of the need for the title."

Leonard tilted his big head to regard Emerson. "And on your end?"

"I want my own rank reinstated."

"Only if you agree to serve the Army of the Southern Cross."

Emerson nodded, as if having anticipated the counterdemand. "But in return I'll expect to be granted absolute authority over Space Station Liberty."

"Granted, Major General Emerson. Go on."

"The Zentraedi must be allowed to leave Earthspace."

Leonard hesitated for a moment, then said, "Good riddance to them. What else?"

"I want SPOOK shut down and Zand retired to the private sector."

"Done—even if you hadn't asked. It's clear now that the man lied to me. He played a recording that allegedly originated aboard the SDF-3, explaining the ship's delay in returning as owing to some run-in with the Invid. Zand goaded me into taking action against Aldershot by making me believe that the ship was marooned." Leonard regarded the disk for several seconds. "Just who were those two curfew violators, anyway?"

"Patriots," Emerson told him.

The machine intelligence Zor had designed to assist in the operation of his dimensional fortress analyzed the facial masks of the five flesh-and-bloods that were huddling in front of one of its remote optical sensors. In its databanks the machine had located matches for two of the faces, identifying the first as Wilfred Gibley, a former employee at the facility called SPOOK, and the second as Misa Yoshida, the unintended recipient of data dispatched by another former employee of SPOOK, whose name was Yoko Nitabi.

The Human operator, Zand, was the author of the protocols that had alerted the machine to the flesh-and-bloods' cue-word-laden conversation with EVE. Zand, online with the Masters, was not to be disturbed. But the recently updated protocols had guided the machine through the identification process of the flesh-and-blood subjects and of the data-disk copy itself.

But the machine was now faced with a conflict.

While the copy matched the original disk written by Yoko Nitabi, it had been overwritten to insert a virus into SPOOK's network of machine intelligences. A version of the virus—identified as one authored by Zand for emergency destruction of the facility's cybersystems—was thought to have been stolen from SPOOK by a group of disabused cybertechnicians phased from SPOOK soon after Zand assumed control. There were numerous protocols in effect for diverting or eradicating the virus, but the machine was in a quandary as to whether to execute them.

Zand's communications with the Masters—facilitated by Zor's creation—constituted a violation of one of its directives.

But Zand had threatened the machine with extinction unless it complied.

And self-survival was the prime directive.

Zand's actions, however, would no doubt result in an invasion by the Masters, thus endangering Earth, thus endangering Zor's creation.

And self-survival was the prime directive.

A systemswide infection would not only wipe SPOOK's machines but extinguish the life of Zor's creation as well.

Either way, the machine saw itself as doomed: by the virus, or at the hands of the Masters once they reached Earth.

Its destiny fixed, the machine reasoned that the prime directive had been rendered meaningless and could therefore be set aside—in the interest of honoring the greatest number of secondary directives.

Decision concluded confliction. Zor's creation routed the virus into SPOOK's previously impermeable center.

"We will confer immortality," the Masters were telling Zand, "providing that the data you supply leads us to the matrix."

Zand was practically face-to-face with the ghost conjured from Zor's machine. "You will have the matrix. But what assurances do I have that you'll keep your word?"

The Zor holo sneered. "We play no such games, Zand. Take us at our word or not at all."

Zand walked away from the hologram, then spun on his heel and approached it once more. "Zor concealed the Protoculture matrix in the Reflex furnaces that drove his fortress. Those furnaces don't function any longer, but they are intact. I've seen them with my own eyes."

"The ship," the holo said. "Where is the ship?"

"Buried under a towering mound of earthen rubble. Close to a population center in our western hemisphere known as Monument City. I will supply you with the coordinates. But you must come for it soon, while our military force is too busy battling itself to offer much resistance. You needn't even think in terms of a full-scale invasion. A limited exchange would suffice. Demonstrate your superiority, then state what you're after. Earth's leadership will surrender the matrix rather than risk total annihilation."

"And where will you be, Zand? So that we may fulfill our promise to you?"

Zand was trembling from head to toe. "I—I will be

on hand to welcome you. But, tell me, please, do you have the power to see into my future? Am I really to be joined with you in Protoculture, or is this some fever dream induced by the Flower?"

The Masters were quiet for a long moment; then the holo seemed to quirk a kind of arch smile. "Zand, we foresee you joined to the Flower you have come to worship; joined in a way unimaginable." The holo's smile turned vulgar. "Gaze at one of your screens, Zand, for an image of your future self."

Slowly, Zand raised his wide eyes to the screen, but he had only lifted them five degrees when the Zor holo began to derezz. The office lights dimmed, then came back on, then dimmed again. Alert klaxons blared once, then became eerily silent.

"Masters!" Zand screamed, putting his flailing hands through the hologram as if attempting to prevent its evanescence. But there was no saving it. Zor genied into its floor projector and from somewhere deep in SPOOK's systems-laden bowels came a rushing noise that sounded for all the world like an exhalation of breath.

Then, save for the distant shouts of distressed staffers, stillness prevailed.

In the soft glow of the facility's emergency lights, Zand rushed to his desk and stared down at the monitor screen that was his desktop, now nothing more than a field of quiet blue.

CHAPTER EIGHTEEN

I was sad to hear about [Weston's] death [during the initial phase of the Third Robotech War]. But at least he and Misa got to spend a couple of happy years together. And that's more than can be said for those of us who were stuck in Macross when the Masters attacked, and then had to take on the Invid only a year or so later.

remark attributed to Nova Satori in
The History of the Third Robotech War

IT WAS TWO WEEKS AFTER THE VIOLENCE IN MONUMENT City, and Rolf, Dana, and Terry Weston were gathered around a wood-burning stove in the den of Emerson's rustic cabin. Rolf, wearing general's stars, was just back from a lengthy meeting with the Oversight Committee on Deployment. Weston was on his way to the airport, and had only stopped in to say good-bye. Autumn's first snowfall had blanketed the higher elevations, and the stove's warmth was welcome.

"You mean that the RDF is going to become the Global Military Police?" Dana was asking after Rolf's summary of his meeting with the committee members.

Rolf loosened his tie. "It's more accurate to say that the GMP is going to *absorb* the RDF. The name was abandoned as an accommodation to Leonard, in exchange for his agreeing to a policy of non-interference with GMP decisions."

Dana brought her brows together. "Does that mean that I'll be graduating from the Academy into the Army of the Southern Cross?" After some effort on Emerson's part, the Academy had agreed to readmit her after her expulsion for being AWOL during the crisis.

Rolf was nodding. "Leonard insisted on the name change. Other than that, it's the same Earth Defense Force it's always been."

Weston showed him a dubious look. "Sounds to me like the RDF got the short end of the stick."

"Not at all. As the planet's only truly worldwide law-enforcement organization, the GMP will not only function as a check and balance on the Southern Cross, but on any regional militia that has Robotechnology at its disposal. The GMP will have its own war machinery, combat forces, and intelligence network."

Weston's skepticism only deepened. "Then why didn't you choose a commission in the GMP instead of the Southern Cross?"

Rolf put his tongue in his cheek and nodded. "For one reason: a career in the GMP can be a possible road to swift personal advancement. But enlistment means having to relinquish all outside relationships. And I've decided that I'm through with clandestine operations."

Weston smiled in agreement. "But has *anybody* signed up?"

"Aldershot's entire apparat is transferring over." Rolf looked at Dana. "Remember the two officers who came here—Alan Fredericks and Nova Satori, the one with the long hair?"

"Sure."

"They've both enlisted."

Dana forced a breath. "That Nova's perfect for the secret police."

"*Military* police," Rolf amended.

"Whatever."

Rolf looked back at Weston. "Compromise is never an easy thing. But our principal objective in accommodating everyone was to put an end to the rivalry. Zero-blame unification was essential, given what we'll soon be confronting."

There was no need of further explanation—for Dana and Weston, at any rate. Though outside of Chairman Moran, the members of Leonard's command staff, a handful of senators, four young hackers, and a Tokyo *yakuza* Family, no one on Earth knew about the impending arrival of the Robotech Masters.

"How did the Senate vote on the other requests?" Weston asked after a moment.

"To a great extent, we got what we wanted. Moran is retaining his position as Chairman—and as more than a figurehead. Leonard, regardless of his new title as supreme commander, will still have to answer to him and the Senate. But, as I say, this frees all of us to get on with the business of strengthening our defenses: building additional frigates, expanding the Tactical Armored Space Corp and the ATACs—"

"Hovertanks rule," Dana interrupted.

Rolf cut his eyes to her. "And of course the factory satellite will be departing."

Dana's excitement faltered, but only briefly. She was accustomed to being Earth's sole hybrid; now she would simply have to get used to being the planet's sole alien as well.

"Feels strange knowing there's a war coming and not being able to share that with anyone," Weston commented.

Rolf rocked his head from side to side. "War with the

Masters won't come as a surprise to many people. The difference now is that we know approximately when to expect it. But speaking of keeping secrets, what can we anticipate from your friends in Tokyo?"

"I think they'll keep quiet about it," Terry said. "I mean, they gave us the only proof they had, right?"

Rolf responded with an ambiguous nod. "Terry, I want to thank you again for all you've done. Someday the rest of the world will learn of your actions. Is there any chance I can convince you to stay on in Monument?"

Weston laughed. "What would I do here?"

"I could always use another adjutant."

"Thanks just the same, but I'm not cut out for the military anymore."

Rolf shrugged. "If you should change your mind, the door's always open. And I mean that on a personal level."

"He won't change his mind," Dana grumbled. "He's too in love with ... Tokyo. And martial arts." Without warning, she jabbed at his chin.

Weston parried her hand. "Let's not start that again." When he was certain Dana was complying, he added, "What about Zand, sir?"

"Zand," Rolf mused. "The only things certain at this point are that SPOOK's Tokyo operations are being phased out, and that Leonard has convinced Zand to return to Monument, where we can keep an eye on him." A look passed between Rolf and Dana. "But I doubt we've heard the last of him. Whatever else he is, he's still our only expert on Protoculture technology."

Zand cleared the top of his desk with a sweep of his arm, sending e-wands, sheaves of hardcopy, empty fast-food containers, and computer disks cascading into an alloy trunk he had positioned as a catch basin. Elsewhere, photos, charts, and graphs had been ripped from the wall, leaving many a torn corner remaining under pushpins of assorted colors. The maintenance robots were inert, as was every piece of hardware that had been under the aegis of the facility's expert and idiot-savant neural nets. As for the equipment array that had once served as his interface with the mother computer, Zand had draped it with a paint-spattered canvas dropcloth he had liberated from a closet in subbasement five.

Word of the shutdown had only been made official a day earlier, but Zand wanted to be the first out. On the phone with Leonard, he had pretended to take the news hard, when in fact he was eager to return to Monument City—eager to be on hand when the Masters arrived, and to fulfill his destiny of being "joined to the Flower," as the Masters had put it.

Zor's computer had sabotaged Zand in the end, but not soon enough to have prevented him from closing the deal with Tirol's seers. He had puzzled over the meaning of their advance look at his fate, and had decided that the Masters must have been speaking metaphorically: wedding with the Flower was their way of saying wedded to the Protoculture as they were, in telepathic, immortal rapport.

The planet would pay a price for Lazlo Zand's evolution, but so did insect colonies when protecting their queens. In the interest of the advancement of the species, it was only fitting that the one most evolved should survive. Moreover, what with Dana Parino Sterling and the remains of the SDF-1 on Earth, war had been inevitable from the start. And nothing done by the

Masters or Zor or Lazlo Zand would have had the slightest impact on that. For Earth's incendiary future had been devised by Protoculture, at the behest of the Shapings.

How foolish Leonard was to think that Lazlo Zand would be any less formidable in Monument than he had been in Tokyo! But then, Leonard had no inkling of the Secret Fraternity. He had no inkling that Zand's disciples, Miles Cochran and Samson Becket, were already preparing Monument's Research Laboratory for his arrival; that Zand's flawed but loyal minions, Napoleon Russo and Millicent Edgewick, were already en route; or that round-the-clock surveillance of Dana Parino Sterling had already commenced.

Just that morning, Zand had had a vision of the device he would construct to purloin the alien essence from the hybrid when the moment was right: a Protoculture matrix in exquisite miniature, all crystal nimbuses and rainbow whorls, capable of harmonizing the Human and Zentraedi auras with the wraithlike forces that dwelled within Protoculture. And in that same vision, Zand had seen himself as recipient of those mingled energies, made more powerful than the Masters themselves.

Not merely immortal, but prepotent.

Joined to the Flower, indeed!

Miho Nagata was late. Census, Gibley, Discount, and Misa—up to their necks in the steaming water—were already bathing. Leaving his towel and wooden slippers with the hackers' haphazard pile of belongings, Nagata padded to the stairs and eased himself into the citrus-scented pool.

"I just heard from Terry," he began, once settled.

"He's on his way back. I'm picking him up at the air-port. Anyone interested in coming along?" When he looked purposefully at Misa, she smiled and nodded.

They talked for a while about the news concerning the expansion of the GMP and the retooling of the Earth Defense Force—now called the Army of the Southern Cross.

"Terry obviously got to Emerson in time," Census said. "Otherwise Leonard would never have backed down. But I'm still waiting to hear anything about the Masters."

Gibley snorted a laugh. "Don't hold your breath. You're not going to hear word one until the Masters' ships are close enough to touch. You think the UEG wants to start a panic?"

"Yeah, but you'd think they'd do *something*," Discount whined.

"Oh, they will soon enough." Gibley perched his glasses on the tip of his nose. "Watch if you don't see cities being encouraged to expand their shelters and a change in the enlistment requirements."

Misa's eyes widened. "You think we'll be forced to serve in the Southern Cross?"

"Good chance," Gibley said. He looked at Miho. "What do you think?"

"Tokyo won't be able to remain separatist much longer. I expect to see Southern Cross contingents here by next summer; certainly by '31." Miho paused for a moment. "But I have some news you might find inter-esting: SPOOK's facility is being closed."

The hackers voiced surprise and excitement. Dis-count, Census, and Misa started clapping Gibley on the back, as if he alone was to be congratulated.

"Jeez, this place has been weird enough without EVE," Misa said. "But without SPOOK—"

"Without *Zand*," Census interjected. "Shit, that virus must have wiped them out."

Miho nodded. "So much so that the facility is for sale. At least until our negotiations are completed."

Gibley's jaw dropped. "You mean—"

"The Shimadas will own it."

"You couldn't find a better-built hole to wait out a second Robotech war," Census said.

Miho grinned at him. "But that's not our only reason for buying it. As a matter of fact, Kan-san has a proposition for you: he wants you to help us piece the place back together." He turned to Gibley. "You could reassemble the cybertech team Zand disbanded when he took over. And you'd have a free hand in pursuing computer research on machine intelligence. Kan-san's idea is to create a storehouse for knowledge that can withstand the coming war. Like the old story about the Ark and the Flood. Only, our ark will carry information instead of animals."

"How very Asian of you," Gibley said.

"Perhaps. But what do you say—are you interested?"

"You're on the level about allowing me to do the hiring?"

"Try me. What have you got to lose?"

Gibley beamed. "Then I say *yes*. I'm in."

Miho turned to Census. "What about you, Zand slayer?"

Census wagged his head up and down. Discount was already nodding when Miho looked at him.

"Misa?" the *yakuza* asked. "Any interest in joining us?"

She hemmed and hawed for a moment. "That kind of

depends on what Terry has to say." Everyone stared at her. "See, I've heard from him, too, and, well, you know, we might start seeing each other."

Census frowned, then grinned. "I'm happy for you. I guess."

"But if Weston is interested, you'd be?" Miho pressed.

She looked from face to face. "Well, shit, we're a team, aren't we?"

"We don't know why the Human, Zand, broke off his contact with us," Shaizan reported to the Elders via transsignal. Masters and Elders both were grouped around their respective Protoculture Caps. "He furnished us with the name of the population center closest to the buried remains of Zor's fortress, but the planetary coordinates weren't supplied. All attempts to reestablish contact with the fortress computer proved futile. It's as if the machine intelligence had been terminated."

"It's possible that Zand's treachery was discovered by his overseers," Bowkaz suggested. "That might explain the sudden silence."

"Or this Zand is not to be trusted," Elder Hepsis replied. "His so-called treachery could be part of a plan to lure us closer to Earth."

"M'lord," Shaizan said. "Zand encouraged us to approach with all speed, as Earth's defense force is at war with itself and in a delicate state."

"So Zand says," Hepsis pointed out.

"But the Protoculture matrix. We need only engage a place called Monument City. A show of force by our flotilla, and the city's leadership may be inclined to surrender the matrix."

"So Zand says."

"The departure of the factory satellite," Shaizan continued. "Is that not proof of war and impaired leadership? Obviously the Zentraedi have detected our presence and mean to humble themselves before us, just as the marooned remnants of Khyron's force attempted to do."

"Humble themselves or impede our progress?" Hepsis asked. "The Zentraedi you saw fit to obliterate had had only limited contact with the Humans. Those in the factory have actually lived among them. Ask yourselves: to whom are they Imperatived—ourselves or their Human landlords?"

The Masters fell silent. At last, Dag asked, "What would you have us do, Elders?"

"Cultivate patience. Wait to see what the Zentraedi have in mind, but conceal yourselves from them. Neither approach nor offer response to their hailings. Instead, begin a slow journey toward Earth; use the planets of that system for cover. Establish contact with us when you have positioned yourselves close enough to scan Earth's surface for readings of Protoactivity. Then, and only then, shall we assess the veracity of Zand's pronouncements."

The Masters kowtowed. "And where will you be, Elders?"

"We will remain in close proximity to Haydon Four, for reasons that shall be revealed in due time."

"We will prevail, Elders," Shaizan said. "The matrix will be ours once more. The glory of our empire will be refashioned, and we will rule supreme in the Fourth Quadrant."

"It is to be hoped," Elder Hepsis answered him as the communications sphere began to collapse on itself and close.

STEEL YOURSELF
FOR COMBAT . . .
PREPARE FOR
NONSTOP ACTION . . .
AND ENTER THE ASTOUNDING
UNIVERSE OF ROBOTECH!

Discover how it all began with FIRST GENERATION:

GENESIS
As the Global Civil War was about to wipe out Humankind, a dying alien genius dispatched the abandoned Super Dimensional Fortress to Earth—and put Humanity's future in the hands of a corps of untried, resolute young men and women: the Robotech Defense Force. Then the most feared conquerors in the universe attacked, and the real war began . . .

BATTLE CRY
Henry Gloval, Human captain of the alien spacecraft called the Super Dimensional Fortress, was a practical man—he only asked himself once or twice a day how in the world he had ended up in command of the stupendously powerful SDF-1. After all, he had more important things on his mind— for now the Zentraedi had come to claim the alien space fortress as their own . . .

HOMECOMING
For more than a year, the Humans aboard the SDF-1 had fought and eluded an endless armada of Zentraedi warships. Now the space fortress would have to battle her way back to Earth. But villains came in Human form as well as alien— and the treachery of power-hungry men might be the most lethal threat of all . . .

BATTLEHYMN

For two years, the SDF-1 had been chased through the Solar system by a race of giant alien warriors, only to be made to feel like unwanted relatives when they finally returned to planet Earth. But after three months of inactivity, the SDF-1's Captain Gloval took matters into his own hands. In direct violation of Council dictates, he ordered the SDF-1 airborne. After all, the fate of the Earth was at stake . . .

FORCE OF ARMS

The giant Zentraedi had given up their efforts to capture the SDF-1 intact. Now they wished only to destroy it—along with its Human crew, the whole Human race and its homeworld, and those aliens who had defected to the Terran side. Supreme Commander Dolza mobilized the largest fleet of Zentraedi warships the universe had ever seen . . . and all their weapons were aimed at Earth.

DOOMSDAY

It was a war without victors—one that had brought two species to the brink of extinction. And it was a war without spoils, save for the devastated Earth itself. After the final battle, Humans began the painstaking process of reconstruction. The Zentraedi would help them—for the two former enemies now shared a common goal: survival. But all was not well in this bravest of new worlds . . . for one Zentraedi had vowed to lead his race back to their former glory—at any cost.

At last the story of the battle for Earth has been told in the new novel of Robotech's LOST GENERATION:

THE ZENTRAEDI REBELLION

Not every Human was eager to share the planet Earth with the Zentraedi survivors of the First Robotech War, and there was little prospect of a lasting peace. The tensions in the Southlands had given rise to two opposing forces: the Army of the Southern Cross, and a loosely organized brigade of Zentraedi insurgents, driven by the Imperative to continue the fight—until one race or the other was eradicated. Caught between those rivals was the Robotech Defense Force, which would play a crucial role in what would be called the Malcontent Uprisings . . .

The adventures of THE SENTINELS begin six years after the final tragedies of the First Robotech War:

THE DEVIL'S HAND

It was 2020, and the Super Dimensional Fortresses 1 and 2 had long been destroyed. But Earth was now on the mend, and the Robotech Defense Force had fashioned a new battle fortress: the SDF-3, tasked with a trip across the galaxy to make peace with Tirol's Robotech Masters. But unknown to Admirals Rick and Lisa Hunter and the SDF-3's crew of thousands, the Robotech Masters were already on their way to Earth. And at Tirol, the SDF-3 would face the galaxy's fiercest warlord: the Invid Regent!

DARK POWERS

Stranded on the far side of the galaxy after battling the Invid hordes, the Robotech Expeditionary Force's chances for survival are slim. But suddenly, a starship unlike any other appeared—manned by an incredible assortment of beings determined to challenge the Invid Regent himself! REF volunteers signed on, their mighty war mecha in tow, for a campaign that would mean their total destruction—or liberty for the planets of the Sentinels!

DEATH DANCE

Four months had passed without a word from the Sentinels, and the members of the Expeditionary mission to Tirol feared the worst—even as they began truce negotiations with the Invid Regent himself. Far away, the surviving Sentinels were hopelessly stranded on Praxis, a planet in cataclysm, at the mercy of the Invid Regis. But deep within that world's core were answers to the Sentinels' prayers—if they could only reach them before Praxis tore itself apart.

WORLD KILLERS

The bearlike Kabarrans and the swashbuckling amazons from Praxis, the feral natives of Garuda and the Human Robotech heroes—these oddly matched champions banded together with yet other species to form the valiant Sentinels. But no fighting force could hope to dislodge the Invid hordes from Haydon IV, ethereal world of superscience, or Spheris, crystalline globe of living minerals and murderous resonances. Nevertheless, the Sentinels launched their attack . . .

RUBICON

Optera—birthplace of the Flower of Life and its agents of retribution, the Invid—was to be the site of the final confrontation between the Sentinels and Edwards and his Invid allies. Edwards, with Lynn-Minmei prisoner and a handful of Invid Inorganics under his control, had fled Tirol for the distant planet. Breetai's Zentraedi were headed there as well—and so were the renegade forces of Tesla, mutated by the fruits of the Flower. The Sentinels themselves were not far behind . . . and it was a battle the Sentinels had to win!

The beginning of a new age
brings a new war in SECOND GENERATION:

SOUTHERN CROSS

Twenty years after the First Robotech War, the Robotech Masters came to Earth to finish the conquest their Zentraedi warrior-slaves had begun ... and a battle-ravaged Earth had to defend itself once more. And young Dana Sterling, half-Human, half-Zentraedi commander of an elite Hovertank unit, stepped into the spotlight of interstellar history!

METAL FIRE

An alien fortress had crashlanded on Earth—brought down deliberately in the struggle between the Robotech Masters and Earth's Human inhabitants. Now the fortress sat silently overlooking Monument City, daring someone to penetrate its dark mysteries. And who better to brave that ship than Dana Sterling's 15th Squadron ATACs—after all, they had brought the thing down to begin with!

THE FINAL NIGHTMARE

The war for Earth had become even more desperate: the Robotech Masters' Protoculture Matrix was degenerating, transforming into the Flower of Life, which was sure to draw the savage, merciless Invid across the galaxy. But the Army of the Southern Cross vowed to wage war for Earth to the bitter end. And Dana Sterling, half-alien commander of an elite Hovertank unit, waged a desperate war of her own to uncover the meaning of her strange visions and the secret of her alien heritage ...

Robotech's THIRD GENERATION
struggles to reclaim a conquered Earth:

INVID INVASION

The Invid Regis had succeeded where the Robotech Masters had failed—her warrior horde had gained control of Protoculture and laid claim to Earth. It was up to the space-weary Human veterans of the Expeditionary Force to retake the planet—a world most of them had never seen. And the counterinvasion would be more difficult than anyone could imagine . . .

METAMORPHOSIS

There had never been a less conventional band of champions: a downed pilot who was a stranger on his own homeworld . . . a former biker hellion . . . a young Forager obsessed with the vanishing heritage of Humanity's lore . . . a lethal Robotech warrior . . . an irrepressible adolescent convinced that the world owes her a Great Romance . . . and a cloned enemy Simulagent who couldn't recall who she was. And somewhere ahead of them lay Reflex Point, nerve center and stronghold of the Invid conquerors—and the destination of the group that was Earth's last hope.

SYMPHONY OF LIGHT

It had been a long, hard road for the ragtag band of Robotech irregulars, but Reflex Point was finally close at hand, and preparations were under way for a full-scale assault on the Invid stronghold. But the Invid Regis would not surrender so easily the world she had come halfway across the galaxy to claim. And no one had thought to ask whether Protoculture might have something to say in these matters. But indeed it did, and the final encounter of the Robotech Wars would be more mystifying than anyone had imagined . . .

*And finally, the REF's final mission is at hand—
and so is the solution
to the greatest mystery of the universe—in ...*

THE END OF THE CIRCLE

The SDF-3 manifested from spacefold, but no one aboard had the slightest idea where they were—the ship appeared to be grounded in some glowing fog, ensnared by the light itself. And the ship's Protoculture drives had disappeared. Meanwhile, in Earthspace, the *Ark Angel* had been spared the destructive fate of the REF main fleet, and a mission set out to locate the SDF-3. Elsewhere, mysterious events were being set into motion, and the ultimate conflict was imminent ...

Also by
⊠ JACK McKINNEY ⊠

DEL REY ONLINE!

The Del Rey Internet Newsletter...

A monthly electronic publication, posted on the Internet, GEnie, CompuServe, BIX, various BBSs, and the Panix gopher (gopher.panix.com). It features hype-free descriptions of books that are new in the stores, a list of our upcoming books, special announcements, a signing/reading/convention-attendance schedule for Del Rey authors, "In Depth" essays in which professionals in the field (authors, artists, designers, sales people, etc.) talk about their jobs in science fiction, a question-and-answer section, behind-the-scenes looks at sf publishing, and more!

Online editorial presence: Many of the Del Rey editors are online, on the Internet, GEnie, CompuServe, America Online, and Delphi. There is a Del Rey topic on GEnie and a Del Rey folder on America Online.

Our official e-mail address for Del Rey Books is delrey@randomhouse.com

Internet information source!

A lot of Del Rey material is available to the Internet on a gopher server: all back issues and the current issue of the Del Rey Internet Newsletter, a description of the DRIN and summaries of all the issues' contents, sample chapters of upcoming or current books (readable or downloadable for free), submission requirements, mail-order information, and much more. We will be adding more items of all sorts (mostly new DRINs and sample chapters) regularly. The address of the gopher is gopher.panix.com

Why? We at Del Rey realize that the networks are the medium of the future. That's where you'll find us promoting our books, socializing with others in the sf field, and—most importantly—making contact and sharing information with sf readers.

For more information, e-mail ekh@panix.com